Berkley Prime Crime Books by Jaqueline Girdner

ADJUSTED TO DEATH
THE LAST RESORT
MURDER MOST MELLOW
FAT-FREE AND FATAL
TEA-TOTALLY DEAD
A STIFF CRITIQUE
MOST LIKELY TO DIE
A CRY FOR SELF-HELP

A CRY FOR SELF-HELP

A CRY FOR SELF-HELP

JAQUELINE GIRDNER

BERKLEY PRIME CRIME, NEW YORK

A CRY FOR SELF-HELP

A Berkley Prime Crime Book
Published by The Berkley Publishing Group
200 Madison Avenue, New York, NY 10016

The Putnam Berkley World Wide Web site address is
http://www.berkley.com/berkley

First Edition: April 1997

Library of Congress Cataloging-in-Publication Data

Girdner, Jaqueline.
    A cry for self-help / by Jaqueline Girdner.
        p.   cm.
    ISBN 0-425-15630-3
    I. Title.
  PS3557.I718C78   1997
  813'.54—dc20   96-31435
                                                CIP

Printed in the United States of America

10   9   8   7   6   5   4   3   2   1

ACKNOWLEDGMENTS

To all the generous people who shared their special bits of knowledge:

Gary Erickson of the Marin County Coroner's Office.

Neal Ferguson, Forensic Specialist.

Betty Golden-Lamb, R.N. and writer.

Bill Gottfried, M.D.

Jacqueline S. Taylor, President of the San Francisco College of Mortuary Science.

Dave Weiss, U.S.A.C.O.E. Park Ranger.

And to my eyes in the days of dark glasses: Lynne Murray, Nancy Kaunitz, Eileen Ostrow Feldman, and Greg Booi.

Thank you so much!

CREATE YOUR OWN WEDDING RITUAL

You've found your perfect soulmate
Now create the perfect ritual to celebrate
I can help

Yvonne O'Reilley (555-1212)

A Metaphor for Two, Forever

MEMBERS OF THE WEDDING RITUAL CLASS

KATE JASPER

Marin County's own, organically grown, reluctant sleuth. And an even more reluctant bride to be.

WAYNE CARUSO

Kate's co-reluctant sleuth. But he's as determined to marry as Kate is reluctant.

YVONE O'REILLEY

Thrice wed, fearless leader of the wedding ritual seminar. The woman knows how to get married.

SAM SKYLER

Human potential guru of the Skyler Institute for Essential Manifestation. He'll lend you a hand if you want to channel your inner essence through finger puppets.

DIANA ATHERTON

Sister to Wayne's employee, Gary Atherton, tantric yoga goddess, and fiancée of Sam Skyler. She makes his puppets pucker.

LIZ ATHERTON

Mother of Diana and Gary. Sam's puppets have not yet grasped her inner respect.

EMMA JETT

Self-styled young woman of the arts . . . all the arts: literary, visual, musical, and melodramatic.

CAMPBELL BARNHILL

Emma's fiancé, a shy grocer with a deep hunger for her love.

NATHAN SKYLER

Often overlooked son to Sam Skyler, and an heir to the kingdom of self-actualized puppetry.

MARTINA MONTEIL

Nathan's dynamic betrothed, and more important to her, Executive Director of the Skyler Institute.

ONA QUIMBY

A woman of size who manages both an office of computer programmers and her own life quite well, thank you.

PERRY KANE

Owner of Kid-Comp, computers for kids, a man eager to be managed by Ona Quimby . . . for life.

Tessa Johnson

The somber funeral director can smile when her sweetie tickles her. But she's not tickled by the prospect of directing *this* funeral.

Ray Zappa

Tessa's intended, a nearly retired veteran cop. He's ready to party. At least, he was.

PROLOGUE

Dead drunk. Still the very presence of the man on the bed seemed to suck all the air out of the room as he snored. All that was left was the smell. Of badly metabolized alcohol and sweat. Even blood. Or was that just my imagination? And the sound. From deep in his chest, the unconscious man let out a low, rasping volley of threats. "Son of a . . . get you . . . get you—" And then, even that volley was choked off by a new snore. And the sight. Red-faced. Red-knuckled. Ugly. So ugly.

The other person in the room stepped closer, looking down, face only a foot or so above the sleeping man's face. And from that view, abruptly a rare moment of dispassion. Of new-found clarity. No fear, no anger. Just reason. A pillow was all it would take. A pillow over that red face, pressed hard. Hard and long.

A quick breath, and hands reached for that pillow. No more fear. No more anger. The plain cotton pillowcase felt like velvet to the hands that grasped its ends.

ONE

"**W**hy the hell didn't you bring a jacket?" I heard someone whisper behind me. Good question.

I wiped my dripping nose with the back of my hand, hoping no one was looking. It was too cold out here on the ocean bluff where we were all waiting for the wedding ceremony to begin below. Far too cold for me in my one and only special-occasion dress. Even with the turtleneck and tights I had thought to add underneath at the last minute. And it was too wet. With that drizzling rain that we Californians like to call "a little fog." I wondered what it was about saltwater molecules that could tunnel so effectively into my stinging sinuses. Not to mention my bone marrow. I switched to rubbing my arms, glaring out into the gray-blue sky.

Was this spring? This morning, there had been pollen sprinkled all over my Toyota like powdered sugar. Greenish-yellow powdered sugar. And late-March winds whipping my early-blooming tulips around like punch-drunk fighters. I wondered if they'd still have their heads on when we got back home. And then wished fervently that we *were* back home.

"They ought to be starting soon," Yvonne O'Reilley assured us all, cheerily pacing back and forth, clapping her hands together as if she couldn't wait. Yvonne, our fearless wedding seminar leader. She didn't even look cold in her cherry-red, shot-with-gold, flowing silk tunic and pants. She had to be at least ten years older than my own forty-some, but everything about her said irrepressible youth. Starting with her curvy face. Curved cheeks, curved nose, curved smile. And an aurora of extravagantly crinkled blond hair pulled up from that curvy face into a series of red and pink plastic barrettes. "They're getting it together at warp speed," she called out, clasping her hands together above her head now. "Cosmic warp speed."

Cosmic warp speed? I turned away from her, too cold for all that cheeriness.

Sam Skyler, founder of the Skyler Institute for Essential Manifestation, dressed in his trademark linen suit over an emerald-green T-shirt, didn't seem to be cold either. Maybe it was something about fiftyish seminar leaders. Only this time Sam was a student at our seminar, not a teacher. He seemed to be engrossed in his conversation with Emma Jett, his deep, sympathetic blue eyes burning into the younger woman's eyes with an intensity few people could muster, even without the wet and foggy cold. Emma danced around in her lace-up boots under the intensity of Sam's stare. Lace-up boots with a tubular spandex minidress. Actually the coppery grommets for the laces seemed to match the brass studs in her ears and nostrils, and the reddish hair cut to the scalp on one side and draping over a narrow cheekbone on the other. I had a short, not unpleasant, fantasy of myself with that hairdo. That's the nice thing about fantasies. You don't have to follow through on them.

"See, it's all this incredible sensation," Emma was telling Sam. "Riding the crest . . ." And then I lost the rest of her sentence over the low roar of the ocean and a new gust of wet wind.

Emma was not Sam's fiancée. Diana Atherton was his fiancée, but Diana was over on the other side of the bluff talking to *my* putative fiancé, Wayne Caruso.

"... Connie the Condom series," was what Emma said next. At least, I was pretty sure that's what she said.

"Empowering concept," Sam commented, bringing his hand out from his chest, fingers first, as if extending his heart. "Monumental vision ..." And then I lost their voices again.

Emma's boyfriend, Campbell Barnhill, was not so talkative. But he was watching Sam and Emma very intently, his arms crossed, a scowl distorting his ginger-bearded, undistinguished face. Did he think Sam was coming on to Emma? *Was* Sam coming on to Emma?

Emma and Campbell were both younger than Sam, Emma probably by more than twenty years. But you never know. Though Campbell's reddening face seemed to indicate that he knew, knew all too well. If it were a choice in looks, Campbell's modest physique and face would certainly lose. Sam Skyler was an impressive man physically. Six foot five, with a body like a lion, his long legs overshadowed by his elongated, oversized torso. A jumbo-pack Pan with shaggy black hair and beautiful eyes. Beautiful eyes focused on Campbell's fair Emma.

I watched Sam Skyler curiously, the man who had become a living legend as a human-potential guru. And the man at least three people were glaring at. Campbell Barnhill certainly was. My own sweetie Wayne's low brows covered his eyes like curtains as he made gargoyle faces in Sam's direction, not hard for a man whose homely face had been enough to win him a position as a bodyguard many years ago. And Liz Atherton, Diana's mother, a no-nonsense type of woman who wore a no-nonsense hairdo and outfit, was sending a no-nonsense scowl at her daughter's fiancé. She rubbed her eyes fiercely and scowled some more. I wondered if her sinuses felt like mine. Then I noticed Ona Quimby was glaring, too. That made four. Ona managed computer programmers for a living. She was a short woman about twice my size around, and about twice my femininity. Her pink and blond soft roundness reminded me of a Persian cat. A Persian cat about to hiss at Sam. Or maybe even claw.

How the hell had Sam Skyler made everyone so mad at him with a bunch of finger puppets? Because that's what the Skyler Institute for Essential Manifestation was all about: finger puppets. Sam's students put these little cloth puppets on their fingers, each puppet purporting to represent an essential emotion, and learned to "reclaim their inner cores," to "revive their heart centers," not to mention "resurrecting their essential selves." All at a minimum of five hundred dollars a weekend at his retreat located not too many miles away in the redwoods of Golden Valley. I had a friend who took Sam's seminar and insisted he was for real. A man of psychic sensitivity and personal genius. A high priest of self-help. But if he was so sensitive, how come he hadn't noticed Campbell yet? Or maybe he had.

Was it purely his physical presence that impressed people? No, I could see a hint of real charisma there. The instant that thought went through my mind, Sam turned as if he'd heard it. Maybe he was psychic.

I jerked my gaze back and stepped up to the hip-high, two-by-four wooden railing that guarded the long bluff. I looked down over the outcropping of rocks below, then stepped back again quickly. The members of the Wedding Ritual class had all met late that afternoon to observe one of the weddings Yvonne had arranged. A scuba-diving wedding. Since we weren't really part of the wedding, our class had met here at the edge of the town of Quiero, in the backyard of what had to be a monstrously expensive but modest-looking house owned by a friend of Yvonne's. The backyard overlooked a deep, growth-covered gully below and also had a perfect view down and off to the right of the cove and enclosed beach located some 2,000 feet or so away past the border of the Point Abajo National Seashore. That was where the wedding would take place. That was where the scuba divers would swim from the sea and climb onto the beach for their evolution from the stormy primordial soup into the windy state of marriage. So far all I could see was what looked like little stacks of colored blocks scurrying around the beach. I assumed they were the wedding guests. I wondered if the black block was the minister.

This was supposed to inspire Wayne and me to plan our own special wedding. So far I hadn't been inspired. Wayne was lost in conversation with Sam's fiancée, Diana. I swallowed a sigh. Diana. Even her name said goddess. Diana was one of the most graceful women I'd ever seen. That's what you noticed about her first. That and her extraordinary beauty. Slender and erect with saucer blue eyes and a long black braid that reached all the way to her trim waist and small but perfect hips. An impressive mate for the impressive Sam Skyler. No way could my own short, dark, and A-line mortal embodiment compete. And on top of it all, Diana was a tantric (read: sexual) yoga instructor, a *young* tantric yoga instructor.

No, this particular part of the seminar was not an inspiration for marriage. At least not for me. Though I couldn't speak for Wayne, who was nodding seriously at whatever the tantric goddess was so earnestly saying.

I told myself to cut it out. Diana was with Sam. And Wayne was not one to be swayed by goddesshood. I hoped.

We'd all come in pairs like Noah's animals to the wedding seminar. Ona Quimby and her fiancé, Perry Kane. Perry's darkly handsome East Indian features offset Ona's pink and white softness perfectly. Tessa and Ray were another study in contrasts. Tessa Johnson was a short and somber gray-haired black woman in her sixties. Her sweetie, Ray Zappa, was a tall, handsome Italian-American (and part Apache, as he kept reminding us) who was far from somber. Hearty, even wild, was a better description. And he was a veteran cop, about to retire. Maybe his wildness was what the quiet Tessa craved. A little smile lit up Tessa's eyes as Ray laughed without inhibition at his own joke. Uh-huh, there was love twinkling in there, deep in Tessa's eyes.

And of course there were Diana and Sam. And Diana's mother, Liz, tagging along for good measure.

And Sam's son, Nathan Skyler, a smaller, less impressive version of his father. I'd almost forgotten him. Nathan was second in command at the Institute. I certainly couldn't see him as first. Nathan was tall and broad through the shoulders, but nothing like his father. His unshaven face made him look like a Wookie with glasses, a professorial Wookie with glasses, actually. It was something about the way his shoulders stooped. But then Nathan's girlfriend, Martina Monteil, displayed the dynamism Nathan lacked. She was tall too, close to six feet and well-built with the cold and perfect features of a model: high cheekbones, bee-stung lips, and large hazel eyes that widened automatically in response to everyone who spoke to her, as if she were instantly fascinated by what each person had to say. Martina was third in command at the Institute. I looked at Nathan, then back at Martina. Nepotism was clearly at work here. Martina was leader material, not Nathan.

I turned back to the triangle of Sam, Emma, and Campbell furtively. Campbell's face was even redder under his ginger beard, and I didn't think it was just from the wind.

"A man like you knows that incredible zing, that *whoosh* when it hits you," Emma was saying. She jumped in place as if the wind had lifted her and set her back down.

"Absolutely," Sam agreed. "That's the manifestation of the essence! Explosive, unstoppable." He pulled something from the pocket of his linen jacket. At first I suspected it was a flask, but then I saw it was a small cloth puppet. "A woman like you must experience the Skyler method. A free session . . ."

Campbell moved in closer, his fists clenching. It was too painful to watch. I turned back to the gray-green water of the ocean.

The backyard ended at a bluff that dropped at least two hundred feet, maybe more, to the gully below. Parts of the bluff were covered with scrub, wild grasses, Scotch broom, and tangled vines. But in spots like this one farthest from the wedding site, the drop was all rock. I shivered from more than cold as I stepped forward again on the overlook and gingerly looked down. Triangular pieces of rock jutted out randomly all the way down the cliff here, like balconies on an overcrowded tenement. Yvonne must have liked this spot. She had set two oversize brass vases filled with wild, wilting buttercups atop this section of the weathered wooden railing. The vases, on bases of large solid brass stars, had to be two feet high.

I imagined them crashing down those rough triangular rocks. Didn't Yvonne's friend realize this was unsafe? The whole overlook railing, winding around the bluff, looked about as effective as a hamster guarding an armored truck. I turned away from the ocean once more, looking for a conversation to join.

Tessa and Ray seemed to be having the best time. And Ona and Perry had joined them. And Liz. And Wayne. My head came up, along with my pulse. Wayne. I looked over my shoulder. Diana was now speaking earnestly to Nathan and Martina. And for once Martina didn't look fascinated.

I walked up and took Wayne's hand, still warm in all this cold. He gave me a smile that warmed me further. No matter what first impression his cauliflower nose, scarred cheeks, and low brows made, his vulnerable brown eyes were beautiful. At least to me.

"Cold?" he asked, his rough voice like a good massage.

My nod turned into a shiver.

He stood behind me and put his strong arms around my shoulders. I leaned into his tall, sturdy body gratefully. Sam might have been a little taller than Wayne, with a bigger chest, but there was nothing like Wayne's body for leaning into. Wayne's face might have been homely, but his body certainly wasn't.

At least no one seemed to be glaring at Sam anymore. I craned my neck around to see for sure. Well, no one except for Campbell.

"Been a court reporter some twenty years," Liz was saying. "Interesting work. See all the best and worst in people. Justice. Injustice." She shrugged her shoulders, then rubbed her eyes again.

"And you're the lovely Diana's mother," Tessa said, her somber voice touched with honey.

"She is lovely, isn't she?" Liz answered brusquely, turning for a moment to look at her daughter where she stood with Nathan and Martina. "Don't know where she gets it from."

But for all of Diana's gracefulness and all her mother's no-nonsense grace*less*ness, I could see the similarity in the two women. In the cheekbones, lips, and large eyes. There was a softness beneath Liz's severe shell.

Her lips curved in a shy smile. "My son, Gary, works for Wayne, Kate's fiancé. That's what got Diana into this seminar."

"And into my tai chi class," I added, keeping the bitterness out of my voice with an effort. Diana had taken a year and a half to master the tai chi form I was still struggling with at year eight. And of course, she looked absolutely gorgeous doing it. It made sense. The woman would look gorgeous doing anything.

"Oh yeah, tai chi," Ona Quimby threw in enthusiastically,

her voice loud. Too loud. Ona's voice didn't match her soft-ness. In fact, it was always a shock to hear that tough, deep voice coming out of that ultrafeminine body. "I took tai chi for a while. But I just didn't have the time to keep on. It's great stuff, stretched my limits. People think someone as big as I am wouldn't have the sensitivity or flexibility for a soft form of self-defense like tai chi, but that's crap." She brought up her leg in a kick as relaxed and limber as any tai chi stu-dent's. "Just wish I could have stayed till we got to the push hands part."

"That's the sparring part," her boyfriend, Perry, translated eagerly. His friendly voice was as loud as Ona's but not as deep. Or as tough. "The rest of the time they just practice the moves by themselves in this long kinda dance form. It's really beautiful."

"Push hands isn't exactly sparring," Ona corrected him. "It's just using the movements and the principles of the form as you interact with a partner."

"And push him over," Ray Zappa said. "It's still fighting. They wanted us to learn it at the police department. Silliest martial art I ever saw. They say it's a big deal, but as far as I'm concerned a good partner and a good gun work a lot better then pushing people over."

"But a gentle way to defend yourself from attack might be great for the police," I put in. I couldn't resist arguing, think-ing about the movies I'd seen where the Master—a small, elderly Chinese man—had lofted burly Marines into the air with those soft pushes. And how those same burly Marines couldn't budge the Master with pushes or kicks or blows. Of course, he was a master.

"Got some crazy kid after you with an assault rifle, you're not going to be using tai chi or any of that airy-fairy stuff," Ray insisted. I shrugged my shoulders. He was probably right. Still . . .

Ray turned to Tessa, a big grin on his face. "I mean, you ever seen a dead body down at your mortuary, killed with tai chi?"

Mortuary?

Everyone's eyes snapped in Tessa's direction.

"Yes, I make a living as a mortician," Tessa admitted quietly, a sigh in her voice. Then she elbowed Ray in the ribs, much less gently than a tai chi push. He grabbed himself as if mortally wounded.

But Liz Atherton looked truly shocked. She narrowed her round eyes at Tessa sharply. And for a moment, Tessa returned the look, tilting her head as if in sudden recognition.

"You buried my husband," Liz declared softly. "Now I recognize you . . ." Her voice faltered. "It's been more than twenty years—"

"And my father," Perry Kane added, his usually high voice low and shaky now. "You buried my father. Because of the race thing."

Tessa turned toward Perry now, one hand raised palm-up in a gentle gesture of defeat.

"I've buried a good many people here in Marin," she said, her voice as steady and unapologetic as her hand was defensive. "I can barely go anywhere in Marin without someone recognizing me. Especially if there was an issue about using the funeral home for mixed races. Our specialty for twenty-five years." She elbowed Ray in the ribs again. "And if someone doesn't recognize me, there's always Ray to make sure they do. Makes me a real popular person everywhere I go."

We all laughed nervously. Or tried to.

"What I really love is my hobby," Tessa said, changing the subject after another moment of charged silence. "I'm a baby holder. You know, for the newborns at the hospital whose mothers can't hold them."

We all nodded, mesmerized. At least I was. Newborns, newly dead . . .

"Well, that's what I do, hold them and cuddle them," she finished, her solemn face softened under her upswept gray curls.

"My Tessa's a great lady, that's for sure," Ray declared, throwing his big arm around her small shoulders, his elbowed ribs apparently forgotten.

Liz took a big breath and threw herself back into conversational duty with an obvious effort. "I do chain saw sculpture myself. Saw a man doing it a few years ago and decided I'd give it a try—"

"You son of a dog!" The bellow erupted from behind us before Liz could even finish her sentence.

Wayne and I turned simultaneously and saw Campbell shaking his fist about a foot from Sam Skyler's face. I didn't see any puppets on his clenched fingers, so I assumed the meaning of his shaking fist was the traditional one. But where did he get his insults? *Son of a dog*? This guy was closer to thirty years old than two hundred.

"Now, Campbell," Sam was saying calmly, "I'm sure that was very energizing, very empowering. In fact, I feel you're on the road to a real turnaround . . ."

"I'll turn your quiffing face around!" Campbell shouted.

"Hey now, sweet-cakes," Emma intervened, physically as well as verbally, inserting her small body between the two men's, and batting Campbell's fist out of the air like a cat with a toy mouse. "Don't be boring. Sam and I were just—"

"Emma, it's not you!" Campbell howled, waving his hands above her head in frustration. "It's that . . . that pompous piece of—"

"Now, I know you're really tinkled," a new voice broke in cheerfully. Yvonne. I'd hardly seen her approaching the trio. I'd been too fascinated by Sam's slow and barely dis-

cernible retreat from the range of Campbell's fist. Talk about
tai chi. This guy was over a yard away now and you could
barely see him moving.

"But you see, it's just the dark side of love," Yvonne went
on. "Channel it now. Channel it into the light of love. Channel
it into loving your Emma."

Campbell was cruelly outnumbered. And outmaneuvered.
Within minutes, he, Emma, and Sam had joined our group and
we were all talking about hobbies again. At least Ona was
talking about Perry's.

"He teaches kids in the inner cities about computers," she
told us, patting Perry's arm firmly as if he were a dog. Perry
turned his head away shyly, a flush reddening his brown skin.
"He says that within a few years the computer illiterates will
be the real have-nots. And he's doing something about it. *He*
really cares."

"Precisely," Sam agreed, putting in his five hundred dollars
worth. "That's what this country needs. More people pushing
their limits. Everything we do, or don't do, can be empowering
or impoverishing, whether we're paid or not paid. All of our
actions reflect the potential to channel higher consciousness
into living grace—"

"Did you say 'leaving grace'?" asked Ray Zappa, cupping
his ear innocently. But I could see the suppressed grin lifting
his eyebrows.

"No, no," Sam answered, a shadow of irritation passing
over his gorgeous face. He stared at Ray for a moment, as if
trying to figure out whether or not he was kidding and then
deciding he couldn't be. I wished I had that kind of ego. "*Living* grace. You see the Skyler method teaches us to turn our
higher consciousness into living grace. Actual living harmony—"

The sound of a conch shell being blown interrupted his

speech. Just in time. Did people really pay five hundred dollars a pop to listen to this man?

"Oh, it's beginning!" Yvonne sang out. She ran to the edge of the bluff. "Everyone get a good place to watch now. You're going to see magic."

Suddenly I was glad the overlook railing extended so far along the bluff. Everyone could get a view without being crowded. We all spread out yards apart, from Sam Skyler alone at the far end by the brass vases to Yvonne O'Reilley alone at the end nearest Point Abajo. Wayne and I cuddled together somewhere in the center, and then the conch shell sounded again.

We peered down at the cove and enclosed beach to our right and waited for the magic Yvonne had promised. The little brightly colored stacks had stopped racing around and were standing in motionless rows now with a space very much like an aisle down the middle of their ranks. Sure enough, the one in black farthest from the water appeared to be the minister. Now that our group had fallen silent, the ocean's roar seemed more rhythmic. Almost hypnotic. The wind even seemed to defer, dying down for the moment. And the misting rain had disappeared. The warmth that radiated from Wayne's body began to seep into mine. Magic?

A lone bagpipe began to play somewhere below. "Briga-doon." Would the fog lift for the ceremony now?

All eyes were on the cove as the surf deposited two sleek black seals onto the beach. Only they weren't seals. The bride and groom? No, no, they weren't, I decided. They were two men. The groom and his best man, I guessed. They stood and walked in the giant, exaggerated steps of those outfitted with flippers and oxygen tanks, making their way down the space in the middle of the stacks of colors until they were in place to one side of the black block that had to be the minister. Just before they turned, I noticed the patches of phosphorescent white that their suits had been painted with, approximating the boiled fronts of tuxedos.

The bagpipe continued to play and then two more seals emerged from the water. These two were easier to identify. At least the one with the long white veil attached to the headpiece of her diving suit and the white train floating from her waist at least three yards out into the water. She and the other seal climbed onto the beach, arm in arm, followed by the smallest seal of all, holding the end of the train. I resisted the urge to applaud as they solemnly followed the awkward path the first two divers had taken through the middle of the crowd.

The bagpipes went abruptly silent as the group of divers arranged themselves before the minister. Then the conch shell sounded again. I wished I could see more, but no one had thought to bring binoculars any more than they had thought to bring jackets.

I wasn't even sure if it was the hum of marriage vows I heard over the ocean and wind. But I saw the ring being transferred and the seals kiss. And heard the cheer from the crowd. All right, it was magical. A magical wedding was possible. At least from this distance.

And then, as the pipes played once more, the two newly married seals duck-walked back to the water's edge and dived, the tip of the bridal train the last vision to disappear beneath the pounding surf.

The conch shell sounded one final note, and another cheer rose from the beach. The wedding was over.

I looked up at Wayne and put my arms around him. His soft mouth landed on mine and I closed my eyes, lost in the moment.

"Sam?" I heard from behind me. Diana's voice. I kept my lips on Wayne's.

"Sam?" again, a little more urgently. "Has anyone seen Sam?"

It was no use. I could feel the kiss lose momentum as certainly as a car with a stalled engine.

I looked around and saw various groups of people, standing and talking, but I didn't see Sam.

"Maybe he went back into the house," Ray suggested.

I took Wayne's hand before he went to comfort Diana directly, and walked impatiently to the place I had last seen Sam, by the vases at the far end of the railing. But the vases were gone.

Had they fallen over the bluff? I looked down over the railing. I didn't see the vases. But I did see the answer to the question that Diana was asking more and more hysterically.

Sam Skyler was spread-eagled below, a guru on the rocks.

ꟼWO

I was looking over the railing at Sam Skyler's spread-eagled body when Diana came up behind me and looked too. In the shallow bubbling water below the body, a life preserver was floating merrily. Not that it would do Sam any good up on the rocks. Actually, it didn't look as if anything was going to do Sam a lot of good.

I was still watching the life preserver when Diana screamed and grabbed my shoulders. And I felt myself tilting forward. The wooden two-by-four railing ground into my hip bones as Diana's screams pierced my eardrums. I wanted to cover my ears, but clasped the railing instead, concentrating on taking the energy that was tilting me forward and using it to tilt myself back again. Like in push hands. But this wasn't push hands. There were rocks down there. I centered myself and rolled my shoulders out of Diana's grip. I wasn't going over that railing. No way.

And suddenly, I felt a new pair of hands on my shoulders, but these were pulling me back. Wayne's hands. Then he picked me up and set me down at least a yard away from the railing.

"Okay?" he asked softly. At least that's what I thought he said.

Because my heart was thumping so hard in my chest, I could barely hear him. Was that what Sam had felt when he had gone over, his heart thumping, his ears buzzing? And then hitting the first rock. Because he had hit a lot more than one of those triangular rocks, the hundred feet or so he had bounced before landing on the large flat one sticking out like an oversized pie-server. His body was smashed and tattered as if . . . I shook the thought out of my head. Sam Skyler had to be dead. And I didn't want to know how his death had felt. Ever.

I forced my stinging eyes to look out at the gray-blue sky and saw that it was shimmering. But five o'clock was still too early for twilight. Or was it? I couldn't seem to think.

And Diana just kept screaming.

Wayne turned her way, his rough face white and drawn. Even in my shock, I could see his shock. And his conflict. A caretaker torn between two needy women. One woman his fiancée, the other having just seen *her* dead fiancé's body smashed on the rocks below. Diana's hands were now clamped over her eyes as she screamed.

I reached for Wayne's hand, but a new thought froze my own hand before it even got that far. Had Diana tried to push me over the edge? No, I decided. No. I shook my head violently. Much as I didn't appreciate the presence of Diana in my life, I didn't think my animosity was returned. At least not enough to kill me. Especially in front of witnesses. *Witnesses.* My mind repeated the word. I hadn't even thought about witnesses.

I swiveled my head around, suddenly seeing the spasming of movement around us. Liz was running toward her daughter now. And Nathan was veering her way, too. Everyone else was moving toward the bluff on different paths. Looking over. Pointing. Exclaiming. Turning away. Turning back.

"My vases," Yvonne's voice came floating over Diana's screams. "Where are my vases?"

And then Liz had Diana's face in her hands and Nathan was patting Diana's back. And finally Diana stopped screaming. All I could hear was ocean and the ringing in my ears as Wayne locked his arms around me.

"Police matter," came a voice into that relative silence. I peeked around Wayne's arm and saw Ray Zappa, no longer looking hearty, his good-time face angular with sobriety. He turned and jogged toward the house.

I pressed my face into Wayne's chest as I threw *my* arms around *him*, hoping I was comforting him as well as myself, breathing in his scent, holding onto his heat. Holding onto his strength. Our strength. He squeezed me back even harder, not quite hard enough to break ribs, but close. And the pain of the embrace felt good. I was alive. But I could still hear the voices that drifted around us on the cold, wet air.

"Police?" asked at least three voices at once. Yvonne's and Perry's, I was pretty sure. And Martina's, I thought.

"The man is dead." Gently. Clearly. That one was Tessa's voice.

"Dead?" That one I couldn't identify. The wet wind took it and twisted it out of recognition. It might have been Campbell. Or it might have been Emma. Or anyone.

And then suddenly, "Was Skyler murdered? Is that what Ray meant?" Ona's voice was too loud to twist, too authoritative. But still her question went unanswered. "Did someone push him?"

I buried my head further into Wayne's chest.

Did someone push Sam Skyler? Or did he fall? Or did he jump? Or—

And then the voice I hadn't thought to listen for came rising over the currents. Nathan's.

"Did someone kill Dad?" he asked, his soft voice high now, incredulous.

I peered around Wayne. Nathan wasn't patting Diana's back anymore. He was looking over the bluff.

"Oh no," he said to himself, shaking his head. "No."

That's when I remembered. Sam Skyler had been Diana's fiancé, but he had also been Nathan's father. Oh God, what was Nathan Skyler feeling now? What—

And then Diana began to sob. "Killed, killed," she repeated, her voice getting progressively higher through her tears. "Why wasn't I standing with him? Killed. Oh why? Why . . ."

I closed my eyes and thought of Sam's huge upper body and the low railings. If they had been hip-high on me, they must have been thigh-high on him. And he was already over-balanced on top. He could have fallen. I had almost gone over from Diana's frightened grasp myself. And Sam had been at the end of the bluff farthest away from the wedding ceremony. No one would have been looking his way. Could someone have pushed him, hoping their risk of being seen was minimal? Was minimal enough to hope for? *Had* someone else seen what happened? The thoughts went through my head even as the horror coursed through my body. I couldn't seem to stop them once they started. Then I remembered all of our talk of push hands, of pushing. And Ray asking if anyone had ever been killed with tai chi.

I shivered in the wet, salty air. Magic had been replaced by something else. Something I didn't want to think about.

And Diana continued to sob.

The federal government, in the person of one Park Ranger Yasuda, was the first representative of authority to arrive on the bluff. He appeared just about the time I noticed the splinters from the wooden railing in my right palm.

Park Ranger Yasuda didn't look much like an official,

though. True, he wore the drab gray and green uniform with the Point Abajo insignia and a name tag, but his long black hair was tied back in a ponytail. His thick, arching eyebrows gave his intense eyes and square features the look of a samurai, a concerned samurai.

Maybe that's why Yvonne hugged him. Because that's what our fearless Wedding Ritual seminar leader did. The first official on the scene and she hugged him.

"Oh, I'm so sorry!" she cried and clutched him as tightly as I had clutched Wayne.

Sorry? Sorry for what? Pushing Sam?

Yasuda raised his eyebrows and pulled out of her grip with some twisting and fancy footwork. But he got away.

And then Yvonne put her arms around him again.

Yasuda's eyebrows went even higher this time. And instead of twisting, he pushed her away, but I could see the effort he made to be gentle in his push.

"Ms. O'Reilley?" he said. Did he know Yvonne then, if he knew her name? Was that why she was hugging him? "What is—"

And then everyone started in at once, telling him about the scuba wedding, and Sam Skyler's body on the rocks, while I tried to figure out just how Park Ranger Yasuda knew Yvonne O'Reilley, if he did know her.

A few garbled moments later, Yasuda put his hand palm up for silence before walking to the edge of the bluff and looking over for himself. When he turned back around, he closed his eyes for a moment. Even when he opened them again, there was a tightness in his face that made me think it was an effort for him to keep his eyes open. He could have probably used that hug from Yvonne about then. I concentrated on studying my hand, trying to figure out if I'd be able to pull out the splinters without a pair of tweezers. It was better than thinking about Sam Skyler.

"What happened here?" Yasuda asked, his voice low and quiet, but strong enough to be audible over the ocean and wind.

"Well," and "uh," and "didn't see," were the only kind of answers he got.

He put up his palm again.

"Did anyone see him go over?" he demanded, a little louder this time.

He got even fewer answers this time. No answers, in fact. If anyone had seen Sam go over, they weren't talking.

A familiar churning started in my stomach. I forgot about the splinters in my hand and glanced up at Wayne. His brows were at half-mast over his eyes. And I would have bet his stomach was feeling a lot like mine. Sam Skyler had not been a well-liked man. And now he was spread-eagled on the rocks. Finding out how he got there wasn't going to be easy. For any of us.

"I want everyone to walk very carefully away from the edge of the bluff," Yasuda was instructing when the second governmental representative sirened up behind us in a car bearing the insignia of the Quiero Police Department.

Both Chief Woolsey of the Quiero Police Department and Officer Fox, who quickly introduced himself and his superior, looked official. It wasn't so much the uniform that Fox had on and Woolsey didn't, but the short haircuts, lack of facial hair, and the disgruntled expressions that they both wore.

"We'll take it from here, Yasuda," was the first thing Woolsey said after he took a look at Skyler's body and asked the same, obvious questions Yasuda had, receiving the same answers. Or lack therof.

But Yasuda wasn't that easy to shake.

"I'd like to stay, sir," he said, straightening his back, military style. "The Park is involved in this one too."

Woolsey turned and glared at Yasuda, finally having found

someone to whom he could direct his disgruntlement. It was a good strong glare, seeming to fit his long, lean face and receding hairline. Fox glared too, his puffy moon-face not quite carrying it off so well.

"This is City of Quiero property and City of Quiero jurisdiction," Woolsey declared. "Your *tourist* park has nothing to do with this." There was something about the way he stretched out the word "tourist" that made me think he didn't appreciate the breed.

"Excuse me if I disagree," Yasuda came back, and they were off and running.

I kept waiting to be interrogated. But we of the Saturday afternoon Create Your Own Wedding Ritual class all stood scattered around the bluff instead, listening to Ranger Yasuda and Chief Woolsey argue about jurisdiction, their voices booming over the rhythmic roar of the ocean below. And the slightly more muted sound of Diana's whimpering.

"Uh, guys—" Ona put in after a good twenty minutes, but the two men didn't seem to hear her, however loud her voice was.

". . . U.S. Army Corps of Engineers will come in if the tides touch the body—" Yasuda was saying.

"The tides aren't going to touch the body," Woolsey argued. "You're a park ranger for God's sake. Look at the ecological situation down there . . ."

I looked up instead of down as the sun began to set, backlighting the gray-blue clouds with accents of silver and apricot. Very subtle. Very artistic. Very cold. My teeth were chattering even with Wayne's arms around me.

It was about then that the Marin County sheriffs arrived. And I probably wasn't the only one happy to see them.

They *did* something about Sam Skyler. I could hear one of the sheriffs as he called in for the Search and Rescue Team that would retrieve Sam's body.

And suddenly Woolsey seemed to remember that he was a chief of police. He turned away from Ranger Yasuda and told Officer Fox to take our names. Once that was done, he herded us all into the house for interrogation.

I heard the clicking of chopper blades as I walked through the doorway, and looked over my shoulder just in time to see the chopper flying in, a basket hanging from its belly. I was glad I wouldn't see the rescue team in action, pulling Sam Skyler's body from its rocky perch. I had seen enough.

Woolsey did most of the talking once we were inside the house Yvonne's friend owned. Inside! A real living room with long, low beige sofas arranged on an earth-gray carpet and equipped with a huge black Swedish fireplace that was unfortunately unlit. But it was still warm in there. Relatively warm, anyway, after the cold and wet outside. We all sat down under Officer Fox's impassive moon-faced gaze as Woolsey led Yvonne O'Reilley into the kitchen for questioning. Woolsey made no comment as Park Ranger Yasuda and one of the county sheriffs followed him. Maybe the sheriffs had embarrassed Woolsey into professional courtesy. Or maybe he was just tired of arguing with Yasuda.

My fingers had just begun to get feeling back in their tips, and my teeth had stopped chattering, by the time Woolsey finished questioning Diana. The warmth had spread to my palms, splinters and all, when he finished with Nathan. And then it was my turn.

The kitchen was even warmer than the living room. I sank into one of the rustic wooden chairs gratefully, happy to be there, interrogation or no interrogation.

But I was out of the kitchen in less than five minutes. Woolsey asked me my version of what had happened. I was ready, and summarized in a few succinct sentences the conversations before the wedding, Campbell's outburst, the scuba wedding itself, and discovering Sam Skyler's body. He asked if I had

known Sam Skyler previously. I told him I hadn't. He asked
if I had seen Sam fall. I told him I hadn't. That was it. He
didn't even ask if I had anything to add before he told me I
could go. Yasuda and the sheriff sat through the three questions and answers without comment, and without expression.
And then it was Wayne's turn.

As I sat in the living room waiting for Wayne, I wondered
if Woolsey actually believed that Sam Skyler had just fallen
onto those rocks. And then I wondered why I didn't.

For all the brevity of Woolsey's interrogations, the sun was
almost completely set by the time Wayne and I were back in
my Toyota with me at the wheel, taking the newly blacktopped
curves of the road home while heat blasted from the dashboard
vents like a blessing. The scuba-wedding party seemed like a
dream.

Wayne and I didn't talk much on the way. I showed him
my splintered hand. He bent over to kiss it. Not quite tweezers,
but good. Definitely good.

Finally pulling into the driveway, we clumped up the front
stairs, shut the front door behind us, and held each other again
so closely you could almost hear the submicroscopic viruses
being crushed between us.

A yowl from the rear broke it up. My cat, C.C. Death,
murder? None of it mattered. Her dinner was late.

Wayne picked her up, burying his face in her silky fur. I
wished I had gotten to her first. But Wayne was faster. C.C.
let him indulge himself for a moment, then turned her spotted
black and white face toward his, widened her eyes, and blasted
him with another yowl. Maybe I didn't wish I had gotten to
her first.

"Cat food or splinters?" Wayne asked quietly as he set
C.C. gently back on the floor. A lot more gently than I would
have.

"Cat food," I answered. "We'd never get the splinters out with C.C. bonking my legs for attention."

We were finally sitting on the living room couch with an open bottle of alcohol (of the rubbing variety), tissues, and tweezers when the doorbell rang.

Wayne screwed the cap back on the bottle, stomped to the door, and reluctantly opened up. Even from where I sat, I could see who our visitors were. Diana Atherton, tantric yoga goddess, and her brother, Gary. For a moment, I studied the two, noting their similarities. Both graceful, erect, and slender, with perfectly symmetrical features and large blue saucer eyes. But at least Gary was balding.

And then I remembered that Sam Skyler was dead. How could I have forgotten, even for a moment? Diana Atherton was in mourning and I was—

I jumped up from the couch and marched over to express my sympathy.

But by the time I reached the doorway, my mouth just opening to speak, Diana had put up her hands as if for silence.

"I've had dreams of violence," she announced softly.

THREE

"What do you mean 'dreams of violence'?" Wayne asked. His voice was low and serious. His face too. Diana's words had tightened the skin over his scarred cheekbones and drawn his brows low over his eyes.

"I...I..." Diana began to sob, higher-than-Everest-pitched sobs that brought my hands up involuntarily to cover my ears.

But I dropped my hands and dived in conversationally before she could get any farther. I knew by now that this woman could cry or scream, or do both at once, endlessly if not diverted.

"Do you mean you've dreamt of killing Sam?" I asked.

That stopped her for a moment.

I took a breath as she raised her now reddened blue eyes to me and stared as if trying to figure out the meaning of my words.

"Is that what you're worried about?" I tried again. "That you dreamt about killing Sam and then you did—"

"No, no!" she wailed and then began to sob in earnest. So much for diverting her.

All through this, Gary Atherton stood by his sister, his handsome face as serious as Wayne's homely one. Without speaking. No "hiya", no "how are you?" Nothing.

Impatiently, I stepped closer to the group standing in the doorway. Just why were the Athertons invading our home anyway? Not to confess anything like murder, I hoped. Were they just here for sympathy? Or for advice?

"Gary," I greeted him.

He shot a quick nod my way and then his eyes bounced back to his sister. Of course.

I knew the two siblings fairly well. Or at least Wayne did. Gary Atherton worked for Wayne, managing his restaurant cum-art gallery, La Fête à L'Oiel. Gary was a good manager. And Wayne took good care of his employees, serving as psychologist, mediator, and mentor as often as boss. And I knew that Gary was very close to his younger sister, Diana. So Wayne was forever advising Gary about his sister, and Gary was forever advising his sister about her life. Their mother, Liz, got in there a lot with her advice too. And her hovering. Liz couldn't stand Sam Skyler, but she still managed to accompany Diana to a good half of the meetings of the wedding seminar.

Everyone took care of Diana. There was something about her that seemed to suck up advice and protection like a well designed vacuum cleaner. Not from me, though. I was too busy being jealous. Because I was forever watching Diana's perfection, whether in tai chi, in simply walking, or in manipulating the world at large into taking care of her. All of which seemed to be unconscious on her part.

But the goddess's fiancé was dead, I reminded myself once more. How could I keep forgetting?

"Come on in and sit down," I said. I couldn't not say it. The phrase is programmed into my genes.

Diana had never been in our house before, but she didn't seem to take much notice of our living room as she followed us in, back still erect even while sobbing. And most people did notice, especially since Wayne and I had built two more four-by-nine bookshelves. Now the room was literally covered wall-to-wall and floor-to-ceiling with bookcases. The only exceptions being the jungle of house plants stuck here and there in the crevices and the two pinball machines holding their own in the corner. And the center of the room. We hadn't figured out how to put bookshelves there yet, only two swinging chairs that hung from the rafters, a futon, pillows, and a denim-covered couch that was a remnant of my former marriage. A remnant just like my antipathy to formal wedding ceremonies. Which was what got me into this mess in the first place, I decided as Diana and Gary took their places on the couch.

"So?" I said, lowering myself onto a swinging chair for two next to Wayne.

Three morose faces turned my way.

"Sam," Diana whimpered. Gary patted her shoulder.

The gesture seemed to stanch her sniffles.

"He was a genius," she declared, her voice a little stronger, though still trembling.

I noticed neither Wayne nor Gary threw in any words or nods of agreement. In fact, I got the distinct feeling that Wayne was rolling his eyes under his lowered brows. I nodded encouragingly for the two of them.

"Oh, Kate," Diana sniffed, turning my way now. "Not everyone appreciated Sam, but he really was a genius at bringing out people's essential selves, their lost selves, their higher selves." She stuck out her ring finger. At first I thought she was showing me her ruby-encrusted engagement ring, but then she intoned, "Grief into growth," and I remembered the puppets. I could almost hallucinate one on her fingertip.

Actually, I was more interested in the people who *didn't* appreciate Sam Skyler, but Diana went on with her fingers before I could formulate the sensitive kind of question that seemed essential to ask someone like her.

"Control into cooperation," she proclaimed, sticking out her thumb. "Denial into determination." Her pinkie popped out. "Grief into growth," she said again softly. Her eyes misted up precariously. But she went on. "I can feel Sam with me now, merging with me." She pulled up her head, middle finger gracefully extended. "Anger into achievement." And finally with her index finger, "Higher self into living grace."

Then she smiled beatifically. Wayne and Gary sat stony-faced. What was wrong with these guys? *I* was beginning to feel protective toward Diana now.

"So that's what Sam taught at his Institute?" I offered as the silence lengthened.

"That's it," she agreed, bobbing her head enthusiastically. "The Skyler Institute for Essential Manifestation." Her round eyes teared up again. "Sam was such a creative, intuitive man. He . . . He . . ."

"Were any of Sam's students in the Wedding Ritual class?" Wayne broke in. Finally, one of the questions I hadn't yet formulated. And Wayne's low voice was gentle enough to give it the sensitivity I'd been searching for.

"Ona Quimby took one of his seminars," Diana answered after taking a trembling breath that seemed to last forever. It must have been all that yoga training that gave her the lung power. "Ona didn't really, well, appreciate Sam, though. They were never really able to merge emotionally."

"Why?" I asked.

"Well." Diana shifted uncomfortably in her chair. "Ona is a big woman, 'a woman of size,' she calls herself, and Sam thought she ought to lose weight to self-actualize. We even argued about it. Ona was that size naturally, organically. But Sam thought she could change if she really wanted to. He always wanted people to push their limits."

The word "push" brought up a picture in my mind of Ona

pushing Sam. Pushing his limits right over the bluff. I shook the thought away.

"Anyone else?" I asked quickly.

"I think Perry Kane came to an introductory class," she answered after a moment. "But he didn't stay."

"How about Emma?" Wayne pressed, his voice still gentle.

"I don't think Emma took any classes, but he might have known her," Diana answered, frowning. Her usually sweet voice had a touch of acidity. Had she been jealous of Emma? Could a woman like Diana feel jealousy? What a delightful thought. I quickly erased the smile from my face, forcing myself to heed the seriousness of the current situation. "And of course he knew me and Mom. And Yvonne, I think . . ."

"And his son, Nathan," Gary threw in from the sidelines.

Diana's perfect skin took on a blush with this information. What the hell was that about?

"And Martina Monteil," she added after the blush faded. "Nathan and Martina both worked for the Institute."

"So what happens at the Institute now that—" I began.

But the ringing of the telephone cut me off. I was just getting to the good part with Diana, so I let the answering machine deal with it.

"Pick up the phone, Kate," the machine ordered in the voice of my friend Barbara Chu.

Barbara Chu. I looked down at my watch. It was after eight o'clock. And Wayne and I were supposed to have met Barbara and her boyfriend, Felix Byrne, for dinner at seven. We'd thought that would give us plenty of time after the scuba-wedding ceremony. I felt a flutter of panic in my chest. Social obligations clearly weren't as vital as death, but my physiology didn't seem to be clear about the distinction.

Nor did Wayne's, obviously, as we both leapt from the swinging chair, leaving it careening haphazardly. I motioned him back down and trotted over to take the call myself.

"Jeez-Louise, what happened to you guys?" Barbara demanded when I picked up the phone as ordered. "We're still at Mushrooms. You guys never showed."

"You're a psychic, you tell me," I answered. I never could tell if Barbara really was psychic. But she did a damn good imitation of it if she wasn't. Sometimes it drove me crazy—because she knew things, but they weren't ever things that did you any good.

"You found another body?" she guessed after a moment.

I sighed. I should have known she'd know.

"Don't tell Felix," I added quickly. Felix was Barbara's boyfriend, but he was also a vampire of a reporter. I didn't want him over here with his fangs out.

"I won't," Barbara promised. Then she whispered, "But he'll find out anyway." She didn't have to be psychic to tell me that. Felix always found out. And then interrogated unmercifully.

"Do you think it was murder?" I asked Barbara on impulse, keeping my voice as low as I could manage, hoping they wouldn't hear me in the living room.

"Yes," Barbara answered calmly after less than a second's consideration. My body stiffened. I hadn't wanted her to say yes.

By the time I'd heard about all the great mushroom appetizers she and Felix had consumed and hung up the phone, I was ready. Ready to ask the obvious question that no one had bothered Diana with yet.

The living room was silent when I walked back in. Then C.C. wandered in behind me and leapt gracefully into Diana's lap. The little fink. A mini-bomb of forgotten jealousy exploded in my chest, flinging up the rubble of all my old feelings toward Diana. At least it wasn't Wayne cuddling up in Diana's lap, I told myself and asked the question.

"Do you think Sam was pushed?"

"I don't know!" Diana wailed, her voice ringing off the rafters. C.C.'s ears flattened against her skull.

Whoops. I'd forgotten to be sensitive. Wayne sent me a look out of the corner of his lowered eyelid as I sat back down next to him.

And Diana began to sob again.

"That's why we're here," Gary explained. "We know you two have investigated these things before. And Diana thought—"

"Oh, no," I said loudly and clearly. "Not this time, not ever again—"

Diana turned her weeping eyes on Wayne. "That's the awful part," she cried. "Not knowing. I can't . . . I just can't believe he fell. He was a feeling man, physically as well as emotionally. And he would never jump. But I can't imagine . . . I can't imagine . . ."

"Anyone killing him," I finished for her.

She turned back to me.

"You see, I have to know, Kate," she told me, bending forward, wrapping herself around C.C. "And you and Wayne—"

I shook my head, opening my mouth to explain why neither Wayne nor I would ever presume to investigate a murder again. Not after the last time, when I'd almost lost Wayne. Not after—

"I'll look into it," Wayne announced from my side.

My mouth fell open even wider, empty of words.

And that was that. As I sat and seethed, Wayne asked Diana more questions. And C.C. purred and rubbed up against Diana's face, licking away her tears. I told myself C.C. just liked the salty flavor. It wasn't true love like the times she had licked away my own tears. Gary was the only one other than me who seemed uncomfortable with the situation. I watched his handsome face as Diana and Wayne made plans, and it was troubled. Did Gary think that asking for help investigating a murder was going just the tiniest bit over the line in employee benefit demands?

Wayne didn't.

He made that clear once Gary and Diana had left.

"Gotta do it, Kate," he told me once the door had closed behind them. "Gary's my responsibility."

Then he took me sputtering back to the couch and grabbed the tweezers and rubbing alcohol to remove the splinters from my hand.

"But Diana isn't your responsibility!" I objected, withholding my splintered hand, a hand I was beginning to think I might withhold in marriage too. "And Sam Skyler certainly isn't your responsibility—"

"No, not Sam Skyler," he agreed, bitterness flavoring his low tone.

"What did you have against Sam Skyler, anyway?" I asked, anger replaced by curiosity suddenly. Because it wasn't just Wayne. Sam had engendered antipathy in too many people. I'd seen it in their faces.

"Sam Skyler abused his wife," Wayne answered quietly, looking away from my face.

" 'Skyler abused his wife,' " I repeated. "What is that supposed to—"

Wayne looked back into my eyes.

"He murdered her, Kate," he told me. "He murdered her."

₣OUR

"Sam Skyler murdered his wife?" I breathed. "But—"

The doorbell rang, bouncing me out of my skin before I could get any farther. Diana and Gary again?

I yanked open the door. But it wasn't Gary and Diana on our doorstep. It was Yvonne O'Reilley, still dressed in her cherry-red silk tunic and pants. And still smiling. Somehow, that smile seemed almost as bad as Diana's sobs. It certainly didn't hurt the ears as much, though.

"Just dropped by to make sure everything was copacetic," she told us, her voice Tallulah Bankhead low. For her, this might have indicated seriousness, but I wasn't sure. She was still smiling. She ran a hand through her crinkly blond hair, snagging a pink barrette. "Really, really cosmic events today."

Cosmic, indeed.

"We're fine," I said, wishing her away.

It was Wayne who invited her in. Personally, I wanted to make Yvonne disappear so I could get Wayne into a hammerlock and interrogate him about Sam Skyler's wife. His murdered wife? I still wasn't sure I'd heard Wayne right. Or if he had meant the word "murder" literally.

Yvonne was sitting across from us in the other swinging

chair before I really tuned in to what she was saying. And
C.C. was long gone. She hated those swings. Not good for
lap-sitting at all.

". . . knew Sam through the seminar circuit," Yvonne said,
her voice still low. She pushed back with her feet and got her
chair swaying. Faster and faster. I knew the woman was close
to fifty, but she could have been eleven at that moment, swinging back and forth. "Sam Skyler, the man was moving at warp
speed." I winced, imagining his descent down the rocks. "His
Institute was cosmically charged. You know all that grief stuff
about his dead wife really worked. He really had it scanned."

Dead wife? Did everyone but me know about this dead
wife? I opened my mouth, but not fast enough.

"Like my Wedding Ritual seminars," she went on. "I've
been married three times so I really know what works. You
gotta have a real sense of wonder in the ceremony. Intimate,
sumptuous wonder." Her eyes moved up to the ceiling. "David was really wonderful about setting up the scuba wedding—"

"David?" I asked.

"Oh." She giggled. "I mean Park Ranger Yasuda. We
worked together on creating the event. He's very concerned
about Sam Skyler's death." Her voice went low again, but
this time it sounded more sexy than serious. Could Yvonne
O'Reilley have a crush on Park Ranger Yasuda? "Very, very
concerned. He takes his responsibilities super seriously."

"Does he think Skyler was murdered?" I asked.

Yvonne's gaze dropped from the ceiling to stare in our direction.

"Murdered?" she repeated, her voice up nearly an octave.

"Pushed," I amplified.

Her eyes got wider.

"Wow," she murmured. "I mean, I thought maybe it was,
like, really bad karma about his wife and everything, but

pushed?'' Her eyes went back to the ceiling. ''What a concept. I can almost see it, though. Someone with that kind of charisma, you know, they just throw out all this energy and sometimes it comes blasting back.''

''But who?'' Wayne put in quietly.

''Wow,'' Yvonne said, louder this time. ''Maybe there's, like, an illegitimate kid. Men like that—'' She interrupted herself. ''Or some kind of scam. Or something from his past life. Or an avenger. Or maybe something not even human. A force that pushed him. What goes around, comes around.''

My head was reeling. This woman had a wilder imagination than my friend Barbara, and that was saying a lot. I was still trying to work out what she meant by the first theory about the illegitimate kid, as she went on.

''Or the wind, you know,'' she whispered. ''Very powerful. Maybe it's a spirit.''

I shivered in spite of myself. The wind had been wild out there. And Sam had been leaning his huge upper body over the railing—

''Who'd Sam know in your class?'' Wayne asked and the picture disappeared. But not the idea. A nonhuman force sounded appealing about now, no matter how farfetched. You didn't have to investigate nonhuman forces.

''Ona's experienced Sam's whole seminar,'' Yvonne answered, landing back on earth. ''But Perry wouldn't. Didn't like the puppet stuff. Too much like religious idols or something, he said. Those poor guys, Ona and Perry. They have a set of kids each. He's got girls and she's got boys and the kids hate each other. We're trying to get the kids involved some way in the Wedding Ritual Class, so they'll feel connected to the process, you know. But it isn't easy. Well, you saw.''

I nodded. The kids had attended one of the meetings and

spent it in separate corners glaring at each other. And that was before they'd started the spitting part.

"I'm on the City Planning Commission in Golden Valley," Yvonne added. "And Perry's on the City Council. And Golden Valley's where Sam's Institute is, but I don't know if that could mean anything. And then there's Diana and her mother. And Nathan and his girlfriend, Martina."

Yvonne shook her head suddenly as if to clear it. Her face curved back into an easy smile as she stood up from the swinging chair.

"But everything's fine," she assured us. "More than fine. Wondrous."

She moved toward the door. Wayne and I jumped up hastily, following her.

She gave us both big hugs before she trotted down the front stairs, shouting over her shoulder.

"Can't say the same for everyone in the group, but Emma and Campbell really do love each other. The Universe will provide."

Then she twirled all the way around to face us, raising her hand in goodbye.

"See you tomorrow at class!" she sang out.

An instant later, she'd jumped into her Saab and was gone.

I strong-armed Wayne back into the house the minute her car lights disappeared.

"Well?" I demanded.

"Well, what?" he muttered, looking at his feet.

"Well, what!" I shouted, grabbing his arm even harder, and abruptly remembering the splinters in my hand. "Did Sam Skyler really kill his wife?"

"Think so," he mumbled. Now I knew he was upset. Full sentences were always the first to go when he was upset. "Might be wrong, though. Shouldn't really say."

"Just tell me, all right?" I said with false calm, resisting the urge to shake him. It's not easy to shake a man as tall as Wayne, anyway. Especially a man with a black belt in karate. No matter how many years I've practiced tai chi.

But I didn't have to shake him. He told me his story, Sam's story, however reluctantly. Sitting on the couch, removing splinters from my hand as he talked.

"I was doing an internship with the Public Defenders Office when Sam Skyler went on trial," he began.

"Ouch," I bleated as a splinter came out.

"Sorry."

"No, go on," I told him as he wiped the spot with stinging alcohol. "Sam Skyler was on trial for murdering his wife?"

"Yeah." He pulled another splinter. I restrained myself from further bleating. "About ten years ago. Sally Skyler, her name was. She fell from the balcony of their house onto the rocks overlooking the ocean in Eldora."

"And Sam fell onto the rocks from a bluff in Quiero," I murmured. Avenging spirits floated through my mind, prickling the hair on the back of my neck with their flight. This was getting too spooky.

"Everyone in the legal community thought the man did it, but people were placing bets that he'd get off." The third splinter came out. Painfully. "Skyler married Sally not long after her first husband died. Her first, very rich husband. Then she was a very rich widow. And Sam became a very rich widower."

"But it still could have been an accident," I argued. "Rich wives can fall by accident, can't they? Why were people so sure he did it?"

"There was a witness, but the defense discredited him, got him to say he wasn't absolutely certain."

"Ah," I murmured. A witness. Then I noticed Wayne was looking down at his feet again. And he'd stopped torturing my hand. He was holding something back. I could tell.

"And?" I prodded.

Wayne sighed and squirmed in place awhile, his eyebrows low on the horizon of his eyeballs.

"Tell me," I ordered, my voice deep with threat. Threat of what I'm not really sure. But it seemed to work.

Wayne turned to me, eyebrows rising. He sighed again.

"You have to promise to keep this part in confidence," he said, his voice deepening, too.

"But what if it has a bearing on Sam Skyler's death?" I asked. I don't make promises lightly. Especially not to Wayne.

His brows dropped again.

"All right, all right," I gave in. "This part in confidence. But the rest is public knowledge."

"Shouldn't even know this myself," Wayne started off, grabbing my hand again. "Had a friend from law school, Joey—" He cut himself off and started over again. "Had a friend from law school who was interning in a prominent defense firm at the same time I was at the P.D.'s Office. He called me one day and we got together for lunch. At his house. He said he had to talk to someone and made me promise never to say anything to anyone."

Wayne turned to me again, glaring. I nodded my understanding.

"He was an ethical guy, more ethical than most, and he was bugged. He'd been in the room when Skyler's attorneys— Skyler had a whole team—were talking with him. For some reason, one of them asked the question you're never supposed to ask: 'Did you do it?' And Skyler answered, 'Does it matter? By the time I'm through with the jury, no one will believe I did it.' Not an actual admission, but still. And my friend was supposed to work on the team defending this man. This man he was sure had murdered his wife."

"So what'd your friend do?" I asked, now lost in his ethical dilemma myself.

"He got himself transferred to another case. But he never forgot the remark. Or Sam Skyler."

And with that, Wayne pulled the last splinter from my hand. That hurt. And it brought me back to the case in point. Even as Wayne bent down to kiss my palm before dabbing on the last of the alcohol.

"But Sam Skyler got off," I prompted.

"You've seen him, Kate," Wayne growled. "He could charm anyone. Joey said he actually used hypnosis techniques when he got on the stand. By the time Skyler finished with the jury, they thought he was a grief-stricken widower, oppressed by an insensitive legal system, who deserved a medal for what he'd been through. Certainly not a man who had pushed his wife off the balcony."

"So that's why you kept glaring at him," I murmured finally.

"Did I?" Wayne asked, brows rising. "Didn't think it was that obvious. But the man gets to me—got to me. Seven months after the trial, his book *Grief into Growth* was published. It was an instant bestseller. He must have been writing it all through the trial. And then he started his seminars based on the book's success." He paused. "Guess maybe I did glare. And Gary. Gary was worried sick about Diana. This man who may have murdered his wife was going to marry his sister—"

"Did you tell Gary all this?" I asked.

Wayne shook his head. "Couldn't decide what to tell him. Skyler had a fair trial. In fact, maybe he didn't do it. Just because my friend thought so, doesn't mean it was true. And Skyler did seem to have real affection for Diana." Wayne stood up from the couch. "It's been driving me nuts. Whether to tell Gary what I knew. He already hated Skyler. And he'd already made up his mind that Skyler killed his wife. Of course Diana didn't believe it for a second."

Wayne threw out his arms in frustration, then dropped them again slowly.

"And now the man's dead," he ended quietly.

"And you still feel you owe Gary," I said just as quietly.

I wanted to scream at him to leave it alone. Sam Skyler was dead. Let the police take care of it. But I knew he never would. I probably wouldn't either in his position.

"Oh, sweetie," I sighed.

Then I just stood up and put my arms around him. And we held each other for a long, long time.

Sunday morning in bed, we were still holding onto each other. But I was having my doubts about Wayne's investigating.

If Gary Atherton really believed his sister's fiancé had killed his wife, then why did he even care who'd killed Sam Skyler? If Sam Skyler had even been killed. Or killed his wife. The words he'd uttered to his attorneys were subject to more than one interpretation. And Wayne hadn't even heard them himself, for that matter. Sam Skyler might have fallen by accident, just as his wife might have fallen by accident. Despite my friend Barbara's psychic opinion. In fact, it was lucky Gary hadn't been on the scene. Assuming Sam *had* been murdered, Gary would be prime suspect material if he'd been there.

I moved my head higher onto Wayne's warm shoulder, snuggling in. It wasn't Gary who wanted to know who killed Sam Skyler. It was Diana. And as far as I was concerned, employee benefits didn't extend to sisters, especially gorgeous, tantric yoga instructor sisters.

"You know," I suggested softly, "I'm not so sure Gary really wants you to investigate this thing."

Wayne's warm body shifted abruptly. My head bounced lightly off his shoulder.

"I think it's really Diana—"

Wayne untangled himself from my arms and legs and sat up, glaring.

"Gary asked me to look into it, and I will," he told me unequivocally.

I rolled over and turned my back on the man I was supposed to marry, the hint of tears pressing against my eyes. This hadn't been the way I'd planned to start the day. But love-making wasn't looking like a very good possibility. Unless I gave in, told him he was right. But damn it, he wasn't right. Maybe he'd told Gary he'd investigate, but Diana was behind the idea. Lovely, manipulative Diana.

By the time Wayne and I were in Wayne's Jaguar on the way to Yvonne's place in Golden Valley, we had exchanged all of ten words. Ten short words. "Yes." "No." "Oatmeal?" "Ready?" That kind of thing. In the perfect mood for the next stage of our Wedding Ritual class. Wondrously, sumptuously sullen.

Even at that, riding up Yvonne's driveway managed to make me smile. Yvonne O'Reilley was an heiress. And oddly enough, a good businesswoman. Besides her wedding seminar business, she owned a company that wholesaled frozen vegetarian meals, and was part-owner of a computer astrology venture that was like going gangbusters. And those were just the businesses I'd heard about. She got the ideas, then delegated the parts that weren't fun. And made money.

If only my gag-gift business would work that way. But of course, it didn't. If anyone was doing the fun parts, it was probably my warehousewomen. And they always got paid, even during the lean times, unlike myself. I closed my eyes for a moment, thinking of all the Jest Gifts paperwork waiting on my desk while I was gallivanting around at a wedding seminar that felt pretty useless so far. Not to mention dangerous.

But when I opened my eyes again, I remembered why I'd

smiled. It was the sight of Yvonne's cow rubbing up against a six-foot wooden statue of some goddess or other that stood on the other side of the chainlink fence. The goddess looked Hindu. The cow looked ecstatic.

Yvonne's house was big and redwood and well-baubled. Chimes hung everywhere, singing their discordant notes next to billowing windsocks. Live animals roamed the enclosed yard, alongside stone Buddhas and marble dolphins and wooden owls. Everything from quail and chickens to pot-bellied pigs and horses. And more. I even spotted a llama munching herbs around the corner of the house.

We opened the chainlink gate, drove in, and closed it behind us quickly. You never knew what might escape from Yvonne's yard, cosmically or otherwise.

The door was open when we got there. And the whole gang was in Yvonne's front room, mixed in among a collection of kitsch and Oriental gewgaws that could have filled Cost Plus Imports, prominent against the metallic madras wallpaper that only Yvonne O'Reilley could have found. Or lived with. Yvonne waved from where she sat on her rattan throne as we closed the tinkling door behind us.

At least all the couples seemed to be together. I wondered who Yvonne had meant the night before when she'd mentioned that she couldn't say that all the couples loved each other. Maybe Wayne and me, I thought with a sigh and looked around, nodding at those who'd acknowledged our entrance.

Ona and Perry shared a white wicker love seat loaded with velvet cushions. Emma and Campbell were seated on neon purple molded plastic. And Nathan and Martina were curled up on a pair of tiger-stripe pillows on the floor. But Tessa Johnson and Ray Zappa were standing.

The first thing I noticed after the initial shock of entering a room vibrating with every color of the rainbow was that Ray Zappa wasn't smiling his affable, good-ole-boy smile. He was glaring. Almost as well as Wayne could. I followed the direction of his glare. Ona Quimby.

"Everyone knows he was an s.o.b.," she was insisting. "So what's the big deal? He killed his former wife—"

A soft voice interrupted her.

"You're talking about my father," Nathan said. It was hard to see if there was any anger behind the glasses and the facial hair. But there was something there, a tremor in that mild voice.

Ona opened her mouth to object, but closed it again. For a moment her pretty, round baby face looked chastened, but I had a feeling the expression wouldn't last long. It didn't.

"Look, Nathan, no offense—" she began again.

The door chimes rang, cutting her off.

Yvonne made her way to the door and opened it, smiling all the way. Was the world wondrous as usual for her?

Diana, Gary, and Liz Atherton walked in, their familial resemblance accentuated by their identical grim expressions.

But even then, Yvonne's smile didn't fade.

It was a moment before Diana spoke, but her question was worth the wait.

"Which one of you killed Sam?" she asked.

FIVE

There was an infinitely long silence after Diana's question. At least it felt infinite, tempered only by the sounds of Yvonne's discordant wind chimes and the various mooings and cacklings and other animal noises from outside. But the humans inside didn't moo or cackle. They just stared silently at Diana and her assembled family, faces slack and as still as if someone had pressed the freeze-frame button on a VCR. Even Yvonne had stopped smiling, her eyes widened in an expression that might have been sympathy. Or maybe just shock. Or guilt? With Yvonne, it was impossible to tell.

And then Yvonne's smile was back. She ushered the Athertons into her front room, flinging out an arm that tinkled all the bells on her many bracelets.

"Come on in and take a seat," she invited cheerfully. "Share your ideas."

Diana, Gary, and Liz came in, but they didn't sit down. Or share their ideas, for that matter. Gary stood, arms clasped behind his back, staring up at the ceiling. Was he as embarrassed by this whole scene as I suspected? I glanced over at Wayne, hoping he would notice Gary's discomfort. (Not to mention noticing that I was right concerning Gary's real feelings about investigating Sam Skyler's murder.) But Wayne's low-browed expression didn't give any more away than Yvonne's open-eyed one had. Liz Atherton's gaze was directed forward, but she didn't seem to see the people in front of her. Her eyes were unfocused as she rubbed her temple absently. Only Diana was really looking, peering into each of the seminar member' faces as if she could read her answer there.

"Did one of you kill Sam?" she asked, her words a little gentler this time, in content and in tone. So gentle, in fact, they were almost a plea.

And then it was as if the VCR button was pressed again, releasing the freeze-frame control. Slack mouths closed. Postures shifted. Ona was the first to speak.

"Honey," she said with a softness I hadn't heard before in her voice. "You know no one's going to answer that question. Especially since Sam Skyler was probably a murderer himself—"

"Sam Skyler had his trial and was found not guilty," Ray Zappa interrupted, glaring once again in Ona's direction.

You could almost see Ona's fur stand up. Once more she reminded me of a Persian cat, pink and blond and round. With claws.

Ray turned to Diana. "Listen, Ms. Atherton, the Quiero Police Department will investigate. No matter what their opinion of Sam Skyler. They are investigating. In fact, right now—"

"The Quiero Police Department!" Ona objected. She threw a hand in the air. "How good is the Quiero Police Department going to be? Has anyone ever been murdered in Quiero before? Besides sea gulls? Listen, I'll be blunt, Diana. I know that you'll miss Sam. I know that you cared for him. But he wasn't a good man. He was a cruel and abusive man—"

"My father was not cruel," Nathan Skyler cut in, gentleness absent from his tone for once. He got up from where he'd been sitting on the tiger-stripe pillow and shuffled his way to

Diana's side, his large shoulders stooped as usual. "And he was not abusive," he finished up, though the gentleness was creeping back into his voice. Maybe the habit was too ingrained to control.

"Oh, Nathan," Ona sighed. She shook her head. "He was your father, so of course you feel you have to defend him. But you don't have to. It's useless. He was put on trial for killing his first wife. And all the cops knew he'd abused her, too. But that doesn't reflect on you. You're a good guy. You know I don't bullshit, and I can tell you you're nothing like your father. He just wasn't a good man. Look what he did to his first wife."

"Sally Skyler wasn't Dad's first wife," Nathan corrected her mildly. I looked into his face for signs of anger, but again the façade of facial hair and glasses was impenetrable. How he kept from screaming at Ona was beyond me. Maybe the Skyler Institute did teach some skills after all. "My mother was his first wife."

"It doesn't matter which wife," Ona plowed on, undeterred. I felt like pointing out it might matter to Nathan which woman had been killed, seeing as one was his mother, but I clearly didn't stand a chance of getting a word in. Ona was talking faster and faster, shaking her finger at Nathan now like a schoolteacher who's disappointed in her student. "I had a boyfriend who was working as a bailiff then, and even he knew Skyler killed his wife. Everyone in the legal community did. And that he abused her—"

"Dad didn't really abuse her," Nathan finally broke in, his tone soft but insistent. "Not in the classic sense. He only fought back. They had a very hard time finding a common ground, those two. And she would lash out physically. And sometimes he'd hit her back. So the doctors had two reports on her, a black eye and a split lip. Two." He stuck up two fingers to underscore his point. "But you should have seen

Dad. He was completely beaten up. He was just too embarrassed to tell the doctor who did it. He went to the hospital
both those times, claiming he'd been mugged.''

He turned and looked at Diana. ''He wasn't a bad man.
Maybe not perfect, but not bad.''

Liz turned her head away from Diana and Nathan, her skin
reddening as her daughter nodded energetically. I remembered
that Liz had disliked Sam too. I wondered if Nathan's words
had changed her mind at all.

''At least he doesn't sound as bad as Dad,'' Gary Atherton
threw in unexpectedly.

Liz swiveled around and looked at her son thoughtfully. I'd
never considered Gary and Diana's father. Somewhere, a
memory surfaced of his dying young. That's right, I remembered. Tessa Johnson had buried him. Liz had said so at the
scuba wedding. I snuck a look at Tessa's immobile mocha-
brown features. Her expression was extremely somber as she
watched Nathan talking. But was that unusually somber or just
normally somber for a mortician?

''And my father really did feel grief when Sally died,'' Nathan went on in a near whisper. ''Natural, deep grief. His
book, *Grief into Growth*, came from his heart. From deep in
his heart. He had to see a grief counselor. He was a wreck.
But he found a way to channel that grief—''

''And a way to make a lot of money with his seminars,''
Ona cut in, still not satisfied. Maybe Persian cat was the wrong
description, I decided. Bulldog was more like it. She wasn't
about to stop shaking Sam Skyler's dead image by the neck
any time soon, that was for sure.

''And he hurt some people with those seminars,'' Perry
Kane added from Ona's side. His dark, soulful East Indian
eyes looked into Nathan's spectacled ones. ''He should have
been compassionate, encouraging Ona as a proud person of

size. But instead he tore her down, tried to make her change her essential nature.''

He put his arm around Ona's soft shoulders. Ona leaned into him. Was the size issue really the hurt that had made her so angry? If so, I'd have bet she would never admit it. Or maybe she would. By her own appraisal, she was no bull-shitter.

''Calling me fat was one thing,'' Ona said. ''And it hurt like hell after all the work I'd done on accepting my size. But that isn't the point here. The man was a murderer. Insensitivity is one thing, but murder is another.''

Nathan just shook his shaggy head and sighed. But Martina Monteil didn't give up that easily. She stood up to her full, almost six-foot height, and looked down at Ona, plucked eyebrows raised, model's face grim.

''If you repeat that lie one more time, I assure you we will sue you for slander,'' she said in a voice of authority that made me believe her without a doubt.

''But—'' Ona began.

''Sam Skyler was a brilliantly empowered man who made a monumental difference in the world. His book and the Institute have changed more people's lives than you can count. And we will find a way to stop you if you continue to spread these ugly lies about this great man.''

''But Sam's dead,'' Ona said, her brows furrowed, probably trying to remember what she knew about slander. Fast. Could dead people be slandered?

''The Institute isn't dead,'' Martina replied.

But could the Institute sue for slander?

I would have asked, but I was too uneasy watching the two women as they scowled at each other. Or maybe ''scowled'' wasn't a strong enough word. There are scowls and there are scowls. These scowls made my scalp prickle, the way it does at the movies when I know there's a man in a ski mask standing behind the door with a hatchet. I turned my head away, remembering why I avoided those kinds of movies.

"Well, I don't know about the rest of you, but I'm famished," Yvonne cut in brightly. "And I have heaps and heaps of yummy food in the kitchen—"

But the sound of Diana's sniffles interrupted her attempt at good cheer.

"I just wanna know what happened to Sam," Diana whimpered in between escalating sobs. Gary, Liz, and Nathan all moved closer protectively, corralling her in their efforts. Liz put an arm around her daughter's shoulders.

"The man just fell," Emma Jett declared brusquely, though there was a hint of kindness beneath the gruffness. She thrust her sharp chin forward, exposing the side of her face that had been draped in red hair. Brass glinted in her ears and nostrils. "Give yourself a break. Don't worry about all this murder crap. Experience it and get over it. Get on with the next part of your life. Don't you think that's what Sam would have wanted?" Those words sounded pretty wise compared to what had been said so far. And from the youngest member of the group. Campbell thought so too, apparently.

"It'll take time, but you'll get over it," he assured Diana, the soothing, musical rhythm of his voice always surprising coming from such a visually unprepossessing man. He stroked his ginger beard lightly. "The thing is not to obsess. Time really does heal." Did he speak from experience? Or from something he'd read? *Reader's Digest*?

"The police will clear it up," Ray Zappa threw in one more time. His face was grim. But not so grim as Tessa's next to him. "Let them take care of it."

Diana shook her teary face. "I have to know," she insisted through her sobs. She stood straighter and cleared her throat. "Please, if anyone knows anything, anything at all. Or saw something. Or whatever. Call me."

"Of course," Yvonne said. Of course? What if you were the murderer?

"And," Diana added, "Wayne and Kate will be helping me too, so please tell them what you know when they ask." A sob filled her voice. "Please," she finished and began crying full force once more.

I was still trying to think of a way to erase Diana's last words from everyone's minds, especially my own, when she turned abruptly and headed toward the door, her back as straight as the columns in the ledgers I was avoiding working on today. Gary and Liz followed her just as abruptly. Even Nathan shambled behind the group, only seeming to remember he wasn't one of the Atherton family when he got to the door. Then he stopped, sighed and closed the door behind them, before turning back to face the rest of us.

"Lunch, everyone?" Yvonne suggested.

No one clapped their hands in appreciation, but at least no one objected. Or started arguing before Yvonne brought out the platters of vegan delicacies. The group was uncharacteristically silent as they dished up the goodies.

As a vegetarian, I probably appreciated the meal even more than most of the others. But even the nonvegetarians were impressed with the garlicky steamed artichokes, the colorful grilled Indonesian vegetables spread out on a star-shaped cut glass platter, the iridescent bowls of Mandarin tofu noodle salad, and the varied homemade breads and spreads that our seminar leader had produced. No wonder her food company was doing so well.

"The perfect wedding must have all the elements of the perfect meal," Yvonne began as we finished off the cranberry linzer tart that had been the grand finale. (Nondairy "ice cream" optional.) Even Ona and Martina were smiling as they dug into the dessert. "Sumptuous, balanced, and simple, but magically extravagant—"

"With or without tofu?" Ray Zappa asked, his good humor apparently restored.

"With tofu, of course," Yvonne replied, her laughter like the tinkle of her high-pitched chimes. "And most of all, with love."

I looked into Wayne's face then and saw a little of that love there in his vulnerable eyes. He reached over and put his hand on mine as I licked the last of the cranberry tart from my lips. Maybe it would work, I told myself. But only if our wedding could be anywhere as good as this food.

"What are your common visions?" Yvonne demanded, standing and spreading her arms, jingling the bells on her bracelets.

Immediately my mind produced a picture of Wayne and me dressed as artichokes, Wayne slipping the ring onto my garlicky outstretched leaf. And then Yvonne was talking again.

"What gets you both cosmically charged?" she caroled. "What is it that brought you together?"

I wished she hadn't asked the last question. Because it was murder that had brought Wayne and me together. Murder, pure and simple, but not magically extravagant. And as the seminar members watched videos of a nudist wedding (with artfully placed flowers), a renaissance horseback wedding (gorgeous but uncomfortable-looking), a clown wedding (even more uncomfortable with all the guests in clown suits, too), and an aikido wedding (the bride and groom sparring to the mat then rising and bowing), all I could think of was Sam Skyler. And his cosmically charged body splayed on the rocks below.

"Look, everything's all right," I was saying into the phone in my dining room-cum office the next Monday morning. "Just send the psychotherapist Uh-huh scarves and Uh-huh ties in separate boxes." I was talking to my warehousewoman, whose name used to be Judy but who didn't want to be Judy anymore. Not that she was sure what her new name should be. Just that Judy wasn't the "real her." I was tempted to call her "hey you" for the time being but resisted.

Jest Gifts didn't work as smoothly as Yvonne's businesses seemed to. Maybe being an heiress to start with helped. But I spent most of my time doing paperwork and clearing up business and employee crises when all I really wanted to do was design gag-gifts. My gaze drifted over to the papers where I'd begun sketching the plans for a line of acupuncturist earrings, all in needles. Sterile needles, of course. I wasn't sure how well they'd sell. After all, how many female acupuncturists are there in the United States? A lot if you judged by Mill Valley, certainly. But that was Mill Valley. Still, the chiropractor's cup with the twisted spine for the handle was one of my top sellers, so maybe . . .

"Damn, how many of them are broken?" I asked, Judy having retrieved my roving attention with the announcement of yet another crisis.

She was fully enmeshed in the details of the bad news when I noticed Wayne sidling his way toward the front door. It was too early for him to go into the restaurant. Way too early. In fact, he didn't even usually visit La Fête à L'Oiel on Mondays at all.

I put my hand over the receiver and asked him where he was going.

"To interview Campbell Barnhill," he muttered and then made his break for the door.

"Not without me, you're not," I objected.

But by the time I got off the phone with Judy, or whoever she was today, his Jaguar was already gone from the driveway.

Still, I knew where Wayne was going. I jumped in my Toyota and raced out after him, popping gravel on the way. Campbell Barnhill managed a family-owned market not very far away in Jacinta Hills. I was about halfway there when I caught up with Wayne. He pulled his Jaguar over to the side of the road. I pulled over after him.

I got out of my Toyota like a traffic cop about to issue a ticket.

"Why were you going to see Campbell without me?" I demanded once Wayne reluctantly rolled down his window. I didn't ask for his driver's license.

"My problem, not yours," he mumbled.

"No," I shot back. "We stick together on this one. It's too dangerous otherwise. Don't you remember—"

"Yes, I do remember," he interrupted. Then his tone softened. "But Kate, you don't even think I should be looking into this."

"I don't care," I told him, crossing my arms. "If you're going to visit a suspect, I am too."

Ten minutes later, we were at the Jacinta Hills Market in our separate cars.

The store that Campbell managed was not a supermarket. It had been owned and operated by the same family for three generations and were still going strong in the nineties. The bright lighting, friendly clerks, organic produce, upscale wines, homemade pasta and sauces, and soft classical music in the background didn't hurt any.

Wayne and I walked in together and asked a woman stocking shelves if Campbell Barnhill was in.

She pointed at one of the front registers where Campbell was carefully packing up a silver-haired woman's meager assortment of groceries. Somehow we had missed him coming in. What was it about his round face under the neatly trimmed ginger beard and mustache that made him invisible?

"Do you need any help getting these to your car, Mrs. Singleton?" he asked in his musical voice. Now, the voice I would have recognized anywhere.

"Not a bit, you sweet man," the silver-haired woman replied, lifting the bag easily and exiting with a wink.

A hint of pink crept into Campbell's cheeks.

"Campbell's such a cutie," the woman stocking shelves whispered to us. It appeared Campbell had his admirers. She stood up, pulling off her work gloves. "Did you want to speak with him privately?"

We both nodded, and she led us to the register, deftly slipping in to take over for Campbell as she rang up a bottle of wine for a well-built man clad in a sleeveless T-shirt and biker shorts.

"Thanks, Candy," Campbell said. "I'll be upstairs if you need anything."

"Anytime," Candy answered and turned to her next customer. Yes, definitely an admirer. I wondered if Emma knew.

Campbell led us through a set of swinging doors, past boxes and boxes of fresh produce, up a rickety set of stairs to a totally different environment. There was no classical music playing up here in the "employee lounge." The walls were bare wood and the chairs were landlord-green vinyl, some repaired with black electrical tape. But there was a table in the center with a potted palm. And a couple of empty yogurt containers. And used paper plates.

"Did you want to talk to me about Sam Skyler?" Campbell asked, his harmonious voice easy as he picked up the yogurt containers and threw them in the wastebasket. But I couldn't see his face as he spoke.

"Yes, Diana asked me to," Wayne answered. No more. No less.

"I thought you might," Campbell admitted, taking care of the paper plates next, then turning to us. "I know I look like the classic serial killer. The guy no one really notices and all his neighbors say he was a nice-enough young man."

Actually, he was right, I thought. What would Jeffrey Dahmer have looked like with a neatly trimmed beard and mustache? And a little more weight . . .

I shook the thought out of my head as Campbell continued to clean up and talk at the same time. Anyway, Campbell's hazel eyes were friendly, not haunted.

"I should've never yelled at Skyler," he told us, wiping off the table with a damp cloth. "And shaking my fist. Ye gods, what a stupid thing to do."

Finally he settled down into a taped chair and began tapping his foot rhythmically.

"Then why did you?" I asked, keeping my voice stern with half a heart. Half a heart because Campbell Barnhill seemed too damn sweet to be dangerous.

"Well, Emma—" He paused and his cheeks pinkened again. "Skyler was always flirting with her. And Emma . . ." He leaned forward carefully. "Emma is actually pretty naive for all her . . . well . . . her striking of poses. She's very creative. And very hardworking. A real Renaissance woman. Performance art. Her rock band, Angie and the Angst. Her Connie the Condom series."

Connie the Condom?

"But she's been really abused by men who don't understand her sensitivity. Oh, she smokes those unfiltered cigarettes and drinks coffee by the gallon, but beneath it all, she's shy and vulnerable. And watching a man like Sam Skyler preying on that vulnerability . . ."

"Did you think he was going to seduce her?" I asked curiously.

"I thought so, at the time," Campbell answered slowly, his eyes drifting up as he considered it. "But I jump to conclusions too fast. And shake my fist too fast, too. I've even shaken it here in the store. I just don't stop to think sometimes. Because if I had, I'd have known that Emma would have just laughed him off if he'd tried. She has her own code of honor."

He sighed deeply. "But there I was, shaking my fist. And now he's dead."

"Irrespective of Emma," Wayne asked. "what did you think of Skyler?"

"I thought he was an arrogant, pompous bull of a man," he declared. "Ona had told me a little about how he treated her and—"

"You knew Ona before the wedding seminar?" I interrupted, surprised.

"Oh, she's shopped here for years," Campbell assured me.

But was shopping at someone's store enough to constitute a friendship? Maybe with a man as seemingly open as Campbell. I began to understand a little more of what Emma saw in him for all her insistence on wild experience and sensation. He seemed to be a sincerely kind man, and an attractive one in his own old-fashioned way. And he *was* old-fashioned for someone who couldn't be very far into his thirties. On the other hand, he hadn't been exhibiting much old-fashioned kindness when he'd shaken his fist at Sam Skyler. I remembered his bellowing voice. And the expression on his face.

"Liz Atherton shops at Jacinta's too," Campbell added helpfully. It was hard to believe he was the same man who had been so angry at Sam Skyler. "And sometimes Diana."

There was a short silence, as I tried to think of another relevant question for Campell.

"Do you think Sam Skyler was pushed?" Wayne asked finally. Well, that was relevant.

Campbell shrugged. "The police do, obviously. They've already been here to see me. As well as some of the local media."

My stomach churned. Police? Media?

Campbell chuckled uncomfortably. "I've really got to stop shaking my fist. Once, someone hit me in the face for it. I thought that was bad enough. But this is the first time I've been accused of murder for the habit.''

"Manager to checkstand two," came a ghostly voice from a grille set into the wall. It sounded like Candy. "Manager to checkstand two."

"Well, duty calls," Campbell announced before standing to shake our hands. Then he led us back down the stairs, through the swinging doors, back into the upscale brightness of the Jacinta Hills Market.

Wayne and I didn't talk much before we got into our separate cars. Maybe we were both too immersed in our own impressions of Campbell Barnhill. But we still managed to arrive home at the same time, ready to pull our cars into the driveway in tandem.

But there was no room in our driveway for our cars. Or on the street for that matter.

Our house was ringed with cars and people and trucks. My brain tried to take in the meaning. A fire? My heart jumped. But these weren't fire trucks. A surprise party? But it wasn't my birthday or Wayne's.

And then I took a closer look at one of the trucks, a big white one, bristling with equipment. It even had what looked like a small satellite dish on the back. The truck said Channel 7 News on the side. My insides curdled.

And then I noticed the people. A couple of them carried hand-held cameras. A few held microphones. And some clasped notebooks.

And finally, as Wayne and I got out of our cars, the people noticed us.

"There she is!" someone shouted.

And I realized they meant me.

Six

My body went rigid. For a moment I felt like a deer caught in the headlights of an onrushing car. Because these "people" weren't people after all. They were reporters.

I should have realized sooner. Sam Skyler was a famous man. And an infamous one to boot. His death had to make great media fodder. I tried to take a deep breath, but I couldn't get past the constriction of my immobilized ribs.

"So how does it feel—" a blond woman in jeans began, launching a small hand-held tape recorder toward my head.

But she was deftly shouldered aside by a more elegantly attired woman with a perfect brown pageboy swinging gently over her ears and a slim microphone in her hand moving much less gently toward my gaping mouth. And behind her, yet another woman, this one in khakis with a steady-cam slung over her shoulder, its lens aimed at my face. I closed my mouth, trying to neutralize what I was sure had to be a look of complete panic contorting the muscles of my face.

"In fact, I'm speaking to Kate Jasper right now," the elegant woman declared, her delivery quick and crisp. "The woman who discovered Sam Skyler's body on the rocks only two days ago. Actually, Kate Jasper has found quite a few dead bodies over the last few years here in mellow Marin. So,

Ms. Jasper, just how do you explain all these grisly discoveries?''

"I . . . I don't—'' I blurted out before I felt the pressure of Wayne's elbow in my ribs.

I shut my mouth again. And heard the kaclunk and whir of a picture being taken. My picture? Wayne's picture? Were we the media event? Not Sam Skyler?

"House,'' Wayne growled into my ear and stepped in front of me, straight-arming the elegant woman with the microphone.

It took me a moment to respond, and by then a big muscular guy with another tape recorder was standing in front of me.

"Did you know Sam—'' he began, holding his arm out to the side, leaving his chest wide open. When he stepped close enough to me that I could smell a combination of smoke and mint on his breath, I shifted my weight back, letting him move even closer, then shifted forward again quickly, my hands on his chest. He stumbled to the rear, a grimace of surprise on his face. I sent a little psychic message of thanks to my tai chi teacher of eight years.

Another woman came up on my side, trying to move herself into place where the big man had been. I turned my body from its center, letting my arm swing with the momentum, and swept her away. Actually, this was kind of fun, I decided, and took a good deep breath, unconstricted now. Push hands in action. Then I took a couple of quick unimpeded steps forward, catching up with Wayne, who was still straight-arming himself through the crowd. He was showing an awful lot of restraint for a man with a black belt in karate. But the crowds were still parting as he moved forward.

I was just beginning to feel in control again when I heard a voice from behind me.

"Do you think the police might have arrested the wrong

people before?" the voice asked loudly. "I mean, look at the body count and always this same woman finding them."

I willed myself not to look behind me and kept moving forward, but now I was beginning to shake with the urge to defend myself, verbally as well as physically. I pressed my lips together hard and kept moving.

"You mean, like, this Jasper woman hypnotizes them into confessing, but she's really the killer?" a new voice hypothesized.

What! *Keep moving your feet*, I told myself. *And don't move your mouth.*

"Yeah, Yeah! Like Bundy or Dahmer. A real serial killer. And the police just haven't figured it out."

"Yet," someone added helpfully.

"You think her boyfriend's in on it with her?"

I stopped in my tracks, and instantly a short man with a notebook and pencil wedged himself between me and Wayne's back. I used the same tai chi movement to dislodge him that I'd used on the bigger man, but it wasn't fun anymore. They couldn't believe Wayne had anything to do with the deaths, could they?

"Or a maybe she's just the Typhoid Mary of murder," I heard as we made the stairs. It was a catchy phrase. So catchy, I could picture it in newsprint. In very large type. Wonderful.

"Or maybe it's some karma thing. Like she attracts murder because of her past life. Or . . ."

By that time Wayne was at the front door with me right beside him. We turned to face the crowd as he unlocked the door behind him. A good trick, which I wondered if I could carry off. But this wasn't the time to think. It was the time to act. A few more pushes and we'd backed inside the house and slammed the door shut. We were safe.

Safe but not sound, not of mind. Scared. At least I was. Very scared.

Wayne put his arms around me and I could feel the trembling in him too.

"Did you hear what they were saying?" I whispered into his armpit finally.

He grunted in affirmation and held me tighter.

"Can they really believe . . ." I began.

"Don't think about it," he ordered brusquely.

Oh, sure.

I was opening my mouth to discuss the low probability of my ever forgetting what I had just heard outside, when I heard a new sound inside. The sound of the flap on the cat door opening. I turned, expecting to see my cat, but what I saw was a hand with a microphone.

That was enough. I made a decision to do something I never thought I would do. Not to stomp on the hand with the microphone and grind it into the floor, however tempting the image was. No, something even more radical. A phone call for help. From the one person I knew who might be able to get rid of these people. And their suspicions.

"Felix," I whispered as I pulled Wayne down the hall into the bedroom.

"Felix Byrne?" he squeaked, his voice almost as high as mine now, if not Minnie Mouse's. A look of horror twisted his features.

I put my finger over my lips and closed the bedroom door behind us.

"But Felix," he whispered hoarsely. "He's a human pit bull when he's on a story. Kate, he'll badger us and badger us. Sometimes I think he's not even human—"

"He can get rid of those people outside," I interrupted, hoping I was right. "He can put them on another track."

Wayne closed his eyes and took a deep breath.

"Maybe," he admitted finally and dropped onto the bed,

his head in his hands. I sat down next to him and put my hand on his thigh.

"Yes?" I asked, then heard the sounds of footsteps on the rear deck and a knock on the back door.

Wayne stood up abruptly. "I'll cook lunch," he muttered and headed out of the bedroom toward the kitchen.

I took that as a yes and made my way slowly to the bedroom phone to call Felix, wondering during the few short steps if the whole idea was a mistake. Because my best friend Barbara's sweetie or not, Felix as a reporter was everything Wayne had said he was. And worse. But not worse than that gang lying in wait outside. I punched Felix's number in quickly before I could change my mind.

Felix was ecstatic once I'd told him the story of the scuba wedding and Sam Skyler's body on the rocks.

"Far friggin' out," he purred. "Kate Jasper, my old compadre, finds another friggin' corpse. And this time, she decides to tell me about it."

"It wasn't just me!" I objected.

"But you were the first one to see him, pal. Right?" he shot back.

"Besides the murderer—" I began, then remembered why I'd called Felix in the first place.

"Felix, the house is surrounded by reporters," I told him, keeping my voice down. "And they're acting like I'm the murderer. How long do you think they'll stay out there?"

"As long as it friggin' takes," he answered, his voice low with something that sounded like pleasure. In fact, I could almost hear him drooling. He was enjoying this.

"An exclusive," he said softly.

"What?"

"An exclusive," he repeated more loudly. "You tell me everything, man, the whole poop. Me and nobody else, you get it? And I'll disappear the reporters for you, zippo presto, pronto. Cool?''

"I guess so," I answered slowly. "But Felix, they think it was me."

"They won't be so sure after a few other rumors get passed around," he assured me.

I didn't even get a chance to consider the ethics of that proposal before he was wheedling again. And wheedling some more. I gave in finally. An exclusive it was.

Then I hung up the phone and waited in the kitchen with all the blinds shut as Wayne cooked. Darkness at noon. And we listened to the mingled voices of the reporters hovering outside. High and low, loud and soft. But all intense. After a while, we heard some shouts and the sounds of a few cars being driven away. Then a few more departures a couple of minutes later. And a few more. Until all the voices had disappeared.

Half an hour later the doorbell rang. I peeked out the window. No reporters in sight—except for Felix Byrne. He was at the front door with a big grin twitching under his mustache. Felix is not an unattractive man, at least physically. Small and slender with a luxurious mustache and soulful eyes.

"How'd you get rid of them?" I asked, opening the door.

"I buzzed in a hot tip to three news rags and two TV stations," he declared in a radio announcer's voice. "Gave them the poop that a prominent state senator was up on Mount Tam to meet the aliens that he believed visited him seven years ago. Said I got it from his deep throat assistant who couldn't handle working for a senator anymore who thinks he's a secret UFO diplomat."

I couldn't help laughing.

"And they bought it?" I asked incredulously.

He nodded, shoving his way in through the doorway.

I instinctively moved to block him, then remembered that I was the one who'd asked him here.

"Then I switched phones and told a bunch of other media geeks that Campbell Barnhill had just confessed to the county sheriffs that he killed Sam Skyler . . ."

Damn. That wasn't fair.

"Then I switched phones again and told a whole different bunch of the boys and girls of the press that Yvonne O'Reilley was busy confessing her little heart out down at the Quiero cop shop—"

"Stop," I told him, putting up my hand. I didn't want to hear any more.

"Hey!" Felix objected, arms outstretched. "You wanted them off your friggin' back, right? And don't get your hemorrhoids in a twist—I spread the rumors around plenty. Now everyone's a suspect. With the truckload of bull puckey I threw out there, they'll need a shovel to get through it all. And they won't have time to be on your case. You know, you'd be deep in doo-doo without a pooper scooper—"

"I know, I know," I conceded. I even forced myself to thank him. I'd worry about the ethics later.

Then Felix raced me to the kitchen to eat the lunch that Wayne had prepared. Wayne cooks when he's nervous. That day, he'd made seitan-stuffed tomatoes, two kinds of cucumber salad, and three kinds of sandwiches on his homemade sunflower-millet bread. Avocado-tahini, marinated tofu, and pesto eggless "egg-salad." And there was leftover carob fudge torte for dessert.

Felix's eyes lit up when he saw the food. If Wayne could cook, Felix could eat.

"Speak," Felix ordered and dug in.

I spoke. I told Felix what I could remember. In bits and pieces. But I kept my own suspicions to myself. Especially of Diana. Wayne even threw in a word here and there so I could take a few bites in between questions. The pesto-eggless was delicious, even if the dining circumstances were less than desirable.

After Felix's third sandwich, I asked the question I'd been wanting to ask. And not wanting to ask.

"Are the police sure it was murder?"

He smiled widely.

"Wouldn't you like to know?" he asked and tilted his head coquettishly.

Wayne rose from the table.

"Hey, everything's cool, big guy," Felix backtracked. "Great food."

"Well?" I demanded.

"Yeah," Felix said, his voice low with lust. He leaned forward as Wayne sat back down. "Nine times out of ten they wouldn't have a clue, but this time . . ."

He paused for suspense.

Wayne stood up again.

Felix came back up to speed.

"See," he told us, "usually when some geek dives off a cliff like that you can't tell what the hell happened 'cause they're all bruised up. But there was this really weird thing, I mean really weird, you know."

He stopped to grab another sandwich.

"What?" I prompted as calmly as I could. My heart was pumping hard now.

"First of all, don't tell a friggin' soul, 'cause my source told me, but no one but the cops are supposed to know. She made me promise not to go public until she gives me the word."

"All right, I promise I won't tell anyone," I agreed impatiently as he bit into his fourth sandwich.

"Well," he mumbled through the avocado-tahini. "All the bruising from the rocks is cool, you know, regular stuff, but there were these really bizarre patches of bruising on the shoulder blades. Even that salami-brain Woolsey could tell they'd been made by a man-made object, not the friggin' rocks. And get this, they were in the shape of five-sided stars—''

"Like the bottoms of Yvonne's vases," I breathed.

"Yeah," he said, his eyes lighting up. "You saw them, right?"

"Great big tall brass vases with brass stars for bottoms," I confirmed.

"Well, they found the friggin' brass vases too, not far from the stiff."

My mind was trying to picture it now. Had the murderer pushed Sam Skyler over with those vases? Maybe grabbed them where they curved in at the top and then slammed his shoulders with the star-shaped bases? That would do it, the way Sam's top-heavy body was leaning. But why? Why not use your bare hands? Fear of fingerprints? Fear of hand prints? Goose bumps rose on my arms as if I were back there on that cold, windy bluff.

"The murderer blew it, man," Felix went on. "If the looney tunes had just pushed with his hands, the cops probably still wouldn't know it was murder, but with the imprints of the vases, it's as sure as dentists suck." He shook his head. "Friggin' vampires."

I had a feeling Felix had been to the dentist lately or not much of the last part made sense. Not that much of any of it made sense.

"And then there's these oily hand prints," he went on. "On the back of the poor geek's jacket—''

"Skyler's, you mean?" I asked. I was getting lost again.

"Yeah, good old guru Sam Skyler. Guru on the rocks. It was some kind of massage oil. They're having it chemically identified now. Technical whiz-bang, you know. Presto, pronto, and they come up with a brand name.''

''But that means two sets of imprints then,'' I reasoned slowly. ''The vases and the oily hand prints—''

''The cops don't have a clue, either,'' Felix interrupted cheerfully. ''Skyler left a will splitting his estate three ways. His tantric sweetie, Diana, gets a chunk. And his nerdy son, Nathan. And his mother, this hot old lady, you wouldn't believe her.''

''So, theoretically,'' Wayne put in, ''the police have motives for two of the people who were actually present.'' His frown told me he wished Diana wasn't one of them.

''Yeah,'' said Felix. Then he bent forward again. ''And I bet plenty of other people had motives too.''

I took my cue. Felix would know everything soon enough anyway. I told him about Campbell shaking his fist and Ona's dispute with Skyler and everything else I could come up with. And then we just sat there eating and talking theories, connections, and personalities until C.C. came in, yowling for food.

I was scooping out cat food when I suddenly stopped to ask myself how come Felix knew so much and hadn't bugged me before.

''Why weren't you out there with the rest of the media pack?'' I demanded.

He grinned so widely his face seemed to disappear behind his mustache.

''Now, what good would that have done?'' he asked rhetorically. ''You wouldn't have talked to me. You never talk to me, your old pal, your compadre. Leave me out in the friggin' fraggin' cold every single friggin' time. But now I have an exclusive.'' Then he leaned back in his seat and laughed.

Had we been had? I looked over at Wayne. His eyebrows

were descending fast. Had Felix sicced the media on us in the first place just so he would look like the lesser of two evils?

Is the Dalai Lama a Buddhist?

Wayne stood up and stepped around the table.

Felix stopped laughing and sat up straight in his chair.

"You're the one who sent the media here in the first place," Wayne accused, glaring down at Felix.

"Well . . ." I could see the war on Felix's face. Part of him wanted to tell us how cleverly he'd worked us. But the other part was afraid. I didn't blame him. I wouldn't want Wayne towering over me with that look on his battered face. I just wished I could pull off the same towering stance myself.

"You're leaving now," Wayne growled and hoisted Felix up by one arm much more gently than I would have. But very effectively. He guided Felix to the door, Felix objecting and wheedling the whole way, and then slammed it behind him.

We waited until we heard the final footsteps down the front stairs, and then Wayne turned to me. I flinched and waited for him to say "I told you so" about Felix. Not that I needed any more blame. I was already kicking myself. My gut had sprung a whole set of miniature flailing feet. But Wayne didn't say another word about Felix.

All he said was, "Time to talk to Ray Zappa."

The Quiero police had just stepped from Ray Zappa's doorway and were heading down the tanbark path when we got to Ray's condo in Sneath Hills. Chief Woolsey gave us a curt nod but said nothing as we passed and Wayne knocked on the door.

"Wondered if I could speak with you," Wayne asked when Ray opened up, his voice low and serious. Man to man. My skin prickled. Damn, I hated all this man-to-man stuff. It was like I wasn't even there. But I kept my mouth shut, because it seemed to be working.

Ray nodded and opened the door wider. Still, his reluctance was clearly evident in the stiffness of his shoulders and the frown on his long, handsome face.

His living room was surprisingly neat and orderly with a blinking computer on a desk next to a neat stack of papers and a couple of bookshelves filled mostly with true-crime books. Ray and Felix. Two of a kind. Ugh.

We sat down on a worn leather couch across from Ray, and Wayne started in.

"Sam Skyler—"

"Police business," Ray interrupted instantly. "I don't talk about police business. You gotta understand something here, buddy. I was a real wild kid. Then I joined the Marines. There's a code, you see. Same with the police. Anyway, the Skyler case isn't even in my jurisdiction."

"I understand," Wayne replied quietly. "But I'm concerned about Kate. How would you feel if the police suspected Tessa?" More man to man. Would it work?

Ray bared his teeth in a shadow of his usual good ole' boy smile when Wayne mentioned Tessa.

"Tessa's a great lady, isn't she?" he said. He pulled a pencil out of his shirt pocket protector and started chewing on it. Then he frowned again.

"I'm with the Sneath Police Department now. Desk job. Got less than a year till retirement. You understand?"

Wayne nodded, but I could see his mouth opening for one more try.

The doorbell rang before he could make it.

Ray answered the ring, opening the door about six inches. I couldn't see who was there, but I could hear.

"Hey, howdy-hi," came the all too familiar voice. "Saw a couple of my pals come in—"

"Is this little weasel of a reporter a friend of yours?" Ray asked, turning to Wayne and me.

"No," came our two voices as one.

"Not today, anyway," I added more fairly. Felix was Barbara's sweetie, after all. Unfortunately.

"Sorry," Wayne said, rising from his seat with a sigh. "I'll take care of him."

And then I followed Wayne out, where he escorted Felix away from Ray Zappa's doorway and down the tanbark path toward the curb where our cars were parked. That was it for our interview with our one possible police contact. So much for the man-to-man approach.

"Hey!" Felix was objecting. "I'm walking, I'm walking. Holy moly, you don't have to be so twitchy, guy. I was just—"

And then we heard the sound of cars driving up. And saw a white truck with the Channel 7 News logo. Reporters came scrambling out of their various vehicles. A recurring nightmare under construction.

Was this more of Felix's work? I turned to look at his grinning face just as Wayne released him. Wayne and I shuffled down the path quickly, passing some of the same people who'd surrounded our house, our faces turned away. But they didn't even notice us, they were so intent on reaching Ray Zappa's condo.

"Corruption in the police department . . ." I heard.

"Cops take care of their own . . ."

"Whaddaya know about this Zappa guy?"

And Felix was nowhere to be seen.

By the time we made it to my Toyota, I felt like we'd run a marathon. It wasn't about us this time, but it could have been. At least that's what my pulse seemed to believe.

"Do you think Ray will be all right?" I asked Wayne as I got out my keys.

But before he could answer me, a whole new fleet of cars

drove up. And the people who got out weren't reporters. I could tell by the puppets on their fingers.

They grouped together at the foot of the tanbark path. Ten or fifteen of them, male and female.

"Grief into growth!" a man yelled, sticking out the puppet on his ring finger in a Nazi-like salute.

"Grief into growth," more voices chanted in unison.

"Denial into determination . . ."

And then they began marching up the path en masse, puppets extended.

I unlocked the Toyota as quickly as I could with shaking hands. And then we were out of there.

Wayne and I were halfway home before either of us said a word. My mind was still trying to detoxify from the media, Felix, and the puppeteers. The puppeteers had to be from the Institute for Essential Manifestation. And they weren't cute. They were spooky.

"Think he's really just worried about his retirement?" Wayne finally muttered.

It took my brain a moment to find the right box. Not the Institute. Not the puppets. Ray Zappa.

"Or himself?" I suggested. "If anyone could carry off a successful murder it would be a policeman."

"But then why use the vases?"

I pondered that one as I took the curves from the highway toward home.

"Maybe he's protecting Tessa?" Wayne offered as I pulled into the driveway.

I mulled that one over as we walked up the stairs. Neither of us noticed what was pinned to our door until we were on the deck, not a yard away.

We both came to a halt in the same instant and stared.

There was a long hollow metal tube pinned to the wood, right where a door knocker would've been if we'd had one.

The thing had to be close to two feet long. And the big fluffy red Christmas bow wrapped around it was almost as wide as the metal tube was long. Worst of all, the tube seemed to be dripping blood from the sharp point at its bottom. Slowly dripping blood down the door, onto our doorstep.

"What the hell is that?" I whispered, totally absorbed by the sight.

"It's a mortician's trocar," a voice from behind me answered.

I whirled around, raising my arms defensively, and then looked into the eyes of Chief Woolsey of the Quiero Police Department.

SEVEN

✢

"A trocar's the tube that morticians use to drain the blood from a body," Chief Woolsey went on as I slowly lowered my arms. And seemed to feel all the blood drain from my own body.

I kept my eyes on Woolsey's lean face as he kept talking. At least I wasn't looking at that thing pinned to our door.

"Dead bodies, that is," he said, throwing back his forearms as if in explanation. Officer Fox, standing a few inches behind him, ducked a forearm. "Part of the embalming process. Not as ecological as some other choices, but commonly used."

Morticians? Embalming? Did this have something to do with Tessa? I wanted to turn and ask Wayne. But if I turned, I might see the trocar again. I reached out with my hand instead and felt his reassuring grip.

"Is that . . . is that real blood?" I asked Woolsey.

"You tell me, Ms. Jasper," he shot back, his voice louder now, hostile. He thrust his face toward mine and I noticed the little diamond stud he wore in his left earlobe. Was Chief Woolsey an ex-hippie? Or did the left side mean he was gay? Then I shook my head to clear it. What was he saying now? "The trocar's pinned to your door, Ms. Jasper. *Your* door."

"Well, I didn't put it there," I snapped. "Do you think it's my idea of a Christmas decoration or something? I—"

"It isn't anywhere near Christmas, Ms. Jasper," the chief informed me.

Damn. Chief Woolsey was not only hostile, he was humor-impaired. Not that there was really anything funny happening here. My stomach could tell you that. It wasn't feeling amused at all, just sick.

"Neither Ms. Jasper nor I have anything to do with pinning that thing to our door," Wayne stated absolutely.

Chief Woolsey shifted his glare in Wayne's direction.

"Do any of your friends have very strange senses of humor?" Woolsey demanded.

Most of them, my mind responded. But I kept my mouth shut. No one, not even Felix, was the type to pull a practical joke this weird.

"None of our friends or acquaintances pinned a trocar to our door," Wayne answered clearly, his low voice sounding calmer than I was sure he was feeling. "Don't you think it's more likely to be related to the Skyler murder?"

"How should I know?" Woolsey shot back. Then he abruptly threw out his arms, to their full extension this time. Officer Fox ducked again, no expression on his round face. Apparently he'd had a lot of practice avoiding Woolsey's arms.

"Fox!" Woolsey shouted, though the man was less than a foot away from him. Poor guy, I thought, he was no fox, not with that doughy round face and recessive chin. But he was quick.

"Yes, sir," he answered promptly, standing at attention.

"Go check out that . . . that thing," Woolsey ordered.

My eyes followed Officer Fox as he checked out the trocar. I couldn't seem to stop them. He drew out a handkerchief and pulled the trocar a little away from the door as if to look at its underbelly. He sniffed the red fluid leaking ever so slowly from the sharp point at its bottom. Then he put out his finger, touched the fluid, and gingerly put it to his tongue.

"Catsup," he announced finally.

We all let out little sighs of relief, even Woolsey.

Unfortunately, that wasn't the end of it, since Chief Woolsey decided the trocar on the door *did* have to do with Sam Skyler's death. But we didn't live in the city of Quiero. We lived in Tam Valley, just outside the city limits of Mill Valley, so the county had jurisdiction over whatever crime had been committed by whosoever had done our early Christmas decorating. Finally, Chief Woolsey asked if he could come inside and call the Sheriff's department.

I took a deep breath and walked up to the door. Woolsey's brain kicked in just as my hand touched the doorknob.

"Don't touch anything!" he bellowed.

"Jeez," Fox muttered under his breath.

Was that "Jeez" supposed to mean I was an idiot? Or did it refer to Woolsey's volume? The former, I decided as Wayne and I led the officers around the side of the house to the back door that led into the kitchen, Fox never farther than a few feet from Woolsey's side.

Once Woolsey had called the Sheriff's, the four of us all settled down around the kitchen table for a nice chat. Chief Woolsey even accepted an offer of herbal tea after first checking the box to make sure the tea was really caffeine free. And once Woolsey had accepted, Fox followed suit.

"Vegetarian?" The chief asked as he scanned the cookbooks and jars of dried grains, beans, and spices on the kitchen shelves.

"Yeah," I answered eagerly, noting the first hint of approval I'd heard yet in his voice.

Wayne kept his nonvegetarian, nonstupid, mouth shut.

"And you?" I asked conversationally, turning the flame on under the teakettle.

Woolsey nodded, then looked off to the side. Was he embarrassed?

"Me too," Fox chipped in. I should have known. I'd have bet that if Woolsey walked on fire, Fox would be there tiptoeing along after him, singeing his little tootsies.

"Notebook, Fox," Woolsey ordered, all friendliness gone from his voice.

"Yes, sir," Fox answered, pulling a spiral notebook and a much chewed pencil from his pocket.

"What were you doing at Ray Zappa's today?" Woolsey demanded.

So much for our nice little chat.

"We wanted to know what was going on with the Sam Skyler case," Wayne answered succinctly.

"Why?"

"A man fell onto the rocks within yards of us," Wayne answered, his tone even. "We'd like to know why. Did he fall? Was he pushed? Did he jump?"

I looked at him in surprise for a moment, because we both knew he was pushed. I even opened my mouth to say so, then remembered that we weren't supposed to know Sam Skyler had been murdered, and closed it again.

Woolsey must have noticed my mouth moving.

"Something to say, Ms. Jasper?" he asked, bending forward abruptly, his eyes glinting as brightly as the diamond stud in his ear.

I sat for a moment and then opened my mouth once more.

"Yeah," I answered. If he could accept my tea at my kitchen table and be hostile, I could be hostile too. "Did you follow us from Ray's house?"

He sat back in his chair and looked off to the side again.

He had been following us! I was sure of it. How else had he ended up on our heels so conveniently when we found the trocar? And if he was following us—

The scream of the teakettle cut off my train of thought.

Wayne motioned me to keep my seat and got up to fill the teacups. I wished he hadn't, because my mind was racing again and I was sure Woolsey could see it in my face. Did he think one or both of us had killed Sam Skyler? Was that why he'd followed us? Or had he just become curious when he saw us go into Ray Zappa's house, and waited for us to come out again? Or did he think we were in on it with Zappa? Or . . .

"Honey?" Wayne offered as the smell of cinnamon, ginger, and chicory filled the kitchen.

Woolsey shook his head violently.

"We don't use honey," Fox put in virtuously. "The bees are oppressed by the honey farmers. The bees work to make their honey, and then it's stolen from them."

I'd heard the theory before. And I was pretty sure we'd just lost our vegetarian points with Woolsey.

It didn't take long to verify the loss. Woolsey began the real interrogation between sips of unsweetened tea. He asked us about everything. And I mean everything. Our interest in this case. Any past associations with Sam Skyler. Our involvement in earlier cases. Even our positions on the environment.

I was trying to explain that I wasn't really against Greenpeace, I just wished they wouldn't ring my doorbell while I was working, when the doorbell rang.

But it wasn't Greenpeace this time, it was Sergeant Tom Feiffer from the Marin County Sheriff's Department. Damn.

I'd known Sergeant Feiffer as long as I'd known Wayne. Longer. And he still looked the same, tall and muscular with curly blond hair and blue eyes. Blue eyes that always brought uninvited lustful thoughts to my mind. No matter how hard I tried to keep them out. I tried picturing a sign that said, No Lust or White Elephants Allowed Here. It didn't work.

It was something about the longing way the sergeant looked at me. (And at my pinball machines. The man was a pinball addict, too.) Even C.C. felt something libidinous for Sergeant Feiffer. She wandered in and rubbed up against his ankles, meowing low in her throat, as I escorted him into the kitchen.

"Got the evidence crew working on the trocar," he told us, his blue eyes on mine, his tone a caress. I turned my head away, blushing from the look and its implications, and realizing at the same time that I hadn't seen the trocar on the front door when I'd let him in. Wayne just glowered.

And then Feiffer started asking his questions, no more blush-provoking caresses in his tone now. And when he was done, Woolsey started in on us again. It was after five o'clock by the time the last representative of law and order left our house.

When the final police car was gone, I dropped onto the living room couch and reached out my arms to Wayne.

But he was muttering something under his breath. "Feiffer," was part of it, but I couldn't make out the rest. That was probably fortunate.

"At least he told Woolsey I didn't do it," I pointed out. No use pretending I couldn't hear anything.

"Yeah," Wayne growled. "The old 'karma' routine."

"Well, it's better than the old 'you look like a murderer to me, Ms. Jasper' routine," I argued, lowering my arms and crossing them defensively.

"The way Feiffer looks at you—"

The doorbell rang again. We both jumped and turned our wary gazes toward the front hallway.

We looked back into each other's eyes as the doorbell rang one more time. Then Wayne got up with a sigh that was about an eight on a scale of one to ten of tragic sighs. (Wayne should have been in the sigh Olympics, he was so good.) Then he trod ever so slowly toward the door, opening it an inch or so and peering out as if for armed enemies.

"Hey, how you guys doin'?" a high, resonant voice asked,

and Emma Jett was past Wayne's guard and into the house, without even pausing to take a breath. Wayne was clearly doing a better job of sighing than guarding at that point. "See, I thought I'd just come right over without calling, you know. More of a surprise that way. Don't you just love surprises?"

She'd danced her way into the living room before she'd even finished her introduction and was patting one of the pinball machines. I would have told her I wasn't all that fond of surprises. If I'd had a chance.

"Wow, this is really cool," she rattled on, fondling Hayburners' side rails, her reddish hair hanging in her face on the side that wasn't cut to the scalp. "I mean this machine's one of the totally legitimate ones. You can shake it, and feel it, and fight with it." She trotted lightly around the side of the machine in her lace-up boots and ran her hand down the colorful backboard. "Not like all that electronic bullshit they make now. The real thing—"

"So," Wayne put in. "You—"

"Anyway, I thought it might be a cool idea to talk about this Sam Skyler thing, you know," she plowed on. When did she breathe? "I mean, that was some experience. Boom, gone. Just like that. And the cops and everything."

And then she spotted the hanging chairs.

"Wow, way cool," she caroled and pranced over in a flash of army fatigues with brass epaulets, her outfit for the day. The epaulets matched the brass studs in her ears and nostrils nicely. A bright touch of theater. Hadn't she mentioned she was in theater or something—?

"Campbell told me you talked with him at the store," she said, lowering herself into the chair and pushing off with her feet to put it in motion. "Campbell's, like, a complete sweetie, you know. The gentlest man I know." Her voice slowed for a moment. And took on weight. "He wouldn't hurt anyone. I want you to know that. And I'm not bullshitting. You can ask anyone who knows him.''

"The police will find that out—" I began. But her mouth was still moving.

"And he's not stupid either," she went on. "He wouldn't shake his fist at the guy and *then* push him over. The person who did it would act like they liked him first." She screwed up her narrow face in a scowl. "If Skyler was even pushed. I don't know why the cops are on everyone's case—"

"What do you—" Wayne began.

I sent him a consoling look as Emma cut him off. He missed it as he sat down in the swinging chair across from her.

"If they're gonna hassle anyone, it oughta be Yvonne O'Reilley. I'll bet she knows—well, knew—Sam Skyler a lot better than she's letting on. And Ona, I mean, all she can talk about is how much she hated the guy. And then there's his space-cadet girlfriend." I found myself nodding at the description, then stopped as I caught Wayne's look. "You ask me, she's more interested in Skyler Junior than she was in Skyler Senior.

"Anyway," she summed up, popping out of the chair like a jack-in-the-box. "This whole thing is getting too intense. I mean, Campbell is put right off his music. He's a wonderful musician you know, traditional stuff. Celtic. And I can't even write, I'm so uptight. It's all too weird. I mean, how can I get into Connie the Condom's mind when all this bullshit is exploding around us?''

"Connie the Condom?''

A smile replaced the scowl on Emma's narrow face as she walked across the living room to the newest of the bookshelves Wayne and I had built. I caught the mixed scent of cigarette smoke and coffee as she passed.

"Oh, Connie the Condom's my children's book series," she explained, picking up a novel from Wayne's futurism section.

That seemed appropriate. "See, she's this cute little pink condom, you know, with perfect blond curls and a little rosebud
mouth. See, it really points up the ambivalence we have about
sexuality, and good and evil. And predestination and all of
that stuff. Anyway, she's, like, this guardian angel and helps
kids who are in trouble. I write *and* illustrate the books. I blew
up some of the pages to three feet by five and had a show at
the Newmind Gallery. People thought it was really cool. But
selling the books is another thing. Since they're for kids, none
of the stores will touch—"

This time she stopped herself.

"Anyway, about this Skyler thing." She put Wayne's book
back on the shelf. Her voice gained weight again. "I don't
like it. And I think it could be really dangerous. Especially to
investigate. You gotta figure it's a lose-lose situation. If the
guy wasn't murdered, what's the point? If he was, who's
gonna stop the murderer from murdering again? You know
what I mean?"

And then she danced back across the living room to the
front door.

"I'll bring you a copy of a Connie book if you'd like," she
offered and was out the door in a flash of brass before either
of us had time to accept or decline the offer. Or say goodbye
for that matter.

"Was that some kind of warning?" I asked Wayne once I
felt able to speak again.

"I don't know," he answered. "Felt more like a random
tornado."

We sat in silence awhile. The silence felt good. A cocoon
filled with non-questions, and non-accusations and non-threats.
I closed my eyes and leaned back against the couch. Think of
flowers, I advised myself. Think of sunsets—

"One thing, though," came Wayne's quiet voice, sidling

into my cocoon. "Emma's scared. Scared for Campbell. Or for herself. But she's scared."

"Do you think she really believes he did it?" I asked.

"Maybe she's just afraid everyone else will," Wayne suggested. "Campbell did shake his fist at the man minutes before he disappeared."

I wasn't through considering that one when Wayne came up with another.

"Could be it's all a ploy to point suspicion at Campbell and away from herself."

I sat up straight on the couch, an objection on my lips. Emma was goofy, but I didn't want her to be a murderer. Or worse yet, to be that treacherous. Could anyone be that treacherous to someone they supposedly loved enough to marry?

"Don't really think it fits either," Wayne said, as if he'd heard my unspoken objections.

I leaned back against the cushions.

"Had a point about Yvonne," Wayne added. "How well did she and Sam know each other? Neither of us has an answer to that question. And Yvonne set up the whole event. Could have been arranging the perfect murder."

"And she brought those heavy vases," I muttered. "But . . ."

"Yeah," Wayne agreed. "Same as Emma. Just can't imagine it." He paused. "Ona, on the other hand . . ."

"Or Diana—"

His glower told me I should have kept that one to myself.

But before the glower could be translated into anything more than a facial expression, our doorbell rang again.

I motioned Wayne to be silent. He nodded in agreement and stood up quietly from his swinging chair, then crept over to the couch to sit next to me. Without a word.

"Excuse me," a voice shouted through the door. Even the shout had an air of politeness to it. I recognized the voice immediately. Park Ranger Yasuda. "Yvonne O'Reilley thought I should speak to you," he went on.

Wayne and I huddled together on the couch holding our breaths, hearing each other's rhythms like drumbeats.

"Excuse me, but I know you're in there," Yasuda said, his voice at normal volume now. We could still hear him clearly.

And we still kept quiet.

And then from behind us a small figure jumped up onto the back of the couch and yowled into my ear.

"Damn it, C.C.!" I yelped.

Wayne gave me one look from beneath rapidly descending eyebrows, stood up abruptly, and strode over to the front door.

His sigh was a nine this time. Maybe even a ten.

EIGHT

I didn't blame Wayne. I could have joined the sigh Olympics too about then. Why couldn't everyone just leave us alone?

I turned to glare at C.C. She yowled one more time and jumped off the back of the couch, slinking off with her own feline sigh. Actually it was more like a grumble, or as close as she could get, considering her vocal cords. I had a few choice replies to that grumble, but didn't have a chance to express them as the tip of her tail disappeared around the doorway.

"So, Ms. O'Reilley suggested I speak to you," Park Ranger Yasuda was saying to Wayne when I finally rose from the couch to be a good host. Well, maybe not a good one, but minimally polite at least. I figured I could handle that.

Within a few minutes Park Ranger Yasuda, or David, as he asked us to call him, was sitting between us on our ratty old denim couch and telling us his problems. I was too tired to do anything but listen. And watch. Which wasn't hard to do.

David Yasuda was a good-looking man, Japanese-American with square, even features and dark, intense eyes under thick, arching eyebrows. And long black hair pulled back in a ponytail. He looked about thirty, but I figured Yvonne's mental age had to be at least half that in any case, so maybe he might not be too young for her fifty-plus real-time years. Assuming she actually did have the crush I was pretty sure she had on him. It was his intensity that was so attractive, I decided as he spoke. And his sincerity.

"Point Abajo doesn't really have any grounds for legal jurisdiction," he was saying. "My boss doesn't think we should get involved." He twisted his hands together, mottling the skin around his knuckles into patches of beige and white. "But I feel involved! If Ms. O'Reilley and I hadn't arranged the wedding, Mr. Skyler wouldn't have died."

"Never helps to say 'if,' " Wayne offered, his voice sounding as stressed as I felt. But at least he was trying. "A thousand things could have gone differently and Sam Skyler might not have died. Not your fault. The only one to blame is the one who actually killed Skyler." He paused for a second. "If someone did," he added belatedly.

I wondered if Yasuda knew what Felix had told us, if he knew that Skyler had been pushed over that bluff.

"I know you're right," Yasuda murmured, still twisting his hands. "At least intellectually. But emotionally and morally . . ." He shrugged his shoulders and arched his eyebrows even further. I had a feeling he knew how Sam had died.

And I found myself nodding.

There is something about having your world touched, however peripherally, by a crime as serious as taking someone's life that breeds an ethical compulsion to find answers, to seek justice. Or maybe not even ethical, maybe just nosy.

And all three of us on that ratty old couch knew it. I finally did sigh then.

"What do you know about Sam Skyler?" Wayne asked.

"Sam?" Yasuda reflected, unclasping his hands. "Well, I admired the man. I know there were those in Marin—and in Golden Valley especially—who didn't. But I did."

"Why?" I asked, genuinely curious.

"He was a generous man, in terms of community," Yasuda told us. "He contributed to the Golden Valley Elementary School after last year's flooding almost destroyed it. Actually, there wouldn't be any Golden Valley Elementary School without him. And he gave personal scholarships out of his own pocket to kids all over Marin who were bright but too poor to go anywhere with their lives. Subsidized a whole graduating class in Southham City one year. Anyone who wanted to go to college, he paid their tuition. As long as they kept up their grades. He was a good man, no matter what he did in the past."

"Then why did people dislike him so much in the community?" I demanded. "Because of the old murder charges?"

"No," Yasuda answered slowly. "I don't think very many people even knew that ancient history. And if they did, most of them figured he'd been mistakenly accused and cleared. It was because of the Institute. Not what the Institute did. But the building itself. Did you ever see it?"

I shook my head.

"It's a huge place. And there was a lot of fuss before it was built. A lot of people didn't think it belonged in the valley at all, which is mostly residential. Lots of accusations of bribery were flying around when its construction was finally approved by the City Council."

"Was this before or after he gave the money to rebuild the elementary school?" I asked.

"Before," Yasuda assured me. He shook his head. "But people still think his contributions were some kind of payoff. Some people, anyway. And lots of these people hadn't even met him. It's really weird how the community was split on the issue of Sam Skyler's worth, and a good half of them didn't even know him."

"But you did," Wayne put in.

"Yeah," Yasuda admitted. "I live in Golden Valley. I met him a couple of times at community meetings. He was a really impressive guy. But people either liked him or they didn't."

That about summed it up. It was a while before Yasuda went on.

"And then there's Yvonne's business to consider," he muttered finally, dropping his gaze, a flush pinkening his tan cheeks. I wondered if he even realized he'd stopped calling our class leader Ms. O'Reilley.

By the time he'd finished telling us how worried he was about the effect of Sam Skyler's death on Yvonne's business, and on her delicate psyche, I'd decided that if Yvonne had a crush on the park ranger, the crush was mutual. And then I started wondering what ritual they'd come up with if they got married.

My extended fantasies of samurai, goddess, and geisha, including a good portion of role reversal and even some cross-dressing, were interrupted when Park Ranger Yasuda got up from our couch.

"Thank you for listening," he said simply.

"Oh . . . um . . . thank you," I responded automatically, embarrassed that I had lost the last half of the conversation while engaged in unscheduled wedding ritual fantasies.

I was in the mood for some cuddling by the time our park ranger had left. Serious cuddling. But Wayne was up, pacing by the front door, jingling his car keys.

"Going out to dinner with the Athertons," he finally mumbled.

"The Athertons?" I repeated.

"Gary, Liz . . ."

"And Diana," I finished for him. "Am I invited?"

This time I couldn't even hear the content of his mutterings. Though I was pretty sure there was something in there about my *not* being invited.

I kept my own mutterings to myself and got up to join him. Dinner with the Athertons it was. I was inviting myself. How gracious of me.

Wayne was meeting the Athertons at Quels Légumes!—the newest, most chichi vegetarian restaurant in Marin County, one Wayne had been promising to take me to ever since it opened three months before. No wonder he was so embarrassed about not inviting me.

"Diana suggested it," he mumbled as he handed over his keys to a valet parking person outfitted in green overalls with an orange carrot embroidered on the breast pocket. "Diana's a vegetarian too, you know."

"Does she use honey?" I asked sweetly.

Wayne flashed me a look from beneath his brows. Did he suspect sarcasm?

I smiled back innocently, linked my arm with his and we marched up to the entrance of Quels Légumes! And that entrance was impressive. Giant green plaster of Paris columns shaped like asparagus spears flanked the wide glass doors. And over the doors was a fresco of brightly colored fruits and vegetables: broccoli, bell peppers, red onions, corn, lemons, and strawberries, just to name a few.

"Wow," I whispered as we entered. Even Wayne's restaurant in the city wasn't this impressive. I noticed him gazing at the decor with a professional eye. Or was it a critical one? Did he think the entrance was a bit overstated?

Inside, the air was cool and the tables and chairs strange, great rounds of orange, red, purple, and green. It wasn't until we were escorted to our table by a maitre d' wearing a green tuxedo with the requisite embroidered carrot that I recognized the shapes of the tables and chairs as oversized replicas of big round vegetable slices.

I ran my eyes over the zucchini, eggplant, tomato, turnip, and beet seats, and chose the eggplant. Wayne placed his bottom on the turnip beside me and we both stared in silence at the carrot-slice table. A vegetarian Disneyland.

"Our soups tonight are gazpacho, eggplant-paprika, and a spicy cilantro-tomato bisque," the headwaiter told us. I shuddered. My taste buds have always thought of cilantro as a poison, not a food.

"Our specials are mesquite grilled vegetable kebabs over couscous with just a touch of Thai-inspired—"

"Wayne, Kate," a slow, soft voice murmured behind me, cutting off the poetry of the specials announcements. Diana's voice, I knew instantly. Who else could send that message of sweet sensuality with just two words? "How good to see you."

Liz took the zucchini chair, Gary the beet, and Diana, most appropriately, the remaining tomato.

We exchanged greetings and I eyed the Athertons for any untoward reactions to my presence. There were none. Liz just looked strained, her no-nonsense hair rumpled and her brown eyes seeming slightly askew. She put a hand to her temple as Gary buried his face in a menu. Diana's face was as serene as usual, her round blue eyes staring into the unknown somewhere behind us.

After the specials were all announced, I took a look at my menu. The prices matched the decor perfectly. They were all oversized.

"We've been very concerned," Diana announced as my eyes meandered by the basil-tofu sushi and clove-scented paella. "Sam's passing has many implications—"

"Not all of them spiritual," Gary interrupted, his voice a muted shout of frustration. Or maybe I was projecting.

Diana nodded and Gary took over, speaking softly but quickly.

"There's this group of guys called Growth Imperatives, Unlimited," he told us, leaning across the table, his handsome features tight with tension. "And they've been bugging Diana wherever she goes. Especially this one guy. They want to buy the Institute."

"I inherit a third of Sam's estate," Diana explained. Then she shook her head gently. "Though the inheritance makes me feel closer to Sam's spirit in a way, I don't really want any money from it. It makes me feel unclean."

"And it makes the police feel suspicious," Gary added with quiet impatience.

Liz's head swiveled in her son's direction, her brown eyes widening, accentuating her resemblance to Diana, for all her cropped hair and Diana's waist-length braid. "The police?" she whispered.

"Yes, Mom," Gary answered, his voice still low, but the impatience in it growing. "The police see an inheritance of that size as a good motive for murder."

"But I thought the police weren't sure of murder," she objected. "He could have fallen. Didn't someone say he did fell?"

Gary sighed. It was a day for sighs. And he had cause. His mother was acting as spacy as his sister. Wasn't Liz supposed to be a court reporter? I'd hate to depend on someone that disoriented to take down my words accurately.

"Mom," Diana explained in her most soothing voice, "I think the police are sure he was pushed. They haven't said so, but intuitively, I can feel their belief. It's best if we assume that's going to be their approach."

"And as if it weren't bad enough with them sniffing around," Gary added, "these Growth Imperatives guys are like something out of the Mafia. They've even been to the restaurant," he added, turning to Wayne.

"Our restaurant?" Wayne asked.

Gary nodded violently, clearly outraged. As much as a usually quiet man like Gary can be outraged.

Wayne's brows dropped contemplatively. I noticed he hadn't divulged to the Athertons what the police actually knew about the circumstances of Sam's death. I was glad to hear it. Or not hear it, actually. Maybe he didn't completely trust Diana after all.

I looked back at my menu, my appetite sharpening suddenly. The artichoke-mushroom focaccia sounded good. And the spinach-pine-nut salad.

Which is what I ordered when our waiter came. Gary and Diana ordered carefully, as if choosing a jewel from Tiffany's. So did Wayne. But Liz just asked for a big salad, "any salad." And Gary sighed again before choosing for her. His mother's indifferent attitude toward her meal appeared to rain down hard on him, a man seriously into the restaurant business. I wondered if he'd picked up his sensitivities, not to mention the sigh, from Wayne.

Then Gary started talking about the Growth Imperatives people again.

"Have you told the police about these men?" Wayne asked finally.

Diana shrugged, slowly, gracefully. "It's up to Nathan, really," she said. "I don't know anything about the Institute."

Then she guided the conversation into less stormy waters. By the time my spinach-pine-nut salad was served, Diana was explaining her holistic approach to tantric yoga instruction.

"So few women really rejoice in their sexuality," she murmured sadly. But then she brightened. "Still, their transformations are beautiful to see. Merging sexuality with spirituality. Passion and compassion in sex—"

"Diana's grandfather was a healer too," Liz interrupted, through a bite of her minted quinoa salad. She was probably about as comfortable as I was discussing tantric sexuality over dinner with near strangers. "He came from Mexico. He was a doctor down there, but not allowed to practice here. But he was still a healer."

"He owned a five-and-dime in San Ricardo," Gary put in. "But people came to him anyway whenever they had a splinter or a rash, or whatever."

"All this prejudice about Hispanic immigrants," Liz said, shaking her head sadly.

"Latinos, Mom," Gary corrected. But Liz just kept going.

"And 'Americans' so concerned about keeping the Hispanics out of California. Who do they think built California?" she said, her voice gaining speed and anger. Her eyes narrowed. "It was the Hispanics who built the roads, the missions, the ranches. The Hispanics civilized this state—"

"And killed most of the Native Americans in the process," Gary muttered. But that didn't stop Liz for a moment either.

"Then once the Hispanics had civilized California, these so-called Americans came in like swaggering hyenas and cheated the Hispanic-Californians out of their land grants. And now they have the nerve to call Mexicans wetbacks. The stereotypes these people perpetrate!" She slapped our carrot table resoundingly. "My father was a Mexican immigrant, my mother English. My father was the epitome of integrity and hard work. He was an absolute gentleman. Never hit my mother in his entire life—"

"Dad could have taken a few lessons—" Gary mumbled.

"Or us kids either," Liz pressed on. No wonder Diana and Gary were relatively quiet, I decided. Growing up, they probably never got a chance to get a word in edgewise. "A completely gentle man. If anyone had a temper, it was my mother. And she came from Great Britain. Not that she hit anyone, either. But she knew how to yell. She was no more the British stereotype than my father was the Hispanic." Liz paused for a moment, her eyes going back to their normal width. "Sorry to climb on the soapbox. But these false stereotypes are truly evil.''

I nodded in agreement. She was certainly right on that one.

We crunched our salads and slurped our soups without speaking for a while. The spinach-pine-nut salad was surprisingly good, very sweet and sprinkled with herbs I couldn't identify.

Liz looked at her watch once she had finished her own salad. ''Gotta go, kids,'' she announced abruptly, and rose from her zucchini. She fished through her wallet for some bills to hand to Gary.

''But Mom,'' he objected, either to her leaving or to the money. I couldn't tell which.

She turned to us with a sheepish smile.

''Sorry about the diatribe,'' she apologized. ''I know I talk too much. Ought to have better social skills at this point in my life. But . . .'' She shrugged. ''Anyway, I hope to see you again. I'll try to keep my lip buttoned the next time.''

''No, no,'' I assured her honestly. ''The stuff about California was really interesting.''

She tilted her head as if to test my sincerity, then smiled crookedly and grabbed my hand and squeezed it.

''Well, thank you,'' she said and then exited Quels Legumes! through its asparagus columns.

''Sorry about Mom,'' Diana murmured once Liz was gone. ''She's been really moody lately.''

''Menopause, I'll bet,'' Gary threw in before I could say I didn't think ''Mom'' had said anything worth apologizing for. ''Not that she'd ever mention it.''

It seemed to me that Liz might actually be a little old for menopause, but I kept my thoughts to myself.

''She's hardly done any chain-saw sculpture in the last few months,'' Diana went on, her round eyes narrowed ever so slightly with concern.

"Yeah," Gary agreed. He looked up at the roof. "The last one I remember was the dolphin. And that had to be four months ago at least."

Wayne and I looked at each other while Gary and Diana continued to discuss their mother's sculptures. How were we going to bring the subject back to murder?

As it was, Diana took care of the conversational direction, just as the waiter brought our main dishes.

"I've been trying to think who Sam knew in the wedding class," she told us as my focaccia was set before me on a giant white china plate. Her voice was perfectly calm, perfectly serene.

I took a bite of the soft white bread smothered in sautéed mushrooms and artichokes. Delicious, but not any better than the take-out at Grace Baking, even considering the giant white plate, the accompanying artistically trimmed raw veggies, and the giant price.

"Sam was the kind of person who'd met everyone," Diana went on, ignoring her own linguine with fresh vegetables and herbs. "Every place we went people seemed to know him. He used to say he was embarrassed because he couldn't remember all the people who remembered him."

"He wasn't a man you'd forget easily," I offered.

"That's true," she agreed eagerly. She bent forward. "He really was bigger than life in many ways. And people felt a sense of intimacy with him, just meeting him." She smiled, then closed her eyes for a moment as if savoring the memory.

I thought of what Yasuda had said—you either liked Sam or you didn't.

Diana's eyes popped open again. I shifted on my eggplant seat guiltily, hoping she hadn't heard my thought.

"Anyway," she said, her voice a little firmer, "I know Sam knew Ona and Perry. And Yvonne. And Nathan of course."

The minute she said Nathan's name her skin pinkened and she seemed to lose track of what she was saying.

Uh-oh. It looked like Emma was right. Diana was more interested in Skyler Junior than Skyler Senior. Talk about motives. Add that little bit of information to the inheritance that she'd probably lose if she dumped Daddy for his son—

"And Martina," she went on, her voice barely a whisper. She was looking down at her plate now. "And maybe Emma." She looked back up again. "Did you know Emma Jett was really born Emma Jones. She changed her name."

"How'd you happen to know that?" Wayne asked. I started at the sound of his deep voice, he'd been quiet so long.

"Oh, I knew her sister in high school."

And that was about it for useful information. It seemed that Diana didn't know much more about Sam than we did. Maybe even less, I thought, seeing Yvonne's brass vases in my mind as we stood up half an hour later.

Now it was time for Wayne and me to offer our apologies, since we had to leave. That is, if we wanted to make the fire-walk wedding that Yvonne had arranged for that evening. And I, for one, did.

I knew people who'd fire-walked, but I'd never actually seen it done. I was ready. To watch, that is. Not to walk.

By the time we got there, the sun had set, and twenty feet of brightly burning coals lit up the backyard of yet another friend of Yvonne O'Reilley's. She seemed to know as many people as Sam Skyler.

"Oh, I'm so energized," she was telling the members of the Wedding Ritual class, who stood in the back of the crowd waiting for the ceremony to begin. It looked as if everyone from the original class was there, everyone but Diana. And Sam of course.

"Such bliss," Yvonne went on. "Raoul and Mary met at a firewalk, you know. And now . . ." She gestured toward the glowing coals. I shivered in the evening breeze, glad for its coolness.

Then suddenly, the bride and groom appeared at the beginning of the molten runway. I was relieved to see that the groom had rolled up the legs of his tuxedo pants and that the bride's white dress only came to her bare knees. On both their faces there was a focus of intention I'd rarely seen before.

The crowd went silent as a man in black joined the couple. The minister. I could see his collar in the glow of the coals.

"Are you ready to prove your commitment to your love by walking together barefoot over hot coals?" the minister asked.

"Yes!" two voices shouted as one.

Then the bride and groom took one last look at each other, gripped each other's hands, and proceeded to walk the length of red-hot coals. They walked at a deliberate, unhurried pace, their eyes directed upwards and their mouths moving, uttering words I couldn't hear.

I could hear the sizzling of the coals though, the mutterings of the onlookers, and from somewhere near the front of the crowd, a female voice sobbing "my baby." The bride's mother, I assumed. Or maybe the groom's.

When they reached the end of the burning runway, cheers rang out from the crowd. And a man with a garden hose washed the bride's and groom's feet.

It was a long time before the minister, now at the end of the runway, could speak over the whoops and ululating of the wedding guests.

"You have both demonstrated your commitment to each other," he finally shouted. "I pronounce you wife and husband."

That brought on more cheers and a surge of barefoot men and women following the fiery path the bride and groom had taken. One by one they walked, looking up and mouthing inaudible words as they strode across the burning coals to hug the bride and groom. A reception line I was not about to join.

This brought more shouts and whoops, and finally everyone who was going to walk the coals had, and the bride and groom were hugging everyone in sight, coals or no coals.

Jubilant cries rang through the air. Even I felt the urge to walk on those coals, to feel what it would be like to challenge the laws of physics. Luckily, someone was hosing down the coals by that time.

As the sounds of celebration caressed the night air, another sound came sliding into my consciousness. Not far behind me, someone was crying.

I turned to see who it was.

Nathan Skyler stood, bent over, weeping into his hands.

And there wasn't a finger puppet in sight.

NINE

✦

"Maybe the groom will walk over hot coals, but will he take out the trash?" Ona joked. Her eyes were ignoring Nathan's distress, but even in the semidarkness I could tell by the stiffness of her soft, round body that she was aware of him. And trying in her own way to defuse his grief.

Perry put his arm around Ona and squeezed as Wayne and I laughed weakly at her joke, keeping our eyes averted from Nathan's sobbing figure.

In fact, most of the members of the Wedding Ritual class seemed to be trying to ignore Nathan, to give him a chance to regain control. Martina Monteil stood up straight and tall, baring her white teeth in her perfect model's smile and made conversation with Campbell Barnhill two feet away from her putative fiancé, just as if he and his tears didn't exist. Campbell wasn't smiling back, though. And Emma Jett shot a look at Nathan and then at Martina before crossing her arms and stomping away in her lace-up boots. Maybe she was looking for Yvonne, who seemed to have disappeared completely. Tessa and Ray were huddled together, Ray's tall figure bent over Tessa's short one. Ray seemed to be whispering into Tessa's ear as he kept his gaze in Nathan's direction.

"Would you walk over hot coals for me, honey?" Ona

asked Perry, her strong voice even louder, but still not loud enough to drown out Nathan's sobbing.

"Any time," Perry answered on cue. "As long as we do it in cyberspace." But I could see his heart wasn't in the fun of it. His deeply shadowed eyes were filled with concern as they furtively flitted Nathan's way.

Nathan's weeping grew even louder. His head was bent into his hands and he was pressing his palms onto his thick glasses so hard I was afraid he'd break them. Even some of the remaining fire-walkers and guests of the bride and groom who had lingered outside were beginning to notice. I couldn't stand it any longer. I turned to go to him. But Wayne was just a little faster than me.

He strode over and put a hand on Nathan's heaving shoulders. Nathan turned to Wayne and threw his arms around him, as if clutching a giant bag of groceries. The scene might have been comical, Nathan's shaggy head slumping onto Wayne's broad shoulders, almost knocking Wayne over in the process. It was so easy to forget how tall Nathan really was, even taller than Wayne. But the crying made the scene anything but comical.

"Nathan?" I began, wanting to make contact. "What's going on—?"

"Nathan!" a sharp voice interrupted. The voice of a drill sergeant. Sergeant Martina Monteil. "What do we do with grief?"

Nathan's head jerked up as if yanked by a string.

"I . . . I . . ." he tried.

"I asked you what we do with grief," Martina reminded him, her voice as cold as her narrowed hazel eyes.

Slowly Nathan withdrew from Wayne and turned to Martina. He stuck out his ring finger.

"Grief into growth," he whispered, the tears still shining in his eyes.

"Louder," Martina ordered.

"Grief into growth," Nathan barked, his voice raw.

I turned away. This was their business, not mine. And if this was the Institute's approach to grief—even just Martina's—I wanted nothing to do with it.

By now, most of the people from the wedding party had disappeared inside Yvonne's friend's house. Bright light shone from its windows, weakly illuminating the backyard. And celebratory shouts and laughter drifted out to the members of Yvonne's class standing outside, nearly alone with the remains of the fire-walk. Even hosed down, there were glints of embers here and there. And the lingering smell of smoke.

Wayne joined me and Ona and Perry once more, his face troubled. Porch lights came on, adding another source of light to be swallowed up by the darkness outside.

"Possible to talk to you about Sam some time tomorrow?" Wayne asked Ona.

"Sure," Ona replied easily. "How about lunch? Perry can cook."

Nice of her to offer, I thought. But Perry just nodded.

Ona looked behind her. I followed her look. Martina had taken Nathan a few yards away, and by the look of his fingers flashing in the air, was putting him through his paces.

"You know, Sam Skyler really was a murderer, no matter what she says," Ona whispered. "There's a big difference between being found not guilty and *being* not guilty. And he really was an insensitive jerk for a man who claimed to be a guru of interpersonal skills. 'Guru' in his case meant bullshitter, if you ask me."

"Skyler kept telling Ona to lose weight," Perry put in. "Even though she'd come to terms with her size. Totally destroying all the work she'd done. Or at least he tried to. But it didn't work. Ona likes her body." He paused to give her soft shoulders an extra squeeze. "I certainly do too," he added.

Ona smiled and leaned into his embrace, looking as fluffy as a county-fair bunny for a moment. I smiled too. Perry obviously adored his fiancée, all two-hundred-plus pounds of her.

"The sad thing is," Perry went on, "Skyler really did have some amazing skills. I've seen him mesmerize people, bring feelings out of them they never knew they had, mediate between them. If he'd been more compassionate, he could have really healed people. And I'm not saying there weren't some who were helped by his methods. Still, if someone didn't immediately agree with him and adore him, they were in big trouble. Skyler could be incredibly destructive then."

I nodded my understanding in the cool night air. I'd known some Sam Skylers before. And hadn't liked them any more than Ona and Perry had.

"And even most of the people who were initially helped by his work became his seminar junkies anyway," Ona added. "Where I come from, mental health doesn't mean following your guru around like a puppy for the rest of your life and wiggling your fingers." Her voice lowered again. "So these suckers' inner feelings were released. Where did they go from there? Did their lives really improve? Did they get better jobs, better relationships?" She shook her head. "Just look at Nathan, wiggling his fingers around while his heart's breaking. Does he look self-actualized to you?"

I turned to look at Nathan but found myself instead staring at Ray Zappa. My heart hopped in my chest. I hadn't heard him step up behind us. I raised my eyes to his long, handsome face. The look on it was not friendly.

"Anyway," Ona threw out, "if you wanna talk about this guy some more, come over to my house tomorrow—"

"What is it with you two, anyway?" Ray Zappa interrupted.

"Are you talking to me?" Ona demanded, her hands on her ample hips, her pretty baby-face that of an angry baby now.

Ray stepped back as if shoved by her glare. But even Ona didn't stop him for long.

"No, I'm not talking to you," he told her. He pointed clearly at me, and then at Wayne. "I'm talking to these two busybodies. Sam Skyler's death is police business and everywhere I go I see these guys acting like they're the police. And they're not. Got it? These two are civilians and don't have any right to be nosing around this Skyler business—"

"Are you telling me I can't talk to civilians when I want to?" Ona demanded. "Last time I heard, the United States of America was still a democracy."

She spread her feet wide and crossed her arms. She might have looked like a fluffy bunny a minute ago, leaning into Perry, but now she'd become a tiger. Perry stood behind her, seemingly ready to jump in if he was needed. But he clearly wasn't. Ray Zappa looked down at Ona's solid figure, a riot of conflicting emotions crisscrossing his long face. Anger. Shame. Frustration. Fear. Conciliation. Then anger again.

"Look, lady," he said finally. I could hear his voice shaking with the effort to keep from shouting. "I don't have a problem with you, okay? We're all in this class together. And up till a few days ago, everything was just fine. But these two."

He swiveled his head toward Wayne quickly before Ona could intervene. "You, Caruso, what's your angle?" he barked.

Wayne stood as firm as Ona had. Only he stood silent, arms at his side, staring right back at Ray Zappa, without saying a word. He'd had answers for Park Ranger Yasuda. But he didn't have a single one for Ray Zappa. Was it because he wanted to keep Diana's name out of the discussion? Or was it some kind of macho posturing? If it was the latter, Ona had already won the prize in that category.

"We just want to know what happened," I explained on Wayne's behalf. "That's all. If people want to talk to us, they can, can't they?" I had meant my voice to be peaceful, reassuring. But I guess it didn't come out that way.

Ray zipped his head back around in my direction.

"And you," he snarled, pointing a finger a few inches from my nose. Maybe Martina had been giving him Institute lessons. But I doubted it. It just looked like a regular old finger of accusation to me. "Always at the scene. I don't care what happened. You're always there. That means something in my book."

"It means I'm unlucky, that's what it means," I objected, feeling the adrenaline rushing through my body now. "Do you think I like—"

"Then, how come you don't just stay out of it?" he demanded, his face swooping down until it was as close to mine as his finger had been. I could smell alcohol and the acid of stomach upset on his breath now. "How come you keep—"

"I don't just keep—"

"Yes, you do—"

"No, I don't—"

And then suddenly, Wayne was standing in the small space left between us.

"Calm down," he suggested quietly. "There's no reason to—"

"Hey, buddy," Zappa snapped then, sounding anything but calmed. "You wanna go for it, huh? Go a couple rounds, huh?"

Bile rose in my throat as testosterone filled the night air. Ray Zappa had a temper on him worse than Campbell Barnhill. And he wouldn't just shake his fist, he'd swing it, I was sure. And Wayne had just put himself in the line of fire. I knew it was for my sake. I understood that. But didn't Wayne realize that I was safe from the worst of Zappa's anger and he wasn't? Zappa would never hit a woman, especially a small woman, but a big guy like Wayne?

"I'm fine," I said in my softest, most soothing voice, trying to wedge my body between the two men. But there just wasn't any space left. Not even air. And sure enough, Ray Zappa's fists were clenched and rising. "I'm sure we can talk this all out—"

"Ray Zappa," came a voice from behind him. It was hushed, but firm. Very firm. "Just what kind of mischief are you up to now?"

Ray's fists lowered slowly, then his whole body seemed to deflate, from the shoulders down. He turned to face his bride to be, an effort at a grin on his face.

But Tessa Johnson wasn't grinning back. I stared at the black mortician in the dimness, shivering a little at the severe expression. She reminded me of a teacher I'd had in the fourth grade. Her name had been Johnson too, I suddenly remembered. Tessa Johnson even looked like the long-ago Mrs. Johnson, different race notwithstanding. Small but erect, there was no way anyone was going to mess with her. Anyone. My stomach began to settle down.

"Just asking a few questions," Ray said defensively.

"In what capacity?" Tessa demanded.

"I . . ."

"You are just as much a civilian here tonight as the rest of Ms. O'Reilley's guests," Tessa pointed out. I wished I'd thought of that one earlier. "And I would expect a man of your caliber to realize that."

"Right," Ray agreed, shrinking just a little more.

"I'm afraid apologies are in order," Tessa said quietly, turning our way, her dark eyes serene and confident.

"Sorry, guys," Ray mumbled.

Wayne mumbled something back.

I even opened my mouth to apologize, then realized Tessa

had probably meant Ray needed to apologize, not us. "At least Wayne and Kate care," came a new voice out of the darkness. A small, trembling voice. Nathan Skyler was back with us now, his eyes swollen behind his glasses, but no longer crying. "Someone should care what happened to my father. He wasn't a guru. He wasn't a fraud. He was a man, my father. And . . ."

And Nathan was crying again, his hands over his face.

Tessa put her hand gently on the young man's arm.

"Of course someone should care," she agreed. The calm sincerity in her voice was enough to bring Nathan's hands away from his face. "Each life is precious in its very own way, your father's no more and no less than anyone else's."

"Yes," Nathan said, his tears vanishing. He looked down at Tessa with something close to awe on his furred face. "Yes, that's exactly it. Thank you."

"Anyway, the guy fell," Emma added, loud and clear, an inch or so away from my ear. My heart did another little gymnastic feat, stopping my breath for an instant. Where had she come from? She glared at us, bits of moonlight glinting off the brass in her nose and ears. "Or else he jumped."

"My father did not jump," Nathan shot back, his voice still trembling, but angry. My mind even supplied the phrase, *anger into achievement*, words I was sure Martina would elicit from Nathan any minute. But when I looked around me, I didn't see Martina. Campbell was there, however, a couple of feet away from Emma, and advancing.

Yvonne was coming our way too. Bearing down on us like a heat-seeking missile.

"Are you all blissed out?" she caroled, her curvy face shining with happiness.

Yvonne's question was greeted with dead silence. She sent a smile at each of us, seeking a happy reaction. Expecting a happy reaction. Had she really missed all the anger seething through our group? If she couldn't see it in our faces and postures, she must have been able to smell it. I certainly could, its acrid scent tainting the night air.

"It was a very moving ceremony," Tessa finally replied politely.

"Oh, it was," Yvonne agreed, one answer enough to get her rolling again. She bent back and spread her arms as if to embrace all the stars in the sky. "So energizing, so cosmically charged, so powerful! Now, can you all imagine the possibilities—"

I elbowed Wayne in his side. None too gently.

He didn't need any more urging. We walked quietly and calmly to the path leading from the backyard, then charged down that path, our hands linked, not stopping until we were safely inside in the Jaguar, traveling down the road toward home.

Once we'd stopped panting and were able to breathe again, we talked suspects against the backdrop of the car's purring engine as shadowed hills, trees, and houses floated by.

"First question," I began, raising a finger to indicate number one. Then I lowered it again. I'd had enough of fingers for the night. "First question. Do we agree that the murderer had to be on the scene?"

Wayne furrowed his impressive brows for at least five minutes. Then he said, "Probably."

"Probably?" I repeated in a much higher voice than his. "That's it?"

"Ninety-nine percent sure," he amplified. "Beyond a reasonable doubt."

"But wouldn't someone have noticed an outsider?" I objected. I wanted one hundred percent.

"You'd think someone would have noticed the murder itself too," he responded.

"All right, all right. Probably," I conceded. He had a point.

"In which case we *probably* have eleven suspects. Yvonne, Campbell, Emma, Nathan, Martina, Ona, Perry, Ray, Tessa . . .''

"Diana and Liz,'' Wayne finished for me. I could feel tense muscles all over my body loosening in relief. And in triumph, since I'd been afraid he'd fight the inclusion of Diana and her mother. But Wayne was a reasonable man. I put my hand on his thigh, feeling warmed by that reason. Warmed by his perpetual sense of fairness.

"How about opportunity?'' I asked next. "Did anyone have better opportunity than anyone else?''

"Yvonne,'' he answered immediately. "She arranged the event. She knew the territory.''

"And Nathan,'' I added. "He probably knew his father's habits better than anyone else.''

"Same for Diana,'' Wayne put in quietly.

"All right, we're up to motive,'' I said, careful not to allow the renewed relief into my voice. Wayne not only knew Diana was a suspect. He knew she was a prime suspect. Wayne still had his reason. Beyond a reasonable doubt.

"Nathan and Diana,'' Wayne proposed. All right! One hundred percent beyond a reasonable doubt. "They both inherit.''

"And they might be in love,'' I contributed.

"Yeah,'' he muttered unhappily. I patted his thigh in sympathy. I wouldn't want the murderer to be my favorite employee's sister either. Whether she was a gorgeous tantric yoga instructor or not.

"Ona was angry,'' I added quickly.

"So was Campbell,'' Wayne said, seeing my suspect and raising me one.

"Liz might have wanted to protect Diana from Sam,'' I put into the pot.

"And Perry might have wanted to protect Ona.''

"Now this is where it gets complicated,'' Wayne murmured

as he pulled into our driveway, popping gravel. "Because all eleven of our probable suspects might have known Sam in other circumstances. Might have had motives we have no idea of."

"Like Sam and Yvonne had an affair thirty years ago and Emma is their illegitimate daughter," I suggested lightly, climbing out of my side of the car.

"Or Yvonne and Sam were *married* before Nathan's mother married Sam and Martina Monteil is a possible heir to the Skyler empire," Wayne proposed, jumping into the game as he stepped from his side of the car.

"Or—"

We heard them before we saw them.

"Grief into growth!" a score of voices chanted.

Wayne and I looked up onto our front deck simultaneously. And the chant became louder.

"Grief Into Growth!"

And angrier.

"GRIEF INTO GROWTH!"

The men and women on the deck waved their hands under the porch lights. Shadow and light battled discordantly as the chants became louder. At this distance, the people looked like monsters, their fingers deformed. Though reason told me we were just seeing the shapes of the puppets they wore.

But that didn't make their appearance any less scary.

Because they were on our deck, blocking our way.

"Anger into achievement!" someone shouted.

And the shout became a roar.

"ANGER INTO ACHIEVEMENT!"

And suddenly, the group on the deck looked less like people and more like a village mob. A village mob ready for a lynching.

TEN

T cast my eyes in Wayne's direction as my heart began to thump in time with the chants of the mob on our deck.

"Control into cooperation!" they screamed over and over again, their deformed fingers still flying in the dim porch light, creating a poorly coordinated shadow play.

Wayne returned my look as one of the puppeteers took a step down the deck stairs. I caught a glimpse of fear in his eyes. Or thought I did. Was it just my own fear winking back at me?

"Denial into determination!" The new chant was repeated.

Maybe we could just spend the night in a hotel. It wouldn't be running away, exactly, I told myself. I just didn't want any more visitors. Ever.

"Wayne, let's just leave—" I began.

"Higher self into living grace!" The voices were getting closer.

I turned and saw the lead puppeteer not a yard away.

"Let's go!" I shouted, turning to dash back toward the Jaguar. But I was too late. Wayne took a fighter's stance as the mob surrounded us. Even if I were to make it inside the car, Wayne wouldn't be in there with me.

I took a deep breath and centered myself. Were we actually in physical danger?

"ANGER INTO ACHIEVEMENT!" they roared. And suddenly I didn't even care about physical danger. I just wanted to be in the house, away from these people.

I considered pushing the closest puppeteer away. I knew I could do it. Sweep the one man away with one turn. But I didn't want to arouse the rest. This was no random sprinkling of reporters. These people were all one beast.

"What is it you want from us?" I asked instead, my tone as loud and as deep as I could make it—compensating for the tiny, shrill whine in my head. Whining to get away. Whining to run.

For a moment, there was silence. Then a single voice took up the chanting again.

"Grief into growth!"

But not as many voices joined in the second round.

"What do you want?" I asked again.

"The killer of Sam Skyler," a voice broke out from the chants.

"We don't know who the killer is," I told that voice as calmly as possible.

The group began to splinter into individuals. Some kept chanting, but some wanted to talk. Some were human.

"My name is Jeffrey Hitchin," said one of the puppeteers, introducing himself. In the dark I could see he was a tall, gaunt man with wild, curly hair. He extended his hand to shake, then seemed to remember the puppets stuck on his fingers and withdrew it. "People say you know who killed our leader."

"What people?" I asked, telling my body to relax. This man was a person, not just a piece of a mob.

It was the wrong response.

"Who cares who told us?" demanded a woman, looming up in the darkness in a voluminous flowing jacket, puppets peeking out the long sleeves. "If it's true."

"It isn't true," Wayne declared, his voice deep and loud.

"We don't know who the murderer is. You've been deliberately misled."

There was a blessed silence then. Were they actually considering his words?

"Grief into growth!" someone started up again.

"Oh, cool it, Simon," someone else said.

"Who do *you* think killed Sam Skyler?" Wayne asked quickly.

Upraised hands dropped as shoulders shrugged.

"Were there any threats made at the Institute?" I chimed in.

"Don't think so" seemed to be the general consensus. Not very helpful, but now they were answering our questions. At least most of them were.

"Who told you we knew who did it?" I asked again.

"Um," said the woman with the flowing jacket, far less confident in her tone now. "I took a phone call at the Institute. Someone called asking to talk to a student, and I was closest."

"Did the person give you their name?" I asked.

"Nooo . . ." she answered thoughtfully. "Actually, they hardly talked. To tell you the truth, I couldn't even tell if the voice was male or female."

So much for that.

After ten more minutes of admissions of ignorance on their side, and denials on ours, the puppeteers departed, waving their finger puppets at us over their shoulders as they walked to their cars parked across the street. I smiled for a moment. They looked like overgrown children, discouraged, overgrown children going home after a field trip. But then I wondered if they had parked across the street on purpose, to hide their presence until we showed up. So they could terrify us all the more effectively from the deck. And suddenly they didn't look like children anymore. I shivered now. Now that they were just people again, not a raging mob.

I felt Wayne's arm around my shoulder.

"Handled that well, Kate," he murmured. "I was ready to fight. Would have been stupid."

I turned to him, astounded by his praise, only remembering how much I'd wanted to run.

"You were the one who turned the questions around," I reminded him.

"We're a good team," he compromised and we made our way up the stairs together.

I felt very old, very fragile, as Wayne opened the front door and we shambled over to the denim couch to sit down quietly, side by side. Alone at last. No puppeteers. No murder suspects. No cops. No one but us.

Except for the blinking light on the answering machine.

Like a well-trained lab rat, I ignored the weakness in my legs and dragged myself over to the machine to let the message tape run.

"Hi, this is Judy," the Jest Gifts' warehousewoman's tinny voice greeted me cheerfully. "No, no, not Judy anymore. Whaddaya think of Blossom for my new name? Too yin, maybe? I thought of Adara. Whaddaya think? Too yang? Maybe Dara-Blossom. Anyway, you know the cat-carrier earrings for the veterinarians, well, there's something wrong with them . . ."

Ten minutes later when the tape finally ran out, I took one guilty look at the stacks of paperwork on my desk and went back to sit on the couch with Wayne. My mind still couldn't seem to focus clearly. C.C. came slinking in and leapt into my lap effortlessly, snuggling up next to my unsettled belly. Without complaining. Had she been as frightened as we had?

"Wayne?" I whispered. "You know what you said earlier about us being a good team?"

He turned to me slowly. I looked under his brows and saw that his eyes were no more focused than my mind was.

"Did you mean it?"

He nodded absently and stroked the side of my face with his big hand, gently pushing my hair back. C.C. purred.

"You and me on this Skyler thing, together," I pressed, resisting my own urge to purr.

He removed his hand and thought awhile.

"Okay," he said finally. "It's not just Diana anymore anyway. Tessa was right. Sam Skyler deserves no more and no less than any other person."

We sealed it with a kiss. A very long kiss, in space as well as time. One that left us both feeling much better a half hour later, woven into a single entity in each other's arms.

$\mathcal{B}$y Tuesday morning, the previous night's events seemed like a dream. Or a nightmare, depending on which piece of tape I ran through the reel in my mind.

Wayne had called Ona early and arranged to meet her and Perry for lunch. Then he'd run off to La Fête à L'Oiel to take care of some things, with a promise to return in time to keep our appointment. I'd been alone for four hours with the reams of Jest Gifts paperwork. And C.C. The towering stacks seemed sinister that morning, almost as sinister as the mob the night before. Almost, but not quite.

I checked off another order and thought about motives as C.C. crouched on the top of my chair and played batting practice with the back of my head. If Sam Skyler had indeed killed his previous wife, or even was believed to, wouldn't there be someone left who'd want to avenge that act? No matter how many years had passed? Was that someone a member of our Wedding Ritual class? The real question, I told myself, was whether anyone in the group had a past association with Sally Skyler.

Yvonne might know, I decided, and dragged my phone over, dislodging C.C., much to her unmuted displeasure. But all I got when I punched Yvonne's number was her canned message, hoping my day was filled with "the energy of cosmic bliss, wonder, and delight."

I slammed the phone back down and thought of calling Felix. If anyone could find out, he could. But still, Felix was Felix.

On cue, the phone rang. It wasn't Felix, of course. It was his psychic sweetie, my friend Barbara Chu.

"Felix doesn't have a clue, kiddo," she greeted me when I picked up the phone.

I still don't know how she does her psychic shtick, but it drives me crazy. Lately, though, I've been trying to be cool, to pretend I don't notice. As if you can pretend with a psychic.

"No clue in general?" I asked her. "Or only as to this murder?"

"As to this murder," she replied. "And he also can't figure out why you guys are so pissed at him."

I opened my mouth to give her the earful I would liked to have give Felix.

"I know, I know," she said before I could even start.

"You probably do know," I muttered. "Any idea who the murderer is?"

"Nope," she replied cheerfully.

I figured that would be her answer. Psychic though she might have been (and I still wasn't totally convinced that she was), she had yet to do anything useful with it, like identify a murderer. Until it was too late—

"I know, I know," she said again.

Then I opened my mouth once more, to ask her why she'd called.

"You don't have to worry about Wayne falling in love with Diana," she informed me. "She's too young, too scatterbrained. And too skinny."

"But—" I began. And heard the front door open.

I whirled around in time to see Wayne walk in. I smiled at him foolishly as Barbara hung up with a parting message, ordering me to give Wayne a great big hug.

Ona and Perry were only minutes away in Cebollas. Wayne and I barely spoke on the way up there in my Toyota. Maybe he was beginning to doubt the wisdom of agreeing to act as a team. Especially with me as his partner. And I was still thinking over what Barbara had said about Diana. But Ona made up for the silence the moment she opened her front door.

"Boy, do you believe that Ray Zappa?" she began as we walked into the house. And kept on talking as we entered the living room, a room filled to the redwood rafters with books and computers and sports equipment. "What a macho creep, telling us who we can and can't talk to . . ."

The walls of the living room sported a couple of paintings of women, large pink women. And a blowup photo of Perry Kane that had what looked suspiciously like dart holes in it. Or bullet holes? I was examining the pitted surface more closely when Ona's voice filtered back into my consciousness.

". . . always try to have at least one lunch together every week. I only work a few miles away and Perry makes his own hours. Perry's a great cook—"

"And a real asshole," a burly looking blond teenager added under his breath. I vaguely remembered seeing him before at one of the Wedding Ritual classes. But I didn't know his name.

Ona introduced him, ignoring his comment. "My son Ogden," she announced, pointing. Ogden snarled some sort of greeting in our direction. "And Orestes," she added as a smaller version of Ogden came running into the room.

"Pammy told me to shove my penis in the blender," he whined.

"Fine, fine," Ona responded. "Are you going to do it?"

"No, but I—" Orestes objected.

"Look, if you're not going to do it, then what's the point?" his mother asked him. "I keep telling you to ignore that kind of bull-crap, okay?"

"I guess so," he answered sullenly.

"These are Kate and Wayne," she introduced us briefly, then turned away from her sons.

"Perry's got two girls, Pammy and Page," she explained. "And I've got these two boy wonders here. And they don't always get along."

"Rather eat shit then live with those two," Ogden muttered in clarification. "And their asshole of a father."

Ona ignored him and went on. Talking *and* walking, leading us toward the kitchen.

"So what's going on with this Skyler fiasco?" she demanded. "Those clowns from the Quiero Police Department grilled me and Perry till they sucked us dry. And we both got some really weird stuff on our doorsteps this morning, papier-mâché daggers covered in catsup." She paused for a moment and glared at her sons, who were following us. At least *she* had suspects outside the Skyler case. "None of the kids would cop to leaving them, and we think we believe them—"

"Wayne and I got a real live trocar," I interjected. "Along with catsup."

"Really?" Ona said, her eyes widening. For a moment she was stopped in her tracks. She really was a pretty woman in all her blond pinkness, especially with her sea-green eyes wide open.

"What's a trocar?" asked Ogden.

Unfortunately, Ona knew and explained in gruesome detail as we entered the kitchen where Perry was decimating something in a blender. Something that smelled of curry. I peeked over at Ogden. He looked a little pale but seemed okay. When I looked back, Perry gave us a little wave, and two new pairs of brown eyes surveyed us. With evident hostility. Or were they glaring at the boys behind us? The boys, I decided, look-ing over my shoulder where Ona's two offspring were return-ing the glare. Oh, the joys of children.

"Pammy and Page," Ona threw out in apparent introduc-tion.

"Hi, there," I said.

The two girls mumbled something back. At least Ona and Perry had matched sets. The oldest girl and boy looked about fifteen, the younger ones about ten. The girls were both slen-der, brown-skinned, and black-haired; the boys wide, pink-skinned, and blond like their mother. At least I could tell the combatants apart.

"Curried vegetables and saffron rice," Perry announced as his hands flew back and forth from stove to tiled counter.

Wayne wandered Perry's way, sniffing and asking about spices.

"Wayne's the cook in the family too," I told Ona, trying for a nonchalant tone, here in the neutral zone between the hostile tribes.

"Not a family yet," Ogden muttered inevitably.

When the meal was ready we served ourselves from the glazed blue tiles of the kitchen counter. The food was good, not as heavy with oil as most restaurant Indian food. The veg-etables were fresh and deliciously undercooked, loaded with spices and coconut and raisins, the saffron rice sweet and full of cinnamon. I was stuffing my face within seconds of sitting down with the rest of the crew, all eight of us crammed to-gether at the expanded teak table.

Even Ona's boys ate hungrily, without comment.

"My father was English," Perry told us after a few minutes of silent feasting on everyone's part. "My mother Indian. It was hard on Mom sometimes, always hard on an outsider. And Dad wasn't very compassionate about her situation—"

" 'Compassionate' " Ogden mimicked, picking up the gushy side of Perry's friendly voice almost perfectly.

"That's enough!" Ona snapped, choosing to hear her son this time. "None of your B.S. while we're eating."

I was surprised that Ogden complied without argument, going back to his vegetables with a minor shrug. Maybe getting his mother's attention was his goal and he was no longer interested once he'd scored. On the other hand, maybe he just didn't want to argue with his mother. I wouldn't.

"You know, Tessa Johnson was the one who buried Perry's mother," said Ona, taking up the thread. "Or at least she worked for the funeral parlor that buried her—right, honey?"

Perry nodded, spooning up some of his rice.

"A real fighter, the guy who owned it then," Ona went on admiringly. "He was white, but he refused to discriminate. His funeral parlor was the first to bury people of other races here in Marin. Before him, if you weren't white, they took you out of county to be buried."

"I didn't know that," I said, shaking my head and wondering uncomfortably what other racial issues had passed me by, living here in all so spiritually correct Marin County.

"Tessa seems like a very caring woman," Perry added. Now that Ogden had done his imitation, I couldn't help but hear the gushing note in Perry's voice as he spoke. "I believe she owns the mortuary now."

"Do you think she knew Sam Skyler before the class?" Wayne asked, getting down to business, even as he stood up to help himself to seconds.

"I don't think so," Ona answered slowly, her baby face pinched in thought. "But I only took one seminar from that s.o.b., so what do I know?" She turned to Perry.

Perry shrugged his shoulders. "Same here," he told us. "I just took an introductory class. A few years back, before I met Ona. The whole puppet routine bothered me too much. Almost like religious idols, you know. And the way he mesmerized people.''

Ogden got up with his plate just as Wayne sat down, mincing his way to the counter and lip-syncing as Perry spoke. Luckily, Ona didn't see him.

But Pammy, Perry's oldest, did. Her brown skin reddened with anger.

"We're gonna do a virtual reality wedding," Ona announced. "We're not clear on the details yet, but Perry and I are both techies from way back, so it'll be supercyber." She paused for a mouthful as Pammy got up from the table. "I gotta say I was surprised to see Sam Skyler at Yvonne's class, though. The man thought he was God. So why would God need a Wedding Ritual class?"

"Probably Diana's idea," I put in.

Grievance must have flavored my tone. Ona shook her finger at me and laughed.

"Well, as long as God is male," she agreed, "I suppose Diana could convince him of just about anything."

I laughed back. That made two of us.

"You know what I wondered," I put in, now that we were laughing together. "I wondered if anyone in our Wedding Ritual class had known Sam Skyler's wife Sally. You remember, the one that went over the balcony—"

But before I could finish my sentence, someone drowned my words out in a scream.

ELEVEN

It was a scream that could have chilled jalapeño peppers. I turned and saw Pammy with her head bent back and her mouth wide open to the maximum effect. This young woman just might have a career in opera, I decided. Ogden had his hands mashed over his ears and was rolling his eyes in real or feigned pain. And Pammy just kept on screaming. What had he done to her?

Pammy took a breath and finished in the fullness of her screaming, "He splashed me, Daddy!"

Getting no immediate response from the onlookers at the dining table, she added in a mere shout, "With water!"

Orestes and Page jumped up from the table then, running to the aid of their respective siblings. Halfway there, they collided. Whether on purpose or by mistake, it was hard to tell, but in the next instant they were down on the kitchen linoleum in a writhing heap of brown and pink anger. Bits of words floated up like wisps of steam from a boiling cauldron.

". . . picking on her . . ."

". . . it's you that . . ."

". . . no way . . ."

". . . moron . . ."

It didn't take Pammy and Ogden long to appraise the situation. And then they were down on the floor too, trying to pry the two younger children apart. Or were they?

The pink and brown writhing mass got bigger and heavier. And more verbiage was added to the steaming cauldron.

". . . don't you call my . . ."

". . . little retard . . ."

". . . you'll be sorry . . ."

When Ona and Perry got up from the table, Wayne and I were the only ones left.

"Um, maybe we ought to be—" I began. Leaving? Running away? Splashing cold water on all involved?

"Ogden, get up this instant!" Ona ordered.

Ogden stood and put his head into his hands, mumbling into his palms, invectives I wasn't close enough to hear. Fortunately. Meanwhile, Pammy jumped up and ran to her father's arms. Leaving Ona to deal with the other two children, which she did handily, pulling each child up from the floor and apart from the other with one hand apiece, and holding them there at arm's length as they yipped at each other. She looked our way apologetically.

"Pammy, now," Perry cajoled his eldest. "You know better."

"Maybe this is a bad time," Wayne tried.

"Just one more crappy day in our soon to be happy household," Ona assured us. Then Orestes took a swipe at Page but missed.

"That's it," Ona announced, her voice now heavy with threat. "Time out for a Talk."

Suddenly everyone looked cowed, including Perry.

Ona looked our way again.

I took my cue.

"Well, it's been fun," I said, pushing back my chair.

"Fun," she repeated, laughing. "That it has been. Thanks, Kate. You're a hoot. We'll see you two later, okay?"

Wayne didn't need any more urging. He jumped straight up from the table like an electrified deer. He didn't even offer to do the dishes.

"Each of us will have a chance to share our feelings," Ona began as Wayne and I made our way back through the living room. "One at a time. No interruptions. No horse hockey. Is that understood?"

I heard a low groan as I shut the door quickly behind us.

"I don't envy them," Wayne muttered once we'd reached the Toyota.

"At least they have their wedding figured out," I replied and instantly wished my words had been on a leash and could be retrieved.

I peered up at Wayne, guilt flooding my bloodstream like a bad drug.

"I still don't envy them," he said gruffly and put his arms around me.

It was his arms that convinced me, not his words. I could still feel the lingering warmth of that embrace as I climbed into the car and Wayne asked me if it was "okay" to make our next stop the Skyler Institute for Essential Manifestation.

In fact, I could still feel the imprint of his arms even as I steered back down the highway and over the curving blacktop into Golden Valley. It was a quiet trip, though, each of us lost in our own thoughts. When we were almost there, I looked over at Wayne. What was he thinking about? Love? Commitment? Murder?

I got considerably more focused once we reached the actual gates to Sam Skyler's domain. The Institute was a fortress.

"Are you sure it'll be all right for us to sit in?" I asked anxiously as I drove my fifteen-year-old Toyota into the compound through the only opening in the encircling ten-foot-high redwood fence. And parked in the nearest space I could find, between a Mercedes and a BMW.

"Talked to Nathan earlier," Wayne explained. "He said it'd be fine . . ."

His words faltered as we took in the Skyler Institute for Essential Manifestation in all its grandeur.

Yasuda hadn't been kidding when he said the place was big. Three stories of rounded redwood with lots of glass and brass and skylights and solar collectors and strangely angled projections that might have been stairways. Or maybe something else entirely. The whole thing had a footprint extending over at least a quarter acre of land, shielded by ancient towering pines. It looked as if a spaceship had landed. Maybe it had. Or maybe the land of Oz had just found a new home.

It certainly felt like Oz when we walked through the electric-eye glass doors.

Wayne and I had collectively taken all of two steps inside when a well-muscled, well-uniformed security guard stopped us short.

"Names?" he demanded.

"Kate Jasper and Wayne Caruso," I answered automatically, resisting the simultaneous urge to salute.

"Purpose?" he barked, scanning the clipboard in his hand.

"In life?" I shot back, automatic obedience on hold.

But he didn't seem to hear me, having found our names on his list by that time. Or maybe mine was a normal response for someone visiting the Skyler Institute.

"Jasper and Caruso," he announced, an abrupt smile cracking his stern face. "Mr Skyler—Junior, that is—said for Alicia to take care of you when you got here," he told us, all friendliness now.

And then suddenly Alicia was there by his side, like a rabbit popping out of a hole. A very attractive brown rabbit with a prominent set of gleaming white teeth. And a very unrabbitlike scent of perfume. Expensive or cheap, I couldn't tell you. But strong and sweet.

"Nathan is teaching the beginner's class right now," Alicia whispered earnestly. "But he said to just bring you on in when you arrived. You'll love it. It's so regenerative. And it'll be over in about a half an hour, anyway. You can speak to him personally then. Will you follow me?"

So we followed Alicia. It wasn't easy. Her high heels made incredibly rapid progress down the plushly carpeted hallway.

"Have a vitalizing day, now," the guard shouted after us as we raced to keep up with our escort.

I waved over my shoulder. Alicia didn't give us any time to slow down for a proper reply. If there was a proper reply.

We passed an open doorway and heard a familiar chant, "Anger into Achievement!" roaring our way.

I shivered, moving closer to Wayne.

"Which class is that?" I asked, nodding toward the doorway which was rapidly disappearing behind us.

"Oh, those are our advanced students," Alicia whispered, barely slowing as she looked over her shoulder. "Very illuminated."

"If someone called, asking to speak to a student, would you choose one of them?" I pressed her.

"Oh, yes," she answered fervently.

"Do you take the calls—" I kept on, but we had reached our destination.

Alicia opened the door and showed us in. And then she was gone, back to her rabbit hole, leaving only her sweet scent behind. The room was impressive, ennobled by a vaulted white plaster ceiling and eight-foot-high windows. Platforms of various heights and colors vied for prominence in the center of the room, encircled by a zone of open space. The sides of the room were dominated by a series of curved, carpeted risers in bright turquoise. All and all, it had the feeling of a small theater . . . a small, experimental theater.

Nathan was standing in the open zone with a few dozen

students, talking to a short young man who was handing out finger puppets.

Wayne and I exchanged looks before we made our presence known. His was a look of martyrdom. I'm not sure what mine was, but my body was sending me tingling fight-or-flight signals.

"Here's your introductory set of puppets," the short young man told me, at my side before I'd even heard him approach. Too late for flight. But not for fight.

"No, no," I objected. "We're just here to observe."

"Wayne, Kate," came Nathan's calming voice. Somewhere under all the fur and glasses, he smiled. "Go ahead and take the puppets. You might enjoy the experience."

Where had I heard that line before? But Wayne and I did take the puppets. They were cleverly made, each knitted so that it was elastic enough to slip on any size finger, color-coded, and two-faced. The anger and grief on one side were easy to recognize. The denial, control, and higher self were a little harder. The face on the opposite side of each was always the same, however, clearly the wise and happy face of a completely self-actualized finger puppet.

Nathan gave us instructions, and we all put on our puppets and sat on the turquoise risers. And I mean all of us, Wayne and myself included. Nathan Skyler's puppy demeanor was just too appealing to resist.

But I didn't chant. I just moved my lips, superstitiously avoiding the real experience. Because there was something too strange about the use of the puppets, something too close to religious, just as Perry Kane had said. I was trying to figure out exactly what it was that was so spooky, when Martina Monteil entered the room.

And I do mean entered, as in Grand Entrance. The light in the room even seemed to grow ever so slightly brighter as she came in. Martina was that impressive. She stepped up onto the highest platform, spine straight, head back and arms spread as if to embrace the room. That's when I noticed Nathan behind her, his hand on a set of controls. Was that what the light was about? True or not, I was still impressed. Especially when she spoke. She began in muted tones:

"You have all come here today to experience your essential core issues," she told us, rhythm and passion already flavoring her soft words. Her voice deepened and her body began to sway almost imperceptibly. "And you will. Those issues will manifest in a way that they never have before." She brought her hand out from her chest, fingers first, as if extending her heart. Where had I seen that gesture before? Sam Skyler, my unconscious supplied in answer. Martina's tone grew louder, a tremolo now a part of it. "You will be illuminated!"

"Yes," breathed someone behind me.

She had them. I turned for an instant to survey the faces around me. They were rapt. Even Wayne looked hypnotized.

Martina continued to speak.

"And when you are empowered," she went on, "when you are enlightened, when you are energized as you have never been before—"

"Amen," someone interjected. But no one seemed to notice.

"Then you will be unstoppable . . ."

The content of Martina's words seemed to me to lack substance, but her delivery made up for that lack in spades.

By the time she was finished, these people would have walked on fire for her. Maybe even taken out her garbage. She had It, whatever it was. The same It as all the great preachers and politicians. The same It that Sam Skyler had possessed.

Even the question and answer period didn't throw her.

"I'm a word processor," a red-haired young man began from behind me, a whine edging his voice. "If each finger has meaning, what happens when you type with them all day?"

"Very good," Martina replied, leaning forward just a bit. "That is the precise reason for the puppets. They enable the manifestation of your essential self through your fingers. But when you're not wearing them, your fingers will become mere fingers once again."

"Which finger represents love?" a much older man wanted to know.

Martina brought her hand out from her chest again. The room grew a little brighter.

"Each and every one of them," she answered, a tremolo in her deep voice once again. "Just as each and every one of us has the potential to be the very essence of pure love."

And with that, she surrendered the platform to Nathan and left the room.

Nathan divided the class into smaller groups. Then they began practicing with their puppets. Suddenly, one young woman began to cry. Nathan was there in a flash, soothing her, bringing her back to herself like a father with a hurt child. He didn't have the It that Martina and his late father possessed, but I'd rather have had him with me on a bad day any time. Or on a good day for that matter.

And finally the half hour was over and the introductory class was herded out of the room by two young women, both of whom bore an amazing resemblance to Alicia. It was something about the gleaming teeth. Maybe they all went to the same dentist.

At last, we were alone with Nathan Skyler.

"Would you like to come up to my office?" he offered diffidently, peering down through his thick glasses at the top of his shoes. I wondered if he had more confidence now, or less confidence than he'd had before his father's training. It was hard to believe that he had more.

As we left the seminar room and were walking back down

the carpeted hallway, a massive man in a blue suit and a red tie came striding toward us, his face set in stone.

"Hey, Skyler," he hissed. "You thought about our offer?"

"I've already told you no," Nathan answered, his soothing voice far more firm than I would have expected. Maybe he had more confidence than I gave him credit for.

But then help was coming. Alicia popped up first.

"If you would please follow me—" she began.

"Yeah?" the man snarled. "Why should I?"

"Because she asked you to," Wayne answered quietly from my side.

A glimmer of recognition flashed in the man's eyes. Recognition of Wayne? Or of Wayne's potential as an opponent? He opened his mouth to speak. And then our uniformed friend from security came striding down the hall.

"Don't know how he got in, Mr. Skyler," he apologized. "But he'll be leaving now."

Nathan nodded, and the man in the blue suit straightened his tie with a great deal of upper-body swiveling.

"Think about it," he growled over his shoulder as he left, flanked by Alicia on one side and the uniformed security man on the other.

"Growth Imperatives, Unlimited," Nathan muttered.

"What?" I asked, still trying to absorb what I had just seen.

"The guy's from some organization called Growth Imperatives, Unlimited. They want to buy the Institute." Abruptly, Nathan started walking down the hall again. Wayne and I bolted to catch up with him. "Not only the Institute but the publishing rights to my father's works. They've even accused me of killing my father. Threatened to frame me for it."

"Who are they exactly?" I asked as Nathan put a key into a brass panel next to the elevator.

He shrugged his perpetually slumped shoulders. "Martina's looking into it. She was the one who hired the security guy.

I thought it seemed a little overreactive at the time. I thought we ought to be able to calm down and work this out without all the hostility. But . . .''

His words trailed off as we rode up in the elevator.

Except for the high ceilings and windows and plush carpet, Nathan's office didn't look anything like the seminar room we had just left. The furniture was like the furniture in any bureaucrat's office. Metal desk and ancient office chair. A half dozen filing cabinets. And a couple of vinyl visitors' chairs which Wayne and I settled into. The only thing out of place was the old Labrador retriever who came waddling out from under the desk to rest his graying muzzle on my hand. I patted his head. He reached up a paw and patted me back.

"Sigmund," Nathan announced, flopping into his own ancient chair which squeaked dispiritedly.

"What?" I said.

"My dog's name is Sigmund," he clarified, his eyes on his desk. A desk cluttered with more paperwork than mine. That cheered me a little, whatever his dog's name was.

"Sigmund Freud," Wayne whispered in my ear.

"Ah," I whispered back.

"Not very many people get the joke," Nathan told us, smiling. His hearing was awfully good. Or else he read lips. I'd have to remember not to whisper anything important around him from now on.

"Anyway, I'm sure you're here to talk about my father," Nathan went on, looking down at the stacks of paper again. "And his death. First, let me say that my father wasn't a great man. And he wasn't a terrible man. All this guru stuff got everyone confused. He was just human."

"Well, we did wonder . . ." Wayne began.

"If he really abused my stepmother," Nathan finished for him, his voice still soft. "The answer is yes and no. He did hit her. But as I said before, she always threw the first punch.

They had a difficult marriage. Though I think they actually cared for each other deeply. His grief over her death was real." He paused as Sigmund trotted over to lay his head in Nathan's lap with a long doggy sigh. I noticed Nathan hadn't answered the real question. The real question wasn't just about abuse, it was about murder. Had Nathan's father murdered his stepmother?

"What Dad really was," Nathan told us, petting the old dog gently, "was a narcissist with exhibitionist tendencies. Actually, he was a lot like Martina."

It was then I remembered that Nathan had a B.A. in psychology.

"He was a man who needed the continuous admiration and adulation of his students. He was addicted to it. And that need grew and grew." Nathan leaned back in his squeaking chair, obviously more comfortable in this abstract professorial mode than in any other. Sigmund repositioned his head. "The ultimate irony is that the more Dad's narcissism grew, the more he lost touch with his true inner core. And manifesting that inner core is the essence of the Institute."

"You're able to analyze your father better than most people could," I said, mostly to fill the ensuing silence.

"Yes, but I loved him too," Nathan answered gently, his eyes misting under his glasses. "I just couldn't help but see what was happening. The way he needed more and more to feed his sense of worth. I even tried to talk to him about it. But he was on his own path." Nathan took off his glasses and scrubbed at them with the corner of his pullover. "I just wish . . ."

Then he rubbed his eyes and put his glasses back on. He sat up straight again.

"Now that Dad's gone, I'll probably go back and get my Ph.D. in psychology. I inherit the Institute jointly with my grandmother and Diana. But the Institute was Dad's, not mine.

I don't want to run it. And I wonder if Martina wouldn't do a better job. She has what it takes. I don't.''

I found myself nodding, and wondered if Nathan expected an argument. But I didn't see any manipulation in his face. At least in what I could see of it under all the fur.

"Martina reminds me of your father," I said instead.

"Boy, have you got that right," he responded, awe raising his usual volume. "Over the years, her voice and mannerisms have gotten more and more like his. They'd become almost interchangeable. Except that Dad was a real innocent. And Martina—"

He cut himself off, shaking his head ruefully.

"Anyway, old Sigmund, the human one, did say all boys want to marry their mothers," he went on with a smile. "Somehow I ended up with my father."

"You're a good observer," Wayne began slowly. "Does anyone in our wedding class look like a murderer to you?"

Nathan frowned and shook his head.

"I've certainly thought about it," he answered. "And I have yet to come up with a single answer. Ona's authoritarian and combative. But I don't think she's a killer. Yvonne and Emma are probably both manic-depressives, though all I've seen so far is their manic sides. Perry's a classic co-dependent. He's lucky he has Ona to straighten him out. I haven't quite gotten a feel for Tessa yet. She's rigid, but compassionate, I think." He frowned again. "But to answer your question, no one's personality cries out 'murderer' to me. I just wish it was that simple."

"Me too," I agreed.

"I can fill you in on a little family background, if that'll help," he offered.

"Go," I ordered. Talk about your silver platter.

"Believe it or not, I had a fairly happy childhood," Nathan began. "My parents divorced early on, when my mom, Helen, discovered she was a lesbian. And that, interestingly enough, worked out well, leaving the 'Dad' slot open for my father— no other man to usurp it. So Dad was always around. And Mom and Dad were really united in caring for me. Dad took me everywhere when I was a kid. And did all the stuff fathers are supposed to: camping and fishing and sailing and all that.'' His voice thickened, and I saw that his eyes were misty again. If he was making all this up, he was doing a mighty good job of it. ''So I was lucky. I even got Dad's mother, Irene, thrown in for a granny.'' He shook his head and rolled his eyes under his glasses. Suddenly, I wanted to meet this Irene.

''Would you give us your mother's and grandmother's phone numbers?'' I asked.

''Sure,'' he agreed easily and wrote the numbers down on a slip of paper torn from a pad somewhere beneath all the clutter on his desk. If he had family secrets to hide, he apparently wasn't worried about our uncovering them.

''By the way,'' he added, ''Dad's memorial service is Wednesday morning. Here at the Institute. I'm inviting everyone from the class. It seems right. Anyway, your visit saves me a call.''

There didn't seem to be a lot left to say after that.

But Wayne wasn't finished.

''What about Diana?'' he asked.

Nathan's phone rang at that point. And he grabbed it. But there wasn't quite enough fur on his face to hide the blush underneath.

''Uh-huh,'' he said to whoever was on the other end of the line. ''That'll be fine. Anyone who wants a refund—''

And then I smelled a familiar sweet scent and Alicia popped up again, ready to escort us from the building.

First, Wayne and I waved goodbye to Nathan. Minutes later, we were saying our farewells to Alicia and the security man as we exited via the automatic doors two floors down. Finally, we were out of Oz.

As we walked to the parking lot, I saw Martina Monteil slide into the passenger's side of the Mercedes parked next to my Toyota. But it wasn't until the car pulled away that I saw the face of the man driving. It was the man in the blue suit and red tie, the man from Growth Imperatives, Unlimited.

TWELVE

"Did you see who that was?" I asked Wayne in a whisper.

But he didn't answer me.

"Wayne, why do you suppose—" I began, turning. And then I saw the reason for his silence. We had company. A man stood at Wayne's side, a tall skinny man wearing a cowboy hat with a blond braid as long as Diana's black one snaking out from beneath the hat's feathered brim.

"Hi!" the man greeted us enthusiastically, extending a hand. "My name's Sky-Guy, and I'd like to buy this here Institute."

I shook his hand automatically. It felt too soft for a cowboy's. Shouldn't it have calluses or something?

"Sorry, but we don't own the Institute," Wayne told Sky-Guy and nudged me in the ribs.

Right. Move it. I began to walk toward the Toyota, speeding up a little as we got closer. We weren't out of Oz yet.

"Well, that's a darn shame," the cowboy said as he followed us, his blue eyes bulging slightly as he spoke. "Man, this place is a virtual light-and-right show, ya know? Techno-magico-emotion, intergalactic-muse, and purification-spirit-location, all sprouting in redwood. And the name of names: Skyler. Mine's Sky-Guy, you know."

"Right," I said, sticking my key in the Toyota.

I backed out of the parking space, still hearing bits and pieces about celestial spirals and cyber-nature through my open window. I rolled it up as fast as I could and waved goodbye through the glass.

Even then, I could still see his lips moving in the rearview mirror. Only he appeared to be talking to the sky now. That made sense, his being Sky-Guy and all.

"Where to next, sir?" I asked Wayne once we were out of the gates.

"Sanity," he replied gruffly.

"I knew you could drive someone insane, but can you drive them sane?" I mused aloud.

He turned and looked at me, brows descending rapidly.

"Yes?" I asked lightly.

"Yes," he agreed heavily.

"Tessa," I suggested halfway home on the road from Golden Valley. Tessa's mortuary was less than five minutes from our house. I'd looked it up in the phone book under Mortuary/Funeral Homes that morning and realized I'd passed it hundreds of times without really registering its presence. But who wants to register the presence of a mortuary, anyway?

"Tessa," Wayne agreed briefly. "Sanity."

There was a funeral party just leaving when we arrived, all in black. Somber black. Formal, somber black. Suddenly, I realized I was in my Chi-Pants and a sweatshirt. At least the pants and sweatshirt were black, though there was a colorful Laurel Burch bird on the front of the shirt. After the grieving party had passed, Wayne strode up to the door with me dragging along behind.

I was still obsessing about my clothes when Tessa arrived and opened the door. And suddenly everything felt all right again.

"Kate," she said, her hushed voice warm and sympathetic.

She reached an arm around my shoulders and gave them a gentle squeeze. "And Wayne," she added, limiting herself to a pat on his arm. Probably these were just the customary niceties extended by a mortician/funeral director. But I still felt welcome.

"I'm glad you've come," she told us then, motioning us inside to the reception area. "I've been feeling that I must apologize for Ray's behavior."

The reception area was decorated much as one might have expected from a woman like Tessa Johnson. Golden-beige walls. Muted gray carpeting with flecks of cream and golden beige. Blond wood benches and chairs scattered about the room. The colors were as somber, yet uplifting and comforting, as the woman who stood before us, dressed in a charcoal suit with a golden-beige silk blouse that was a perfect accent to her mocha-brown features and upswept curly gray hair. She stared at us for a moment, serene deep-set eyes the only noticeable feature in her long, narrow face.

"Are there any more funerals going on here?" I whispered anxiously. If there were, I didn't want to be caught with the dead in my sweatshirt and Chi-Pants.

She glanced at her watch. "Not for at least another hour," she assured me and then went on, a hint of a smile curving her sensual mouth. A mouth whose sensuality was invisible until she smiled. "I'm afraid Ray has a tendency towards the dramatic. When it's the drama of romance, it can be very appealing, but regrettably the drama of hostility doesn't work nearly as well."

There was something about that hint of a smile that made me feel as if I were the recipient of an intimate gift.

I smiled and nodded back.

"I can assure you, however, it's all drama." She paused, her serene eyes suddenly intense and searching. "He's a breed of dog that doesn't have nearly as much bite as bark."

"Guessed that," Wayne replied, his tone one of embarrass-ment. I wondered why. Did he feel that he'd brought on the encounter with Ray? And then I wondered why Tessa was apologizing for Ray, instead of Ray himself.

"Well," Tessa said briskly, "I'm sure you're here to talk about Sam Skyler. Unless you have any loved ones . . ."

I froze guiltily, then saw the subtle smile on her face once more.

This time I laughed. A little hysterically, actually, register-ing the fact that we were indeed in a funeral home. Or a mor-tuary. Or whatever they called it.

"Would you like the grand tour while we talk?" Tessa of-fered.

"Sure," Wayne agreed, though I wasn't so sure myself.

"I'm not certain what I can tell you about the 'loved one,' " she said, leading us into the chapel. It took me a moment to realize that Sam Skyler was "the loved one." More funeral humor? I looked into her face and saw a glint of laughter in her eyes.

I was beginning to wonder if Tessa was really a standup comic in the sober clothing of a funeral director. Or maybe it was the constant gloom that pushed her to these little jokes. And I began to understand her attraction to Ray Zappa, Mr. Life of the Party. That is, when he wasn't angry.

"I didn't know Sam Skyler before the Wedding Ritual sem-inar," she told us. "And I didn't really get to know him then. He seemed to have enough to say to himself. I didn't feel the need to intervene."

I laughed again, the sound bouncing off the walls of the chapel eerily. I knew I was in a funeral home here, with the gold-leaf pews and maroon carpets and gray walls. And tall brass candlesticks everywhere.

"Look up," Tessa ordered.

We did. And saw a magical painted sky of midnight blue, sparkling with golden stars and moons in various phases.

"Beautiful," was all I could whisper.

"I painted it myself when I bought the funeral home from Mrs. Olcott, my former boss's wife," Tessa said quietly. "My boss was a wonderful man, the man who trained me."

"You were the one who buried Perry Kane's father, weren't you?" I asked, suddenly remembering, my eyes still on the ceiling. "And Liz Atherton's husband?"

Tessa's answer was a little slower this time. And there were no jokes either.

"Yes," was all she said. I brought my eyes back down from the magical ceiling and saw that she was no longer smiling.

Had I broken some kind of rule of funereal etiquette? Did funeral directors have confidentiality considerations like lawyers and doctors?

Tessa led us to the casket room before I had a chance to ask. The room was far too spooky as far as I was concerned, filled with painted coffins that looked like overgrown bassinets, overflowing with fluffy silken linings and little ruffled pillows. And the incongruous smell of lacquer floating over it all.

"Nice," Wayne commented, patting one of the larger models. Was he serious? "What are they made of?"

"Most of our caskets are metal, steel, or copper. Only a few are wood anymore these days," Tessa answered. "A lot of them are made by former auto companies." The smile came back in her voice. "Recognizing a need and filling it."

"Well, if either of us needs any funeral services we'll be sure and use yours," Wayne announced cheerily. "Our house can't be more than two or three minutes away. Literally."

"Oh my, you do flatter me so," Tessa replied flirtatiously, a Southern belle for an instant. "I'll keep a casket warm."

Ugh.

"Did you notice anything odd about any of the members of the Wedding Ritual class?" I cut in. I'd had enough casket jokes.

Again, Tessa didn't answer right away. But this time I was watching her face. And her eyes were troubled.

"I don't think so," she answered slowly.

"'Don't think so,'" I repeated. "Tessa, is there something you noticed that you're not telling us?"

"No, no," she answered finally, shaking her head. But there was something. I was sure of it. Something about Ray? Or one of her former customers? Or—

"You'll really enjoy the embalming room," she announced brightly.

And all other thoughts left my mind. If that had been her intention, she'd done a great job.

The embalming room was actually two rooms, neither of which was decorated tastefully. Or decorated at all. Unless cement was the new look. The first room was the staging area where the bodies were received and sorted. Gurneys and hoists dominated, along with a couple of respectful lab-coated assistants and two, well . . . bodies. With toe tags. The room got all shimmery and liquid for a moment as Tessa explained the necessity of the toe tags to avoid any confusion. I took a couple of deep breaths and wondered if there was anything to this karma business. Was my karma somehow entwined with corpses? Eternally? The room began to shimmer again. And I told myself to cut it out. Thinking, that is.

The second room was where the actual embalming took place. Now, that was a great place to be dizzy. First off, it smelled of disinfectant, a smell that always makes me think of doctors' offices. And everything was already slanted, including the floor and a large white porcelain fixture mounted on a pedestal, that looked like a cross between a bathtub and a serving tray. I directed my eyes away as Tessa's hushed voice explained the uses of the hoses on one end and the hoses and drain on the other. And the trocar—

"Trocar!" I interrupted, zapped out of my dizziness by the word. "Did you put the trocar on our front door?"

This time Tessa's eyes looked really troubled. But more as if she was worried about my sanity than anything else.

"No, Kate," she answered evenly. I recognized the tone. It was the same one I'd used on violent patients when I worked in a mental hospital. "Did someone really put a trocar on your front door?"

I nodded emphatically.

"With catsup," Wayne added. I gave his warm hand a squeeze. I was glad he was there to back me up.

"But why would anyone do such a thing?" Tessa demanded, her usually serene eyes squinting with what looked like outrage.

I really wanted to answer her. Actually, I really wanted to get out of the embalming room. I got my second wish when one of her assistants came and whispered in her ear.

"Oh, dear," Tessa murmured, looking down at her watch. "John is absolutely right. I'm afraid it's time to prepare for the next service."

Then she graciously hustled us out and down the hall, taking the time to tell us about E-mail funeral options on the way.

"What do you do then?" I asked as we got to the front door. "Fax the body?"

She threw me that subtle intimate smile one last time before showing us out of the Olcott Johnson Funeral Home.

It wasn't until we were in the car that Wayne and I noticed that neither of us had ever managed to turn the subject back to Sam Skyler. Not to mention interrogating Tessa as to what she might or might not have been telling us.

It took me two and a half minutes to get home. On the dot.

"Well, does she know something?" I asked Wayne as I opened our front door.

"Probably," he replied slowly.

"But what?" we both said together.

Unfortunately that left no one to answer the question.

Not that we didn't chew on it awhile, anyway. A long while. Along with all the other questions.

"Publishing rights," I blurted out after a moment, my brain synapses speeding up. "Do you think Sam Skyler was publishing another memoir?"

"Interesting possibility," Wayne answered.

"Maybe I could call his publisher," I suggested.

Wayne shook his head. "They're not going to tell you anything," he told me. "Even if we knew who they were."

My synapses were slowing back down to their usual "duh" state when the doorbell rang.

To answer or not to answer, that was the question.

I looked at Wayne. He looked back and shrugged his shoulders. When the bell rang a second time, he got up and answered it.

Wrong choice. Even C.C. was suddenly in the room scolding when the massive man in the blue suit from Growth Imperatives, Unlimited barged in. I was wondering why Wayne didn't just push him back out, when I saw the bulge in the man's pocket, my eyes drawn there as he stuck his hand in that pocket. A gun? It had to be.

"Okay, you guys," the big man hissed. "Someone told me you two know more than you're telling—"

Great, I thought and started back-stepping in the direction of the phone. It seemed like a good time to try out the 911 button.

But before I even got to the phone, I heard Police Chief Woolsey's booming voice "... ecological disaster, but does anyone care?'' and the sound of footsteps up our front stairs. That was fast.

I stepped back to the front door just in time to see the man from Growth Imperatives, Unlimited turn and slither away. Quickly. Very quickly for a man of his size.

"Did you see the guy going down the stairs?" I demanded of the chief excitedly when he made it up to the front door.

"The man in the blue suit?" he asked back.

"Yeah, I think he had a gun—"

I stopped when I saw Chief Woolsey roll his eyes in his companion's direction.

"Maybe the guy was an overzealous solicitor," Officer Fox suggested, and they both had a good laugh.

"But—" I began.

I felt a gentle hand on my shoulder.

I looked up to see Wayne shaking his head ever so slightly. He was right. These guys would probably think the bit about the gun was just a ruse to make us look less guilty. In fact, they probably thought we put the trocar on our own door in the first place.

"So, Ms. Jasper," Woolsey said, no smile on his lean face as he thrust it forward, "I understand you and Mr. Caruso are asking a lot of questions."

I just nodded. I wasn't letting these guys in my house this time. Much less offering them any tea. Woolsey had already asked enough questions to last me a lifetime or two on their previous visit.

I was thinking about telling him so when I heard the clatter of someone else's boots coming up my stairs. I peered around Wayne and the police officers and saw Park Ranger Yasuda approaching.

Woolsey turned to follow my gaze. Yasuda stopped for a moment, then took a deep breath and another step.

"I thought you got the message, Yasuda," Woolsey snarled,

spewing hostility and the fragrance of mint tea. "You're not a part of this investigation."

"I'm not here officially," Yasuda muttered, clasping his hands behind his back.

"Then what are you doing here?" Woolsey demanded, throwing his arms out in apparent exasperation.

"Yeah, what are you doing here?" Fox parroted, as he dodged the chief's arms.

It was then that I heard the sound of the chants.

"Anger into achievement!"

"Grief into growth!"

The voices were coming nearer.

"Oh, Christ," Woolsey snapped. "Not the Merry Musketeers again. I told them we didn't know who did it."

I turned to Wayne. Were the students of the Skyler Institute for Essential Manifestation bugging the police now? I worked hard to keep the smile off my face as Woolsey, Fox, and Yasuda all retraced their steps to their respective cars and took off. A couple of the puppeteers gave Wayne and me little knitted waves over their shoulders and then got in their own cars and followed the representatives of authority. I wondered how they gripped their steering wheels with their puppets on. And then I let myself smile. If there was any truth to be had from Woolsey, I felt sure the advanced students of Sam Skyler's Institute were just the puppeteers to squeeze it out of him.

"Let's get out of here," I said to Wayne.

"Feel like some vegan asparagus mousse?" he asked. "White bean pâté, roasted eggplant with pine nuts . . ."

My mouth was too busy salivating to answer. But I could still nod. It was early, five o'clock, but I was ready if he was.

"Get dressed," he whispered suggestively. "We'll go to the restaurant."

Since "the" restaurant was his restaurant, La Fête à L'Oiel, I understood why he didn't consider me "dressed" already.

Silk and jewels were more common there than Chi-Pants and sweatshirts. I packed my body into my one and only velvet jumpsuit while Wayne dressed in his own suit, and we were on our way to San Francisco within minutes. There's a rainbow painted on the tunnel leading into Marin from the Golden Gate Bridge. For once, I was glad to see it disappear behind us. The only person who hadn't shown up on our doorstep in the last half hour was Felix. Well, actually Diana and Sky-Guy hadn't either. I sank deeper into the passenger's seat of Wayne's Jaguar with a moan of pure pleasure.

Wayne and I were still chortling over the thought of the puppeteers pumping Woolsey when we arrived on the doorstep of La Fête à L'Oiel.

A giant plaster cockroach was pinned to the restaurant's front door where the Open sign usually was.

And this time there was a note attached to the red bow.

It said, "Yum, yum. I'll investigate you if you keep investigating us."

⟨HIRTEEN

⟨ heard a sound next to me, a low rumbling like the first warning growl of an earthquake. It took me a minute to realize it was coming from Wayne. Then the rumble took the form of words.

"No," he declared, his voice deep and vibrating. "Not here."

He stood, staring at the thing on the door, his whole body trembling. But why was he so upset by a plaster cockroach? And then instantly, I knew, and I was trembling too. Wayne had inherited La Fête à L'Oiel from the man for whom he had acted as bodyguard for years. The man whose murder he had failed to prevent. At least, that's how Wayne saw it. For Wayne, this restaurant/gallery and the others he had inherited were a sacred trust. And that sanctity had been violated.

I took his hand in mine. It was cold with shock. I rubbed it between my own hands, not knowing what else to do.

"It's all right," I whispered. "We're alive. We have each other."

He swiveled around to face me so quickly that I stopped breathing for a moment. There was real anger on his homely face. The face that had given him a job as a bodyguard. A frightening face, a frightener. And then, just as quickly, his anger dissolved. And he took me in his arms, so gently I might have been a pile of fallen leaves and not one leaf would have moved. Too gently, I thought. How much was he holding back? What was he holding back?

"Thank you," he whispered gruffly.

And that was all. He released me from his arms as gently as he had embraced me and turned back to the door to remove the plaster cockroach.

"The police?" I asked once he was done.

He shook his head, his eyes on the cockroach in his hands. He was still angry, no matter what he wasn't saying or doing. I could smell it on him. Just a scent, but I had lived long enough with this man to identify it.

We opened the door and entered the foyer-cum-gallery of La Fête à L'Oiel to the muted orchestration of Vivaldi and the not-so-muted aroma of sautéed garlic. But the art that met the eye overshadowed sound and smell. La Fête à L'Oiel was as much about art as it was about food. That was one reason Gary Atherton was so useful to Wayne. Wayne knew how to cook, but he was probably no more attuned to the contemporary visual arts than I was. Not that either of us was disinterested, but neither of us were art experts. Or enthusiasts. Wayne had inherited another man's passion, and he kept it alive. Vigilantly. But he never really felt it, much to his constant guilt and shame.

Gary Atherton, on the other hand, was the real thing. A real artist. He'd met Wayne while trying to place his paintings in La Fête à L'Oiel's gallery. They were strange disturbing paintings in layers, the top layers like gorgeous sunsets complete with pastel luminosity, but beneath that luminosity always a glimpse of hard, backlit objects in stark primary colors. The paintings sold fairly well for all their strangeness, but Gary was still a starving artist, at least until he became the manager of La Fête à L'Oiel.

The art gallery today displayed the work of three almost major artists. One was a sculptor whose headless torsos had hearts that you could peek into, like the sugar easter eggs I'd received as a child. Except that the scenes in the torsos' hearts were much less sweet. The other was a "composite" artist, or maybe a compost artist, whose works used bits of city artifacts like discarded beer cans, bus transfers, shoelaces, and smashed Styrofoam. The third was a black-and-white photographer whose subject matter seemed secondary to her extraordinary sense of light and dark. And then there were two of Gary's paintings. That was in the contract.

Wayne and I were early enough that only two couples were viewing the works. Well-dressed and quiet, they stood and peered, occasionally exchanging hushed comments. These four must have been real supporters of the arts, six o'clock being far too unfashionable an hour for a San Francisco dinner.

Wayne glided silently through the gallery, through the dining room, and into the kitchen with me gliding a little less silently behind him.

"Gary," Wayne said softly, and Gary Atherton turned from supervising a woman and a man in tall chefs' hats as well as a troupe of lesser players, chopping, slicing, and pulling foodstuffs from giant refrigerators.

"Wayne," greeted Gary, his handsome face registering surprise at his boss's presence.

Wayne pulled the plaster cockroach from beneath his arm and held it out in front of him. Did he suspect Gary of putting it on the front door?

Gary's head reared back and then came forward again to scrutinize the thing.

"What's that?" he asked. "Someone's idea of art?"

Not Gary, I decided. Wayne seemed to come to the same conclusion.

"No," Wayne answered quietly. "Probably someone's idea of a joke."

Then he threw the plaster cockroach in the garbage.

"Kate and I thought we'd eat here tonight," Wayne announced, his voice a little less strained. Everyone else's shoulders in the kitchen seemed to stiffen though. A challenge.

This was the reason I didn't eat very often at La Fête à L'Oiel. I knew as a vegetarian that I was a royal pain to these people who had their hands full keeping the restaurant's four-star reputation alive and well without having to cater to a woman who didn't eat animal products. True, there were a few items on the regular menu that were vegetarian, but they were mostly salads and appetizers. However, when Wayne brought me, here he expected the best. My sweetie became a tyrant. And I knew better than to argue. I inhaled garlic to keep the vampire of guilt at bay and decided to enjoy my meal.

The food was a gustatorial delight, complete with the silken asparagus mousse as promised, white bean pâté with the flavor of basil and thyme, and something that might have been brandy on crisp rounds of toasted French bread, as well as roasted eggplant. Yum. And more.

But conversation left something to be desired. I'm quite capable of handling both sides of a conversation by myself under normal circumstances. But these weren't normal circumstances.

Wayne picked at the vegetarian food he shared with me and ignored my oohs and ahs of pleasure.

"All right, Wayne," I hissed finally. "Spit it out."

My timing might have been less than perfect, since his mouth was full of blueberry sorbet right then, but he did at least answer me. Or try to.

"Can't do anything right," he mumbled through the blueberries.

That's what I'd thought. In a crisis, Wayne always blamed

himself. For everything. He was probably busy blaming himself for not solving Sam Skyler's murder, for the appearance of the cockroach, for our not being married. Not to mention the depletion of the ozone layer.

I jumped up from the table, scattering linen and silverware.

"God damn it, Wayne!" I threatened. "I won't let you start this, this . . . stuff again."

At least I got his attention. Not only was I threatening him in a public place, it was his public place.

He made frantic sit back down motions with his napkin, turning his head to see if any patrons or waitpersons had heard me.

"Not till you promise," I told him, my voice back into normal but easy to hear range.

"Promise what?" he whispered, an entreaty for mercy in his vulnerable brown eyes.

"That you'll stop beating yourself up," I told him, lowering my voice so only he could hear me now. "If you want someone to beat you up, I will. But nobody else."

"Okay" he muttered, his eyes on his plate.

"What was that?" I demanded, drill-sergeant style.

"Okay," he enunciated, quietly but clearly. "I will not beat myself up. I am a good and worthy person. I know so because you've told me." His voice went almost subvocal again as he added, "about a million times."

We were halfway back to Marin under the orange spires of the Golden Gate Bridge when he asked, in his slinkiest growl, "Would you really beat me up?"

"You betcha," I growled back and in a few minutes we were discussing the possibilities of a primal scream wedding. Progress. Real progress.

However, by the time we drove through the rainbow tunnel, Wayne was serious again.

"Should talk to Sam Skyler's ex-wife, Helen," he reminded me.

I looked at my watch. It was a little before eight.

"How about now?" I suggested. "We can stop at a pay phone and call her."

Helen Skyler was in. And she was perfectly willing to talk. She told us Nathan had called to let her know we might be visiting. Her deep, musical voice was welcoming over the phone, a voice that sounded as if it had laughed a lot.

"I already like her and I haven't even met her," I told Wayne as I slid back into the snug decadence of the Jaguar.

"At least she isn't a suspect," he pointed out. "You can let yourself like her."

But I couldn't allow myself to like any of the people who might have murdered Sam Skyler, I reminded myself, wiggling my aching shoulders, not so comfortable anymore despite the snug seat. No wonder I felt so cranky. It was hard to talk to people you couldn't allow yourself to like. And we'd had a day of it. It would be a good antidote to visit Helen Skyler, I assured myself. At least I hoped so.

We heard Helen's house as much as saw it, a small architectural gem on a hill in Tiburon. Somewhere inside, a cello was being played and a dog was howling. The dog was winning.

The woman who answered the door still had her cello bow in hand. Her brown hair was pulled back in a severe knot at the nape of her neck. The eyes that peered out at us from beneath thick glasses were her son Nathan's eyes. But now I could see what all his fur probably covered—if he'd inherited his mother's lovely, perfectly oval face with clear, radiant white skin.

"Come in, come in," she ordered tossing her head theatrically toward the room behind her.

Within minutes, Wayne and I were seated on a too-plush

red velvet couch, while Helen Skyler and her Great Dane, Huzza, perched across from us, their respective hands and paws crossed in an amazingly similar manner, on what appeared to be a former park bench sprayed in gold paint. Whimsy was the theme of Helen's decor. Upside-down romance novel covers, pop star posters, jeweled scepters, and Van Gogh reproductions all shared space on the lavender-tinted wall across from us.

"If you want the story on Sam," she told us, "you've come to the right place." She shook her head for a moment, sadness in the gesture, but then threw her head back again. All her gestures seemed limited to her head and neck. Maybe everything below was saved for the cello.

A stocky red-haired woman came into the room, holding scissors and smelling of fresh rosemary and something roasting. Potatoes, maybe? And chicken?

"Ah, you must meet Mary," Helen told us with another toss of her head. "My reason for living."

"Oh, hell," said Mary, her skin pinkening beneath freckles. "Music is your reason for living."

They laughed in unison and Huzza howled in agreement.

"Has Helen told you she's the lead cellist with the San Ricardo Symphony Orchestra?" Mary asked then.

We both shook our heads. I felt a twinge of guilt. I was far too ignorant of the music world thrumming around us. I didn't even know San Ricardo had a symphony orchestra.

"And that she's the director of the Zantano Music Workshop in—"

"Enough, enough!" Helen cried dramatically, but I could see the happy squint in her eyes underneath her thick glasses as Mary went back to the kitchen.

"Mary writes romances," Helen whispered once her reason for living had left the room. "She makes a lot of money doing it too, but she won't talk about it." She winked largely. "Sam wrote romances too, before he made it in the human potential movement. But he wouldn't talk about it either. Would you believe I was married to a man who wrote romance novels for a living, and now I'm married to a woman who writes the same kind of books for a living?''

"Romances?'' was all I could say.

I guess Wayne was stunned too. I hadn't heard a word from him since we'd been swallowed up by the red velvet couch.

"Sam was into every New Age movement that came around the sacred peak. For years,'' Helen continued cheerily. Maybe she was used to stunning her guests. "TM, Ram Dass, Open Encounter, est. But he was always a bridesmaid, never a bride. He 'assisted.' He wrote pamphlets. He even ghosted biographies for some of the biggies. But he never really got his career off the rocks until Sally died. So he wrote romances for the money.''

"Sally—'' I began.

"Oh, all that stuff about Sally,'' Helen admonished, lowering her head and rolling her eyes over the rims of her glasses. "Sam never hit me. He wouldn't have dared. But Sally! Jesus, that woman was mean. Always swinging her fists at him. That doesn't really excuse Sam's swinging back, but hell, what do you expect? 'Course, it served Sam right. He married Sally for her money. Her inherited money. Sally sparred with her previous husband regularly, but he was some twenty years older than Sally, and in a wheelchair. He certainly died conveniently enough. But Sam, Sam was a lot bigger than Sally. He could have restrained her without hitting back.''

"Did Sam—'' I began again.

"Push Sally over the balcony?'' Helen finished for me. She furrowed her elegant brow. "I was never sure. But he did really grieve for her. He even went to a grief therapist.''

She bent forward, winking once more. Huzza bent forward

too, for the punch line. "A grief therapist who used puppets to express grief."

"Grief into growth?" I whispered.

"Got it in one," she replied and leaned back again. "When Sam got the idea, he ran with it. He stole some of his shtick from his grief therapist, with a little from Tony Robbins, a little from John Bradshaw, and a little from Richard Bandler. Not to mention Werner Erhardt. Then he stirred it all together, wrote *Grief Into Growth*, and became the Skyler Institute. Finally, he was in the spotlight."

She paused and sighed. Huzza put a paw on her knee.

"I liked him better when he was hostile. He used to carry a chip around on his shoulder the size of my cello. When we first met I asked him if his cologne was Eau Contraire."

She laughed then. I joined in along with Huzza, who emitted a brief hoot in appreciation of the pun.

"See, the poor guy was the son of a failed evangelist," Helen added, more seriously now. "That man beat Sam every day of his life. And kept his wife, Irene, beat down too. Irene completely neglected Sam. And Sam loved her so. Sam was so damn Oedipal, it hurt. Poor kid had no one to love him back. I always think that's why he craves attention so much. 'Course, Nathan could tell you more about Sam's psychology than I could. But Sam's an adoration junkie now, that's for sure." She put her face into her hands. "Damn, I mean he *was*. It's so hard to believe he's dead. Sam Skyler, his own Institute."

I saw tears leaking from beneath her glasses.

"You liked him, didn't you?" I asked, stunned once more.

"Couldn't help it. The man was so damned needy." She pulled out a handkerchief and blotted her eyes.

Wayne made throat-clearing noises and stood up. I stood up with him. It wasn't easy. The red velvet couch was eating me alive. I just hoped it had taken the biggest bites from my thighs.

"Sorry," Helen mumbled, standing too. She gave us a half-hearted grin. "Bad 'heir' day. I found out I wasn't in the will."

Then she showed us out.

"Come back if you have any more questions," she said as she closed the door behind us.

Moments later, we heard the sound of her cello. And Huzza begin to howl.

Our ride home in the Jaguar was brief. And quiet. I was lost in the life of an abused kid who was so needy that he built an empire. And was murdered. Was he murdered for his empire?

It was dark when we shuffled up the front stairs. Neither Wayne nor I noticed the slender figure waiting for us, sitting silently on a porch chair.

It wasn't until she rose gracefully from that chair, the sudden sight of her goosing my feet into an impromptu hop and my heart into extended gymnastics, that I recognized Diana Atherton. My pulse was still thumping in time when she spoke.

"Gary and I have thought it over," she whispered in place of a greeting, her saucer blue eyes wide under the porch light. "We think you should stop investigating."

FOURTEEN

⊤

"Are you serious?" I asked, still shaken by Diana's unexpected ghostly appearance under the porch light.

It was a stupid question really. Diana was always serious. If not serious, then earnest at the very least.

"Um . . . yes," she answered, tilting her head, her hands folded neatly in front of her.

"But why do you want us to stop investigating?" I demanded. Now that my pulse was getting back to normal, my mind was too. I wanted to throttle her.

"Because it's causing everyone so much pain—"

"Who's everyone?" I cut in impatiently.

"Oh . . ." Her eyes widened again and she turned away from me, her long black braid whipping along behind her. I had a feeling we were in for the crying routine.

We were.

"Because . . ." She gulped back a sob. Loudly. "Because my dreams are my own, and Gary says if it is a murder, it could be very dangerous. And . . . and—"

Her own sobs brought her to a choking stop. Then she really began to cry, alternating long, gulping sobs with piercing wails. Tantric yoga definitely does something for the lungs, I decided, putting my hands over my ears.

I turned to Wayne. His eyes were invisible in the weak light. Especially with his brows at half mast. But at least he wasn't rushing forward to comfort her. Or to invite her into the house.

"You want us to quit investigating?" Wayne asked again once Diana's sobs and wails had tapered off into sniffling. I thought I caught the tang of anger in his low, quiet tone.

She turned back to face us, looking waiflike under the light.

"Uh-huh," she whispered finally.

"Need to talk to a few more people tomorrow at the memorial service," he warned her.

All right, Wayne! My inner cheerleader did a few twirls and kicked out her legs as Diana shrugged and lowered her head. If I'd had a puppet, I would have wiggled it.

I crossed my arms instead, just in case Diana stooped to make a request of me personally to stop investigating. I wasn't going to agree to stop looking into Sam Skyler's death now. It wasn't about Diana anymore. It was about Sam.

C.C. came out onto the deck and stared at Diana through slitted eyes. Without a sound.

That made three of us.

"Well . . . um . . ." Diana tried. She peered into Wayne's eyes, then mine, her own eyes scrunched up as if she'd been physically beaten. Then she just shook her head sadly and walked past us and back down the stairs, her long black braid flapping against her erect spine.

Long after she'd driven off, and Wayne and I were tucked into bed, I began to feel guilty. I remembered Diana's hurt look before she left us. Talk about your whipped dog. And if I felt guilty, I could bet that Wayne—

I turned to look. He lay with his eyes wide open, staring up into the skylight. But I'd have bet he wasn't seeing the sky.

I moved closer to him and put my head on his chest.

"Hold me?" I suggested.

And he did.

Wednesday was Sam Skyler's memorial service. I got up at six and worked on Jest Gifts until ten. Then Wayne and I got ready for the services. We hadn't discussed Diana's request to stop investigating. That would have opened a can of worms that could wriggle across the Golden Gate Bridge. We'd told each other we were too tired the night before. And too busy the next morning. So I ran scenarios through my head solo as I paid bills and checked invoices, assuming Wayne was doing the same as he worked. And I waited for him to bring it up. He still hadn't by the time we drove up to the Skyler Institute For Essential Manifestation where the memorial service was to be held. The reception would come later, at Skyler's home, farther up the road in Golden Valley.

I was surprised there was still any room for my Toyota in the mammoth parking lot at the Institute. Even though the event hadn't been publicly announced, the lot was almost full, and there were rented buses at the gates, for what purpose I wasn't sure. The building was still three stories of rounded redwood, but it looked a little less like a spaceship this time since it was surrounded by people and vehicles in motion. Lots of people and vehicles in motion.

My friend Barbara made her way through the crowd to meet us as we joined the line of people snaking in through the doors. Almost as if she'd known we'd be arriving at that very instant. She probably had.

"Felix is here," she whispered as she gave me a hug. Then she got in line behind me, in front of Wayne. A man with knitted puppets on his fingers and tears in his eyes took his place behind Wayne.

"Any murderer vibes?" I whispered to Barbara over my shoulder.

"Not yet," she answered, "but the woman at the door—Jeez Louise, I wouldn't want to share a mind with her for very long. Not even a room." She made a fairly subtle gagging motion and then turned to hug Wayne.

The woman at the door was, of course, Martina Monteil. I should have guessed after the gagging routine. Martina greeted each of us with a special word and a well-practiced wistful look on her model's face. She was flanked by two guards, the one we had met before and a new, scarier-looking one.

"Fantastic," she murmured as she shook my hand.

I had no idea what she meant.

"Monumental," she told Barbara.

I never did hear what she said to Wayne.

Two Alicia look-alikes were herding everyone down the plushly carpeted hallway into a room at the end. How were all of us going to fit?

I shouldn't have worried. The room was an auditorium the size of a stadium. Or as near to the size of a stadium as it could be and still remain tasteful. And tasteful it was, right down to the three-story vaulted ceilings, shimmering skylights, beige walls, and teal multitiered seats. Seats that were close to full.

Felix had saved a few for us near the front. Wayne wasted no time, plopping down next to Felix and making rumbling noises in his direction. Felix started wriggling in his seat as he hissed back. The two of them sounded like my stomach on a bad day.

I was too busy scanning the crowd to even try to eavesdrop as they argued. It was easy to spot Diana's long black braid in the front row. I assumed Liz and Gary Atherton were the two heads to her left. And I was pretty sure I saw Nathan's furry head on her right. And next to him, the woman with her hair in a knot at the back of her neck had to be Helen Skyler. I couldn't identify the French roll next to her, though. And I wouldn't have been able to spot Chief Woolsey and Officer Fox if they hadn't turned to glare behind them. Of course, that black ponytail behind *them* had to be Yasuda. And seated right beside *him*, an aurora of curly blond hair—was that Yvonne O'Reilley? Yep, I decided as she began waving her hands. Did she just happen to sit there or—

Sound issuing forth from loudspeakers shook the room.

"Grief into growth," came a voice, Sam Skyler's voice.

And then the puppeteers joined in.

Damn, it was cold all of a sudden. I shivered in my seat.

Even Wayne and Felix settled down as the loudspeakers continued the litany. I went back to my eyeball search of the crowd, easily finding Emma Jett's oddly divided red hairdo next to Campbell's conservative cut. And an upswept mass of gray curls that had to be Tessa's next to Ray's smoother gray hair.

Quite a turnout for a Wednesday morning mourning, I thought, and saw Ona and Perry slinking in, with guilty expressions. Guilty for attending a funeral of a man they didn't care for? Or was it the sound of "control into cooperation" on the loudspeakers? Or just that they were late?

Suddenly, the lights dimmed and the loudspeakers went silent. As did the crowd.

Then Martina Monteil entered the room, lights shining around her, brighter and brighter, as she climbed to the podium at the front, back straight, her arms spread wide as if to envelope the whole room.

"Sam Skyler was a monumental man," she said. And suddenly I understood her words at the door. Each was an homage to Sam. Her voice deepened and the crowd leaned forward en masse. She swayed slightly. "He was an empowered man, a passionate man." She paused and brought her hand out from her heart. "How shall we grieve for his passing?"

"GRIEF INTO GROWTH!" the crowd bellowed.

I might not have joined in the chanting, but I was mesmer-ized as much as anyone else by Martina's performance. And a performance it was, right up to the presentation of a plaque made from Sam's ashes (and other organic ingredients). And after.

"And we will continue as Sam would have wished," Mar-tina finished up. "We will be unstoppable!"

"Yes!" the puppeteers agreed in unison.

Then she leaned forward and held out the plaque to the whole room. It was a home run. The crowd roared. The pup-pets rippled.

And then the lights dimmed once again as Martina Monteil disappeared. With the plaque.

I saw Sky-Guy and the man from Growth Imperatives, Un-limited on the way out of the Institute. Luckily, neither man seemed to see me in the crowd that surged out the doors and hurried toward their cars to follow the blacktop road up the next couple of rolling miles to Sam Skyler's home.

I saw the reason for the hurry when we got there. Sam's home had a parking lot too, but not as big as the Institute's. Lots of people had opted to leave their cars at the Institute and ride in the rented buses I'd noticed before. But I hadn't even thought to ask about the function of the buses, so Wayne and I, along with half of the rest of Marin, drove to Sam Skyler's. I ended up parking in the first legal space I could find, nearly a mile away.

As Wayne and I huffed and puffed back up the long, wind-ing road, past all the illegally parked cars between my Toyota and Sam's driveway, I couldn't help hoping the Golden Valley Police Department had been informed. They could probably make their year's revenue in parking tickets this afternoon alone.

The exterior of the house looked a lot like the Institute, a slimmer version of the redwood spaceship, complete with the glass and brass and skylights and solar collectors and oddly shaped projections.

But inside it was different. Very different.

Once Wayne and I muscled our way through the crowd outside, past the front door and into the living room, we both looked up. And up. Sam's living room was a cathedral. Golden light streamed down from a ceiling at least four stories high, illuminating the candelabra, the velvet and gilt furnishings, the rows of bookshelves filled with leather-bound books, and the grand piano. Not to mention the gilt-framed works of art work on the walls. And I mean Art with a capital A. The horde of humans crowding in hardly seemed to put a dent in the room. Vertically that is. Horizontally, it was getting hard to breathe in there.

Nathan and Diana stood together near the door, forming an impromptu receiving line. At least it looked as if neither of them had planned any such thing. Both seemed dazed as people shook their hands and offered condolences. Wayne and I moved toward them, propelled by the crowd. Diana pulled out a little bottle of oil and rubbed her hands during a lull. I could smell the scent of honeysuckle floating on the air.

Martina stood a few feet away, momentarily ignored. There was a chilly expression of anger on her face as she looked over at Diana and Nathan. But then a woman with puppets on her hands approached Martina and bowed. If there had been more room, I'm sure the woman would have prostrated herself. Martina's beautiful face took on a look of solemn concern. And then she was lost in a swarm of puppeteers.

"Hello there, Kate," someone whispered in my ear and I twisted my head far enough around to see Tessa, her small frame as upright as ever, though I could smell a faint whiff of alcohol on her breath.

I couldn't blame her. This must have been a real busman's

holiday for her. But at least she didn't have to direct Sam's memorial.

"How're you doing?" I greeted her back, but before I got any further, my attention was diverted by a mourner I hadn't seen before. The woman who stepped up next to Nathan with a smile on her face was probably in her seventies. But her bouffant hair, done up in a French roll, was jet black with tendrils of curls softening her wrinkled forehead, and her skirt was at least six inches above her knees. She had great legs.

"Sam's mother, Irene Skyler," Tessa informed me, her voice a little louder. It had to be, to be heard in this crowd.

Though I could certainly hear Irene.

"So I bet on this big ole stallion named Samson, and sure enough he came in first," she was telling Nathan. "Neck and neck, then, boom, Samson just goes blazing ahead. Won by a nostril. Just like my Sammy . . ."

The receiving line was breaking up, Diana sneaking off toward the buffet set up at one end of the room. I'd follow her soon, I promised myself. I wanted some answers from that woman. Real answers.

"The daily double had a gorgeous chestnut, name of Horizon. So I said to myself, 'Horizon is like sky, right?' And I put a hundred on that one too," Sam's mother went on.

"She doesn't seem too upset," I said to Tessa.

"You'd be surprised how often joy and relief are the dominant feelings of the so-called mourners," Tessa replied, a hint of laughter in her voice.

Just then, the woman in front of us swiveled her head around. It was Liz Atherton. And she wasn't smiling. She narrowed her eyes in Tessa's direction, rubbing her temple at the same time.

"Oh dear, I am terribly sorry if I've offended you," Tessa murmured immediately, and sincerely, I was sure. "I had no call to say such a thing on this serious occasion. Sometimes the wine makes my tongue sloppy.''

Liz's expression softened. "No, no," she assured Tessa. "No problem. You're only being honest.''

"Well, please accept my apology in any case," Tessa insisted.

I slunk off, leaving them to swap courtesies. I'd lost sight of Wayne, and I wanted to corral Sam Skyler's ex-fiancée on my own, anyway. I saw Diana across the room, her face blank as she nibbled at a cracker from the buffet.

The eavesdropping opportunities were plentiful as I crossed the room. It was well worth the trip.

I passed Emma Jett right off. "Life's a bitch and then you get murdered," she was expounding to Ona Quimby.

Ona threw back her head and laughed, slapping Perry on his shoulder at the same time. He smiled weakly along with Campbell.

I kept on moving.

And found myself cutting around a knot of people in the center of the room. A man in a tweed jacket and a polka dot tie was addressing a rapt group of puppeteers.

"He finished his final work right before his death. It was almost as if he knew," the man said solemnly. Was he Sam's attorney? Editor? Agent?

Puppets and puppeteers nodded.

"It'll be a blockbuster. *Higher Self-Help* by Samuel Skyler.''

"Higher self into living grace!" the puppeteers chanted.

The man in the tweed jacket stepped back in alarm for a moment, then seemed to remember something, and stepped forward again.

"*New York Times* Bestseller List," he chanted back as I moved on.

"Yvonne O'Reilley and David Yasuda were pocketed

against a wall, whispering to each other, but I didn't detour. I had my prey in sight.

I was only a few yards away when Diana spotted me. She looked around for a moment, her eyes even wider than usual, as if seeking help, then sighed and picked up another cracker. Ready to face the inevitable?

By the time I made it to the buffet, I'd decided on the direct approach. I knew I had to get my questions in before she started crying.

"Why did you ask us to stop investigating?" I demanded, blocking her body with mine, cutting off her only path of escape. Unless she decided to crawl across the buffet table. The scent of honeysuckle and acrid fear floated over the ripe smells of food on the buffet table.

"Um . . . I . . ." she faltered.

I decided on a multiple choice approach.

"Has someone threatened you?" I asked.

She turned her head away, mumbling something I couldn't hear over the noise of the crowd.

"It's all right to tell me if someone has," I said to her, more gently. "We've been threatened too." If a trocar and a cockroach weren't threats, I didn't know what was.

But all she did was shrug her shoulders. Her gorgeous shoulders. Even her shrug was sensuous. I mentally slapped myself back into clear thought. Her shoulders weren't getting me anywhere.

"Are you trying to protect someone else?" I prodded.

She shrugged again.

"Damn it!" I shouted as softly as I could. "Did you kill Sam Skyler yourself?"

"No," she answered, her blue eyes wild. "I . . . I . . ."

Time had run out. The tears had begun.

"The whole thing's such a mess," she sobbed.

Well, that was something. A statement of sorts. I was about

to ask her exactly how things were "a mess" when I heard the sound of voices behind us, arguing male voices.

I turned, just as one of the voices shouted above the noise of the crowd.

"All right, bud, you're carrying a gun. Why?"

FIFTEEN

⚓

It was easy to see where the argument was coming from. The man with the gun peeking out of his pocket was the Growth Imperatives guy in the blue suit and red tie. The man who had him in a hammerlock was Ray Zappa.

"Hey, I gotta permit, okay?" the Growth guy objected. His voice was stringy and congested now.

He didn't seem to be struggling, though. It may have had to do with the position of Ray's arms, one across the man's throat and the other jerking his arm behind his back. If Ray jerked much harder he'd break the man's arm. I'd learned that much when I worked in the mental hospital. The man's face was getting red, too red, verging on purple. But then so was Ray's.

"Doesn't explain why you're carrying a gun here!" Ray shouted, not loosening his hold. In fact, he seemed to be tightening it.

I was beginning to sympathize with the Growth Imperatives man. Thug or not. Did he have to explain his gun? I thought that was what the permit was about. But Ray just kept increasing the pressure on his arm and throat. The noise level in the room plummeted as everyone watched what was going on.

"Un-cool," came a new voice from my side. I whipped my head around.

It was Sky-Guy, of course. Cowboy hat, braid and all. But I agreed with him. It was un-cool. I even thought of intervening, but rejected the idea. I'd only make the situation worse.

"Guns stun, thunder asunder," Sky-Guy declared softly. "No function, no compunction, stunning isn't cunning . . ."

Sky-Guy's words drifted away from my ears as a couple of hard-looking men moved in on Ray and the Growth guy. More Growth Imperatives men? No, I realized as they flashed badges.

"Golden Valley P.D.," one announced.

"We'll take it from here," the other one said and gently pulled the Growth Imperatives man away from Ray Zappa the way you might take a favorite toy away from a two-year-old.

The man from Growth Imperatives was led toward the door, a Golden Valley policeman on each side of him. He sputtered about his permit and his rights, but even his sputters sounded relieved. Ray Zappa, on the other hand, looked angry and frustrated. Tessa approached him with a glass of something that might have been wine. He downed it in one gulp. She put her hand on his arm and began whispering in his ear as a procession began to form behind the three men leaving.

Chief Woolsey and Officer Fox were first in line behind them. Then Park Ranger Yasuda. And Felix. And a whole bunch of people who must have been media. Notebooks and microphones began sprouting like a fast-spreading mold. The noise level rose again to a massive braying as the air filled with the varied scents of the bloodhounds.

Everyone seemed to be leaving. Not really, but enough of the crowd was gone in those few moments so that you could breathe in that huge room. Finally.

It wasn't until then that I turned back to look for Diana. But she was gone. Completely. Maybe she'd crawled under the buffet table. Even Sky-Guy was gone.

But Wayne wasn't.

He came up from behind me as I was gazing up, hypnotized, at the golden light streaming down from the ceiling. I never saw him. I just heard him from my golden trance.

"Let's go," he growled in my ear.

And once my heart climbed back down from where it had lodged in my esophagus, we did.

Even at that, it took us a mild forever to traverse the room, saying our goodbyes to Nathan and Emma and Yvonne and all the rest who were left. We'd just made it out the door when I noticed that Perry Kane was exiting in front of us with Ona. And he was limping.

"Did you see Perry's limp?" I asked Wayne excitedly as we huffed and puffed the mile of blacktop back to my Toyota.

"Perry's always limped, from the first day," Wayne informed me. He took another breath for the hike. "He had polio as a child."

"What?" I objected. I stopped in my tracks, panting. "But I never noticed."

"Perry told me about it the first day of class. Said it was one of the disadvantages of not being born in the United States."

"Oh," was all I said for the rest of the mile. But only because I'd run out of oxygen.

Ten minutes into our drive back in the Toyota, it was a different story. I had my breath back. And my spirit. I told Wayne all about how I'd accosted Diana. When he didn't say much in reply, I just figured he was impressed with my report.

"So then she starts going on about what a 'mess' the whole thing is," I babbled on. "But what does she mean by a 'mess'? That she killed Sam herself? Or that she was threatened? Or maybe she's protecting someone else. Like Nathan? Or Liz? But then why would she be so obvious?" I stopped for a quick thought break. Far too quick a thought break.

"Though I bet if she *was* threatened she'd cave. She's such a wuss—"

"Kate," Wayne interrupted gently. "Did it ever occur to you that she might be protecting us?"

"Huh?" I replied. Translation: No.

"The cockroach on the door," Wayne reminded me. "And I told Gary that Ray Zappa's not happy about our investigation. Gary may have asked her to call it off."

"But—" I sputtered.

"And he may be right," Wayne went on quietly, but inexorably. I pressed my foot down on the accelerator. I knew I didn't want to hear what was coming next. "This whole thing *is* a mess. None of our business. Haven't garnered a single clue so far as I can tell—"

"And you're going to let that stop you?" I demanded. I had to say something or crash into the back of the slow moving car in front of us. Or just explode.

"Yes," Wayne answered.

"Yes?" I parroted. "What about us being a team? What about it being about Sam, not Diana anymore? What about—"

"Kate, it's dangerous," Wayne insisted. "Maybe to you. I forgot that for a while, but I remembered today. You mean a lot more to me than Sam Skyler. You shouldn't be involved in this—"

"But it's fine for you—"

"I didn't say that," he cut in sullenly.

But he meant it, I was sure.

Wayne would keep looking into things in secret so he wouldn't involve me. Well, so would I. Mentally I crossed my arms. I'd be careful, but I wasn't going to be scared off any more than he was.

Wayne sighed as if he'd heard me.

"Kate, I love you," he explained when we finally pulled into our driveway.

The words were nice, but his voice was too high as he spoke them.

"Well, I love you too," I pointed out. And somehow my words were exasperated too.

So we hugged when we got through our front door. Because exasperated or not, the words were true. And then we let the subject of Sam Skyler's murder die a natural death.

Wayne fixed us a quick lunch, then told me he had some work to do in the city and left. I didn't even ask him if the work involved his restaurant or Sam Skyler.

I looked at my watch. It was after two o'clock. I approached the stacks of Jest Gifts paperwork on my desk carefully, and abruptly the image of the guy in the polka dot tie at the reception popped into my mind. He obviously had something to do with publishing Sam's new book, *Higher Self Help*. Just what had Sam written in that manuscript? Talk about a safe place to hide clues. If Sam's work had been the least bit autobiographical, and I had a feeling a man like Sam Skyler couldn't resist the autobiographical, it might be loaded with clues. Damn. What if he was killed because of something in that book? Now I was really agitated. I marched across the room with C.C. following me in lockstep, yowling.

But I needed a name for the polka dot tie man. Not to mention a phone number. I marched back across the room to the phone and punched the number of the Institute, hoping Nathan would be there. But he wasn't. And he wasn't at his home number either. But Martina Monteil was at her home number. And surprisingly enough, she was agreeable to an afternoon meeting, an immediate afternoon meeting at her home. I'd work up to the name and number of the polka dot tie man subtly, I decided. After a nice long talk with the woman who was the clear successor to the throne of the Skyler Institute For Essential Manifestation, Nathan Skyler or no Nathan Skyler.

Twenty minutes later, I parked my Toyota in the visitors' lot in front of Martina's condo in Larkspur.

"Kate, how are you?" Martina asked, her voice deep with what sounded like genuine concern as she opened the door to her living room. She stared down into my eyes from her near six feet of model's perfection, her own hazel eyes widening as if in fascination.

"Fine, fine," I replied, looking off to the side, embarrassed by her intensity. Martina's condo was clean, white, and crisp. And loaded with success books. I saw *Swimming With the Sharks*, *Winning Through Intimidation*, and Trump's *The Art of the Deal* on the nearest shelf. Along with *Grief Into Growth*.

Martina stepped away from the doorway and touched my shoulder lightly as I entered her living room, murmuring something about a seat. The touch seemed caring, too caring. What did she want?

I glanced up quickly and caught a slight narrowing of the eyes that didn't quite match her voice.

"Nathan and I were appalled by Ray Zappa's behavior today," she said. I could have soaked in the warmth of her tone, like soaking in a hot bath. I gave myself a little shake and felt imaginary droplets fly. "And you and your Wayne so unstoppable in your search for the truth, in your search for the real core issues . . ."

I hardly remembered sitting on her clean beige sofa as she continued. All I could seem to see was the movement of her gleaming white teeth as she spoke. Swimming with the sharks, indeed.

"So what have you learned?" she asked quietly, bending forward, the intensity in her hazel eyes like a penlight now.

"Not much," I mumbled. Wayne had been right on that score. "Sam Skyler was loved by some people and hated by others. But we don't know why he was killed. Or who killed him."

Martina sat back in her easy chair, the look of concern instantly gone from her eyes. Of course, she wanted information. That's why she'd agreed to see me. But she was a narcissist-exhibitionist too, I reminded myself. I ought to be able to hold her attention with a show of my own interest.

I bent forward now.

"You're so much like Sam," I murmured, my eyes on hers. They widened again. My mind searched for the buzzwords that would move her. "Your energy, your presence."

Martina Monteil smiled my way, a real smile this time?

"When you speak, I can almost see Sam again," I went on shamelessly.

She brought her hand out from her heart. "Thank you, Kate," she said and dropped her eyes modestly for a moment. "I feel Sam's essence with me daily now. His gift. I only hope I can carry on for the Institute."

"Oh, I'm sure you can," I told her. And I wasn't lying. "You have the charisma." I held my breath for a second and took a guess, "And the backing from the Growth Imperatives group."

"Yes!" she exclaimed, uncharacteristically slamming a hard fist into her palm. The tension went out of my body. My guess was on the mark.

"The people from Growth Imperatives, Unlimited are real power people," she enthused. Not only had I guessed right, I'd pushed her button. She was on now. "They can pump in real money. We can make the Institute an unstoppable force." She straightened her back. "Personal genius can be duplicated. I've proved that already with Sam. We could have branches all over the United States. The movement would be explosive. *Will* be explosive!"

"How does Nathan feel about that?" I asked as gently as possible.

Martina frowned, but only for a moment.

"Nathan is a very sweet boy, but he lacks the monumental insight his father had," she replied. "Still, he's beginning to understand what I could do with the Institute. He's beginning to understand the incredible possibilities." She leaned back in her chair. "Even Diana has begun to understand. But she's so . . . so . . ."

I could see the struggle in Martina's face as she tried not to say anything negative about Diana. The Institute was about positivism too, after all.

"Wimpy," I supplied for her.

"Yes, wimpy," she agreed, molding her expression into concern again. "I'm afraid not all of us are manifesting at the same rate. Dynamism can be taught, but the energy has to be there. And Diana . . ." She shook her head.

"Slow manifestation material," I suggested.

Martina nodded, then pointed behind me.

"See those trophies," she ordered, her face suddenly serious in a way that seemed more real than all the other expressions she'd worn.

I turned and did see them, a whole mantelpiece of trophies I hadn't noticed before. A brass figurine shaped like a mermaid swam out of the granite base of the middle one.

"I could have been an Olympic swimmer," she announced. "But my parents lacked the vision. To them, making a living was enough. A house in the burbs mortgaged to the hilt. They couldn't see any further." Anger tensed the muscles in Martina's face, real outward anger. She didn't need a finger puppet to access it now.

"I almost made it," she went on, her voice low and fast. "Almost. I kept my grades up and swam every day. I would have swum every minute if I could have. But my parents owned a dry-cleaning shop and expected me to help out in the afternoons and on the weekends. They thought I would never make the Olympics, no matter what my coach told them. They thought it was all a dream.''

She paused for a moment, then declared, ''Never again.'' Her eyes were somewhere else now. But I believed her.

''And that's what you teach your clients?'' I asked, trying to bring her back from wherever she was. There were goose bumps on my arms. All that intensity focused on a world that I couldn't see was frightening. ''That vision?''

And then Martina brought her eyes slowly back to me. And winked. If I hadn't seen it, I wouldn't have believed it.

''I never call them clients,'' she informed me, her lips curled in something bordering on a sneer. ''They are seekers.''

Seekers or suckers? I kept the thought to myself. And reminded myself I was here to find out the name and number of the man with the polka dot tie.

''Sam had just finished another book, hadn't he?'' I led in slowly.

Martina's eyes narrowed a bit with the change of subject.

''Yes,'' she admitted, her words slowing. ''It's a brilliant book. Full of insight. We're not sure yet how to integrate it into our programs, though.''

''Too autobiographical?'' I asked casually.

But Martina's doorbell rang before she could answer me.

A voice shouted out, ''*Golden Valley Press!*''

And Martina's face lit up like a flashbulb. The media had arrived.

''Did you kill Sam?'' I asked quickly.

I had to ask. If anyone ever had motive, it was this woman before me. She would be the new leader of the Skyler Institute For Essential Manifestation. I was sure of it. Nathan and Diana couldn't last another month against the force of her will. Probably not even a week.

Martina's smile deepened at my last-ditch question. And then she rose from the easy chair to her majestic height.

"No, I didn't kill Sam," she answered as she walked to the door, glowing. "I didn't have to."

I watched her as she opened the door to the press. Martina Monteil was star material all right. As a child I'd been on an elevator with the man who'd played Tarzan in the TV series. Even at twelve years old, I'd recognized that glow of stardom. A star is dead, a star is born, I thought, and then tried to think of how I was going to slink by the media while Martina mesmerized them. Because they were all there, cameras whizzing and microphones thrust forward.

"Yes, Sam Skyler has passed on," Martina declared, her hazel eyes misting over. "But his monumental presence will not be forgotten at the Institute. We will continue with the passion and the energy we can bring to his memory—"

I took that moment to sidle out the door.

"Isn't that Kate Jasper?" one of the less mesmerized reporters asked as I moved by him.

Martina nodded solemnly.

I kept on moving and heard the next question from behind me.

"As a psychologist, what's your opinion of the Jasper woman's mental state?"

I swiveled my head around to hear Martina's answer, wondering if she even *was* a psychologist. And doubting it.

She looked over the heads of the reporters in my direction, with an expression of immense sympathy on her face.

"Kate's inner feelings are her own," she announced. "I just hope some day she will learn to manifest them in an appropriate way."

Sixteen

I'd manifest my feelings in an appropriate way, all right!
As I took the highway on-ramp home I imagined my puppet-
less fingers around Martina Monteil's swanlike neck and
squeezed the steering wheel. Hard. But not hard enough to
stop the burning in my face. Or the burning in my veins. And
I hadn't even gotten the name of the polka-dot-tie man! Or
his number.

Was Martina really a psychologist? And just what had she
meant by "I didn't have to," when I asked if she'd killed
Sam? That she was already better than Sam as a master hyp-
notist, or whatever the hell she was? Or that she knew someone else would eventually kill the man? Someone specific?

Did she know who that someone was? Was it Martina herself?

The steering wheel wasn't answering my questions. It
hadn't even begun to crack. I let up on the pressure and tried
to think as a red Mercedes passed me in a puff of diesel.

Was Martina really the murderer? I wanted to think so, I
realized. And that was affecting my judgment. But she did
have motive. And an intensity of ruthlessness that made goose
bumps jump up on my arms again, just remembering.

But so did Nathan have a motive. And Ona. And Diana.

Diana as murderer. I let out a little contented sigh. The thought was almost as appealing as casting Martina in that role. But just because Diana was young and beautiful and manipulative wasn't enough for a murder conviction. Not quite. And just because Martina Monteil had embarrassed me in front of the reporters didn't make her a killer either.

I punched the steering wheel with one hand. I needed more information. And then I remembered that there was one person I hadn't talked to. One person Wayne hadn't talked to either. Sam's mother, Irene Skyler. I wished for the hundredth time that I had a car phone. I'd have to stop at home to call if I wanted to visit Irene Skyler. Somehow, despite her apparent lack of concern over her son's death, I didn't think that dropping in unannounced on a bereaved mother on the day of her son's memorial service was quite the thing to do.

So I drove home and called. And Irene Skyler told me to come on over. As long as I could make it quick. She wanted to go to the racetrack soon.

Irene's house was art deco beautiful and located on prime waterfront property in Sausalito. I doubted if she'd earned the mortgage at the track. My guess was that the pale mauve building I was looking at was an example of Sam Skyler's legendary generosity.

I pushed the doorbell and heard not only ringing, but chirping and cawing and scrawing as well.

When Irene opened the door I saw the reason for some of the noise. Irene was still wearing her miniskirt. Her black bouffant hair was still done up in its elaborate French roll with the loose tendrils softening the wrinkles of her forehead. But something new had been added to her ensemble: a parakeet on one shoulder and a parrot on the other.

"*Scree-scraw*, a real winner," the parrot greeted me.

"Are you Kate?" Irene added in her carrying voice.

"That's me, Kate Jasper, a real winner," I answered them both.

"Whooee, you're a stitch!" Irene cawed, slapping her leg just above her hemline. The parrot just squawked.

I sure hoped my legs would look that good when I reached whatever year she was celebrating. I took her to be around seventy, because for all her makeup, and there was plenty of mascara and crimson plastered on, I could still see the age in her face.

"A stitch in time," I offered.

That elicited another caw and a screech. And got me inside the house, where I saw the rest of the noisemakers. And smelled them. There must have been close to ten or fifteen cages lining the walls of Irene's living room, with noises coming from all of them. I saw parakeets, mynas, toucans, and parrots, their intense colors a moving counterpoint to the flashy artwork and brightly colored sofas.

Irene made kissy noises at the cages and then at the birds on her shoulders as we sat down.

"Thought we might talk a little about Sam," I finally shouted over the cacophony.

"Friend of Sam's?" Irene inquired back, just as loudly. Now I knew why she had that carrying voice. She had to, to make herself heard in her aviary.

I nodded, wondering if nodding counted as lying.

"Friends of Sam have been dropping over ever since the memorial," she told me. "Kinda strange service, but my Sam was always into some weird thing or another. Real go-getter, my Sam. Took good care of his ol' ma after his pa died."

"How did Sam's father die?" I asked, suddenly curious.

"Of holiness, I guess," Irene answered and laughed at her own line, slapping her leg again.

"Whooee!" the parrot added.

I smiled encouragingly and Irene went on. She wasn't hard to jump-start.

"Honey, my husband was an impossible man, and I mean impossible! Never wanted to have a good time. He was so damn holy he got booted out of his last church. That much sanctimony can be a pain in the rear even to parishioners."

I shook my head in sympathy and wondered how she'd acted in those days. Hadn't Sam's ex-wife, Helen, said something about this woman being "beat down?" I was having a hard time imagining it right now. Something screeched behind me as if in agreement.

"Sam was no Holy Roller, at least," she added. And for a moment I thought I saw a shadow of sadness pass over Irene Skyler's brightly painted face. Maybe this was how she had to act to keep going. Or maybe not. "He bought me this house. I got me an annuity too. And an inheritance. Sam was a good boy. Strange, but good to his ma for sure."

"What did you think of his Institute?" I asked.

"Whooee, that place was weird," she answered, shaking her head.

"Whooee!" the parrot echoed.

"But I guess it made good enough money," Irene went on. "Not quite sure what those folks thought they were getting. I went to a few of Sam's 'sessions.'" She shook her head again.

"Weird?" I suggested.

"Got it in one, honey," she agreed. "Lots better places to go for a good time, that's for sure." She looked down at her watch. "Like the track. There's a pony I've got my eye on for this evening—"

"*Scraw, caw*, a real winner," the parrot put in. Then it whistled.

I had a feeling time was running out.

"So, Sam was about to publish another book," I yelled.

"Yeah, some goofy kinda thing," Irene said, her eyes taking on a distracted look. Thinking about a horse?

"There was a guy at the memorial reception, wearing a polka dot tie," I hurried on loudly. "Was that Sam's editor?"

"Don't know, honey," she replied. "Guess I didn't follow that part of Sam's career too well."

I resisted telling her that was an understatement. *Whooee, honey*, it was an understatement.

"Going across the bay to Golden Gate Fields," Irene brayed, looking at her watch again. "Don't mean to hurry you or anything—"

I gave up and got up, wishing her good luck on the way out the door.

"Thanks, honey," she said. "Anyway, Sam was a real good boy."

I was feeling pretty sorry for Sam Skyler as I drove home from Sausalito. His mother hadn't been interested in his Institute or his book. Or much besides his money, I guessed— the money that she equated with his being "a good boy." Damn, no wonder he craved adoration, I thought as I guided my car into the driveway. I couldn't even begin to imagine his childhood.

Mainly because a car pulled in behind me before I got a chance to. A turquoise vintage '57 Chevy. Felix's car.

Scowling, I got out of the Toyota and placed my hands on my hips. Felix had a lot to answer for.

"Hey, howdy-hi," Felix greeted me, a Cheshire cat grin on his pit bull reporter's face as he closed his own door behind him carefully. He loved that old Chevy.

"Yeah?" I growled back, imagining Wayne's spirit guiding me.

"Jeezus H.," Felix replied, still smiling. Not to mention advancing on me one quick step at a time. "You're not P.O.'d at me or anything, are you?"

"What do you think?" I snapped back, wishing I had a better answer. Something witty and cutting. "You sicced the media on us."

"Hey," he advised, "don't get your hormones in an uproar. Those potato brains at the Quiero cop-shop wouldn't have done diddlysquat on the case if someone hadn't goosed them."

I was about to tell Felix what I thought of his hormone crack when I suddenly wondered if he knew what the Quiero police knew. That was the problem with Felix. Just when you were ready to kill him, he usually came up with some information.

"Woolsey cares more about the friggin' dolphins than he does about Sam Skyler," Felix went on, his mustachioed face inches from mine now. "And—"

"And I suppose you know all about the Quiero police investigation—"

The sound of another car pulling to the curb jerked my head up. I hoped Felix hadn't brought the rest of the media with him. Or the puppeteers, for that matter. Or the police. Not to mention the guy from Growth Imperatives.

But it was my friend Ann Rivera who got out of the blue Volvo parked by my mailbox. She gave me a wave and a toothy smile that streached clear across her brown face. Ann ran a local mental health facility. I was glad she was here. A little mental health might be a refreshing antidote to Felix.

So after a quick exchange of greetings all around, Ann and Felix having met each other enough times to be brief, the three of us went inside. I put on a kettle for tea and brought out a loaf of homemade sesame-millet bread. And a bowl of the wonderful bread-spread glop that Wayne made out of tofu, tahini, maple, lemon, vanilla, and some other ingredients I'd never quite figured out.

"So what's the newest scoop?" Felix asked as I sliced some bread to toast.

I'd filled him and Ann in briefly by the time tea and toast

were ready and we sat down at the kitchen table. Ann had taken the most filling-in, having missed the earlier parts of the saga. But Felix made up for any preferential treatment by stuffing his face.

Even C.C. made her yowling appearance and got some Friskies Senior for her trouble.

"So who do the Quiero police think did it?" I asked after Felix had swallowed three slices of well-glopped bread.

"Campbell Barnhill," he told us, grabbing a fourth slice.

"Oh damn," I muttered, my hand squeezing guiltily on the teacup's handle. Poor Campbell. I took another sip of peppermint tea. "Somehow I just can't believe it was Campbell Barnhill. Why do the police think so?"

"No friggin' imagination," Felix informed me. "The guy yapped at Skyler and shook his fist, so now he's a murderer. They don't put Diana Atherton or Nathan Skyler much further down on their doo-doo-dunit list either."

"Why?" I asked again, not feeling any less guilty. Wayne and I hadn't helped Diana much, that was for sure. Whether I liked the woman or not.

"Moolah, the green stuff," Felix answered, rubbing his fingers together. "The inheritance, remember? So who do your little gray cells think dunit?"

"Not for publication?" I said first.

"No way," Felix promised, making a big show of crossing his heart. "What kind of lousy geek do you think I am?"

He almost lost me with his last protestation, but I answered anyway. I wanted to toss this around with someone, anyone. And Wayne wasn't available.

"If I had to place a bet, I'd say Martina Monteil," I told him, watching his face.

His eyes widened as he bent forward, mouth open like a fish. Now he'd press for details, I was sure.

But Ann beat him to the auditory punch.

"Martina Monteil," she murmured tentatively. I turned her way. She was twiddling a dark curl around her finger. "I could imagine that."

"You know Martina Monteil?" Felix and I both asked at the same time.

"Yeah, I know her," Ann shot back. "That's why I came over. I took a Skyler Institute seminar last fall. I met Sam Skyler. And Nathan Skyler. And Martina Monteil." She chuckled. Both Felix and I had our mouths hanging open now. I shut mine on a piece of bread. Lemon and vanilla flavors filled my mouth. Maybe orange rind too, I guessed. "I talked to Barbara Chu this morning," Ann went on, "and she said you and Wayne might like to hear my impressions—"

"My sweetie, Barbara!" Felix objected, rising halfway from his chair. "My Barbara told you to tell Kate and Wayne. Not me, her doll-baby, pumpkin-pie, sweet-lips—"

"She said to talk to you too," Ann assured him gently. And just in the nick of time. I didn't want to hear another one of Barbara's endearments out of Felix's mouth. Ugh.

Felix sat back down, smiling again. No wonder. Now he had another informant.

"Martina had an ambitious streak the size of the Skyler Institute for Essential Manifestation," Ann offered. "Both she and Sam struck me as narcissists, but at least Sam seemed to care. But Martina . . ." She shook her head. "Talk about dysfunctional."

"Is Martina a psychologist?" I mumbled through bread and spread.

"I don't think so," Ann said. "At least it didn't say so in any of their promotional materials."

Huh! I thought.

"But boy, is Martina a good manipulator," Ann continued. "She could convince you that you needed help if you were the most self-actualized person since the original Buddha. After filling out that questionnaire of hers, you begin to think you really do have serious problems. Or as she put it, under copyright no less, 'unresolved core issues that need expression.' Or 'manifestation,' or whatever.''

"Did the seminar help at all?" I asked, genuinely curious. Ann was one of the most grounded people I knew, Adult Child of Alcoholic notwithstanding.

"Yeah," she answered slowly. "A little. Gave me a sorta glow of confidence. Sam Skyler could really inspire that in people. He was really mesmerizing, in a truly positive way. Though he clearly didn't do it for everyone. Some people were just turned off by him. I guess . . . I guess I fell somewhere in between. I got something from the seminar, but not enough to want to go back."

"And Martina?" Felix murmured.

"Martina had that charisma too, but not the kindness to go with it. At least it seemed that way to me."

"And Sam was kind?" I pumped her.

"Yeah, I think he truly was. Or could be. I've seen him take time with people with such apparent love." Ann shook her head. "But he could be pretty nasty to people who argued with him."

"People who didn't adore him?" I suggested.

"Right," she agreed, pointing her finger. "That's it exactly. I think Sam would have done anything for someone who really needed him, who really adored him. But if they didn't"—she spread her hands—"he just lost interest, I guess."

We threw around a lot of pop—or maybe not so pop—psychology, after that. Ann did work in a mental health facility after all, even if it was as administrator. I told them about Sam's mother, Irene. And about the purported beatings Sam had taken from his father as a child.

After a lot of oohs and ahs on Felix's part, and a lot of toobads and too-sads on Ann's, I turned back to Felix and asked who he'd bet on for murderer.

"Don't have a clue," he said and my heart sank. "But I would lay odds on who wants a publishing contract out of this whole mess." Then he grinned again.

"You?" I guessed.

"Naah," he said, shaking his head. Though a little blush told me he wouldn't mind one. If he ever got around to writing one of the true-crime books he kept saying he was going to. "Ray Zappa," he announced.

"Zappa!" I objected, but then I remembered the blinking computer and true-crime books in the policeman's living room. The about-to-retire policeman's living room.

"Zappa's already trying to sell his friggin' memoirs," Felix added smugly. "A friend of mine knows his whiz-bang agent. So Zappa's hoping this Skyler corpse will cap off his pile of memories like a friggin' marble gravestone."

"But the murder's got to be solved, right?" I said.

"Not necessarily," Felix argued. "If he handles it right, he could make it the Great Unsolved American Mystery or some other hot-shit thing."

"He wouldn't have killed Skyler for the publicity, would he?" I asked, thinking of Tessa. I liked Tessa. I didn't want her sweetie to be a murderer.

"Nobody but Oz knows," Felix replied. And then I thought of something else.

"Hey, remember the guy in the polka dot tie at the memorial reception?" I asked.

"Sam's agent," Felix fired back, nodding. "Sam had a new manuscript too . . ."

And then Felix's eyes lit up. I could almost see the same thoughts going through his little story-riddled mind as had gone through mine. Sam's manuscript, repository of possible clues.

"You don't happen to know his name?" I asked.

"No, but I'll find out," Felix assured me.

"And tell me when you do?" I demanded.

"Oh, sure," he agreed absently.

I wondered if Felix already knew the agent's name. But even that was all right, I decided. If Felix could find the agent, the manuscript, and the clues, we would all be that much closer to solving the mystery. I told myself it was just ego that made me want to be the first to know. I had to tell myself that, or I'd be reduced to choking the facts out of Felix. And then I reprimanded myself for the escalating violence of my thoughts. We were talking real murder here. And all I could think about was strangling people. That was, if Felix counted as people.

Our little tea party broke up not long after that.

Ann gave me a good long hug before she left and my strangulation urges left me. Mostly.

Once I was alone in the house, I thought of making dinner. But I was full of bread and glop by that time. I'd wait for Wayne, I decided. His dinners were better than mine anyway. Then I sat down to my stack of Jest Gifts paperwork.

The telephone rang the minute my bottom touched the chair. Someday, I'd find the magic button that caused that phenomenon. But not now.

"Hello," I said, hoping for Wayne's gruff voice on the other end.

But the voice that answered was soft and weak. And close to hysteria.

"Kate," the voice whimpered. "This is Tessa Johnson. I think someone may have just tried to kill me."

Seventeen

✠

"Kill you?" I repeated, my mind a few fibrillations behind.

"I'm not sure, but I think so," Tessa whispered. "Here at the funeral home. Kate, I'm so scared—can you come—"

"Have you called the police?" I interrupted, my mind almost catching up with my heart.

"No . . ." she said, sounding confused. Tessa confused was not normal, not good. "Wayne said you were a couple of minutes away . . . and I . . . I . . ."

"I'll be there," I assured her, keeping my own voice from shaking with an effort.

I hung up, trying for less than a second to remember if Tessa's funeral home was in the actual city of Mill Valley or outside of it and under Marin County jurisdiction. Then I just dialed 911. Whoever was on the other end would just have to sort it out.

The dispatcher seemed to keep me on the phone forever, but then time was moving in a very strange and disconnected way. It was probably only moments.

"Not at my house," I repeated one more time. "The woman in danger is at the Olcott Johnson Funeral Home." Maybe this sounded like a prank to him. Attempted murder at a funeral home?

"Do you have that address?" the dispatcher asked again.

"It's in or near Mill Valley. Look it up in the phone book," I advised and slammed the telephone down. They'd figure it out, I told myself, and ran.

It took me less than two minutes to get to Tessa's funeral home. I should have attracted the police just by the way I was speeding, but I didn't. Unfortunately.

Because the Olcott Johnson Funeral Home was very quiet when I got there. Dead people don't make a lot of noise. But Tessa wasn't dead, I reminded myself. I hoped.

The door to the reception area was unlocked. That was good, right?

I centered myself, then opened the door slowly, jerking my head around, looking for Tessa. And/or her assailant. But all I saw was an empty, tasteful room in gray and cream and golden beige, silent except for the pounding in my ears.

I turned toward the casket room, but then I heard a small cry.

"Kate?" the voice questioned. "Is that you?"

The voice came from the chapel. But what if it wasn't Tessa's? I tried to shut the idea out, but it clung, holding me there for an agonizing few seconds. Was this a trap?

"Tessa?" I called back softly.

"Kate!" she cried again.

Of course it was Tessa, I told myself and rushed through the doors to the chapel, faster than my own fears could follow.

I cursed the time my fear had cost when I came to the back of the first pew. Because Tessa was there in the center, alone, her head bent down, an ooze of blood highlighting her gray curls.

"Oh God, are you all right?" I whispered stupidly. Or maybe I was praying. I was in a chapel.

And then Tessa lifted her head.

"Thank you," I muttered to whoever or whatever was watching over the chapel.

And then I ran around to the front of the pew, tripping over a brass candlestick in the aisle as I went, a brass candlestick with blood on it. My mind took in the blood, but I kept on going until I was crouched next to Tessa, holding her clammy hand, and wondering what kind of medical treatment I should be giving her that I didn't know about. What if she had a concussion?

"What can I do?" I asked her in desperation. She was a funeral director. Maybe she knew the right first-aid procedures as well as embalming techniques.

"Just stay here," she suggested distantly, her breathing shallow, way too shallow to my buzzing ears. "I'm okay, just a little dazed."

"Someone hit you," I said, as if she needed that information.

"I know," she answered. At least she was talking. I said another thank you, this one silently. "I was doing my evening reflections. I thought I heard someone behind me. And then . . . I think I might have been unconscious for a minute."

Where were the police and the paramedics? Damn. What if the dispatcher *didn't* sort it out? I had given the right name of the funeral home, hadn't I?

"I went and called you," Tessa continued, her voice still a whisper. "Then I came to sit again—"

"Why me?" I asked. I couldn't help asking.

I realized that Tessa probably shouldn't be talking if she had a concussion, but I had to know. Her calling me instead of the police just didn't make sense.

"I thought . . . I thought it might have to do with Sam Skyler's murder, but . . ."

"What? What might have had to do with Sam Skyler's murder?" I squeezed Tessa's clammy hand but got no reply.

"Did you see the person who hit you?" I tried.

"No, it's just that . . . well . . ." Her voice faltered to a stop.

"Tessa?" I asked as gently as I could. "Is there something you know? Something someone knows you know?"

"I . . ." Her voice suddenly got firmer. "No, it can't be related."

"What?" I demanded, barely able to control myself. It wasn't good to shake a possible concussion victim, I was sure, no matter how strong the urge. "What can't be related?"

"Nothing," she told me. "Thank you for coming, Kate."

"Tell me, for God's sake," I ordered. "Someone tried to kill you—"

And then the police and the paramedics arrived.

"Okay, move away from her slowly," a tall police officer holding a gun told me.

It took a minute for his words to sink in. Did he think *I* was the one who'd attacked Tessa?

"But I—"

"Just move away," he ordered again.

"Kate's okay," Tessa told the officer. "She's the one who called you."

But I moved aside, anyway. And the paramedics moved in.

"You can put down your gun," I assured the officer, the way I would have calmed a mental patient some twenty years ago. "My name is Kate Jasper. I'm the one who called 911."

"That's right—" Tessa began, but the paramedics shushed her. And here I'd been pressuring her to talk.

I was certainly glad the paramedics were there. But I wasn't so sure about the police officer with the gun. Because he wasn't putting it down, no matter what I said.

A couple of hours later, the officer had put away his gun and the paramedics had assured Tessa that she would be all right. That was the good news. The bad news was that various police officials were still asking me why Tessa had called me, not them. First the Mill Valley Police had asked me, then the county sheriffs, and finally Chief Woolsey, all the way from Quiero. And as far as I was concerned, I was the wrong interrogatee.

Because Tessa was the only one who could answer that question, and she'd just told them I was closer when they'd finally received permission from the paramedics to ask her. An inadequate and suspicious explanation, even to my mind. Tessa had wanted to tell me something, but what? I never got to ask. I was the one being questioned, and by the time I was hustled out of the Olcott Johnson Funeral Home, Tessa Johnson was nowhere to be seen.

At least I hadn't picked up the murder weapon, I told myself as I drove home slowly in the dark. They'd only find my Reebok sole prints on the bloody candlestick.

And then my shoulder muscles stiffened. Wayne. I had never thought to leave a note, and he had to be wondering where I was. Worrying about where I was. Going crazy about where I was. If he was home.

He was home. In fact, he was at my car door by the time I pulled in the driveway, his brows so low they almost touched his cheekbones. Concern or anger?

"You okay, Kate?" he asked gently. My shoulder muscles relaxed a little. Concern.

Could I lie? Should I lie? I got out of the car and he put his arms around me. And those arms sucked all the truth out of me like a pump. I couldn't seem to stop babbling every detail of what had happened at the funeral home. I just kept on talking as we walked up the steps, through the front door, and into the kitchen. Then Wayne fixed me dinner. Silently. He didn't ask any questions. He didn't offer any observations. He didn't smile. I kept waiting for the recriminations, but they never came. After dinner, he just lifted me in his arms and carried me down the hallway to the bedroom.

"Any wedding ritual," I murmured a while later, wrapping all my limbs around him like an octopus. "Any ritual at all."

And finally, under the moon's glow that floated down through the skylight, Wayne smiled.

*B*y the next morning, Wayne was talking again.

"On this Sam Skyler thing," he reminded me gruffly, "wherever you go, I go."

"Ditto," I answered, as smugly as one can answer through a mouthful of Granola-O's and soy milk.

Then, across the table, his face produced an evil leer I'd never seen on it before.

"*Any* wedding ritual?" he asked, leaning forward.

"Ulp," I answered. But I had promised. "Ulp, yes," I amended.

Not that he'd give me any idea of what he had in mind. No. He just kept directing that evil leer at me as I alternately begged him to give me a clue and gulped down the rest of my cereal. Just what had I promised?

I still didn't know by ten o'clock, though my imagination had processed infinite gruesome possibilities, mostly involving lots of white lace and red faces. All I knew was that I couldn't concentrate on Jest Gifts paperwork. And that I wanted to talk to Sam's ex-wife, Helen, again. She might know the name of Sam's agent.

And whither I went, Wayne did too, flashing that same evil leer every time I turned to look at him in the Toyota. It wasn't until we got to Helen's that I realized that maybe the leer was the recrimination I'd been waiting for. If it was, it was a doozy. I opened my mouth to tell him to stop it, then closed it again. He must have really suffered last night, waiting for me. In his place, I probably would have been yelling and screaming. He had reason to give me a hard time. Maybe.

So I kept quiet, opened the car door instead and marched up to Helen Skyler's house, Wayne glued to my side, hearing the sound of Helen's cello and Huzza howling louder and louder as we got closer.

They both stopped abruptly when I pushed the doorbell.

Helen answered the door, cello bow in hand. Her eyes were friendly, though, under her thick glasses.

"Still sleuthing?" she asked before I had a chance to apologize for interrupting her.

I nodded, suddenly embarrassed by my own arrogance. Why was it that I was still sleuthing? For a moment, I couldn't remember.

But when Wayne and I sank into Helen's plush red velvet couch and she began talking about Sam again, I did remember.

"Sam wasn't a hate-able man, not really," she said sadly, throwing her head back in a dramatic gesture that might have been designed to indicate grief. I wasn't sure. "He could be a jerk, but he didn't deserve to be murdered."

"No," I said and turned to Wayne. He wasn't leering now.

"Whenever Sam acted like a real jerk, I'd tell him he was having a 'heeling' crisis," she went on. Huzza emitted a hooting bark. "Get it, a real heel?"

I got it. A low chuckle from Wayne told me he did too. And that his sense of humor was in better shape than mine about then.

"Sam had just written another book," I interjected.

"Right, *Higher Self Help*," Helen said, rolling her eyes. "I was the one who suggested the title. As a joke. But he loved it. And his agent loved it. And his editor—"

"His agent was the guy in the tweed jacket with the polka dot tie at the memorial reception, right?" I cut in, trying to lean forward as the plush velvet couch pulled me back. Now we were getting somewhere.

"I don't know, I never met him," she answered. I swallowed my disappointment as I let the couch eat me.

Helen pursed her lips. "Nathan might know, though," she said, pausing, her eyes directed downward as if in thought. "You're thinking the manuscript might tell you something about his murderer."

I nodded again, letting her think. Helen Skyler was a good observer. A good thinker. Maybe she would come up with something.

"Knowing Sam, the book had a lot about himself in it," she said slowly. "But I doubt if he'd write about anyone who reacted negatively to him. He preferred to think everyone loved him."

"You're probably right," I agreed, feeling my expectations sink along with my body into the cushiony velvet.

Still, even positivism can be deciphered, I told myself. There was always a chance of a clue.

"I'll miss him, damn it," Helen told us, her eyes misting behind her glasses. Huzza put his big paw on her knee. "Sam was just a scared little boy inside, craving attention. It was like he had this postdated reality check. And he never had time to cash it."

At this point both Wayne and I were nodding frantically. Neither of us wanted to cause this woman any more sadness. Sam Skyler's ex-wife, who seemed to care more for him than his own mother did.

"And Nathan understood that and loved his father all the more for his vulnerability," Helen went on, lifting her eyes to ours. "He would never do anything to harm his father."

The phone rang and Huzza began to bark before Wayne and I had to nod anymore. So we struggled our way out of the red velvet couch and left, whispering and waving little goodbye waves to Helen on the way out as she talked to someone about an upcoming concert. I just hoped her concert would take her mind off our visit.

"Doth the mother protest too much?" Wayne said once we were back in the Toyota.

Now, that was an interesting question. Just why had Helen felt the need to mention Nathan's feelings for his father? To assure us that patricide wasn't on?

I pulled out into traffic and thought awhile. When we got to a red light, I glanced at Wayne to ask him more. And he leered back at me.

"All right, all right!" I yelped. "Are we back to flower girls now?"

He just shrugged. And leered some more.

"Do you want me to dress up as a steak?" I demanded, sweat forming on my brow as awful possibilities coursed through my mind. "A lamb chop, maybe? You're not going to make me sing, are you? You know I can't sing—"

"Kate, the light's green," Wayne pointed out.

"What?" I answered as someone behind me began to honk.

"Kate, I'm just teasing you," Wayne assured me, the leer gone. "I haven't thought up anything specific."

"Really?" I said, putting my foot on the gas, lurching forward gratefully.

"Yet," Wayne added.

I didn't check to see if the leer was back. I didn't want to know. I took the next highway entrance instead, heading for the Skyler Institute For Essential Manifestation in Golden Valley. Someone had to know who Sam Skyler's agent had been. Nathan or Martina. Someone, anyone.

There weren't as many cars as before in the parking lot at the Institute. Not nearly enough cars to feed the three stories of rounded redwood, glass, and brass that faced us. But the well-muscled, uniformed security guard was still in place as the glass doors glided open to admit us.

And he still had his clipboard in hand.

"Names?" he asked as he had before.

"Kate Jasper and Wayne Caruso," I told him. "But we're not on your list. We just dropped by to see Nathan Skyler."

"Mr. Skyler isn't in," he told us, turning away.

"Or Martina Monteil," I added quickly.

The guard frowned as he turned back.

"Oh, well," I said to Wayne, ready to give up.

But then the woman who looked like a well-dentured brown rabbit popped up by the guard's side. Alicia, that was her name. The woman who wore high heels and a lot of sweet perfume. I breathed cautiously, trying not to cough. Alicia, the woman who had been kind enough to guide us through the Institute before. Maybe she would do it again.

"Hello, Alicia," I greeted her, infusing my voice with a friendliness that wasn't entirely feigned. "Could we ask you a few questions?"

"Of course you can," she answered with just as much friendliness. What a nice woman. Even her perfume smelled better to me now. "Just follow me to my office."

Alicia's office was more like a cubicle, but it did have a nifty brass-framed porthole in the outside wall. And a desk and three chairs.

"I'm sorry to have missed Nathan," I began as soon as we sat down. "We're looking into some things for Diana Atherton."

I didn't dare look at Wayne as I said it. Which was good because I was watching Alicia as her gleaming white smile faltered.

She shook her head. "Poor Diana," she murmured. "You're here about Sam's death, aren't you?"

"Yes," I confessed.

"I'll do anything I can to help," she assured me. And then I realized that I was probably looking at another person who had sincerely cared for Sam Skyler.

"I've been trying to find out something about Sam's last manuscript," I told her honestly.

"Uh-huh," she mumbled, nodding her head eagerly.

"You don't happen to have a copy of it, do you?" I asked, going for the gold. It must have been the influence of all that positivism floating around the Institute.

"No, I've never seen it."

I suppressed a sigh.

"Do you know the name of Sam's agent?" I tried.

"I don't think so," she muttered, her eyes half closed, as if trying to force the unknown name into her head.

"Would Martina know?" I asked desperately.

"Maybe," she replied, opening her eyes again. "But Ms. Monteil . . ." Alicia's nostrils flared. I had a feeling she liked Martina about as much as I did.

". . . probably won't tell me," I finished for her.

"Yeah," she acknowledged. "Ms. Monteil, well . . . she's not like Sam, you know."

"I know," I concurred fervently.

"But we can always try," Alicia offered. Her white teeth were gleaming again as she pushed a button on her telephone.

"Ms. Monteil," she said crisply. "This is Alicia from Reception. I was wondering if you had the name of Sam's literary agent."

A long silence followed. Alicia's teeth disappeared again.

"For some people who are interested," she finally put in. And then, "Kate Jasper and Wayne Caruso."

A shorter silence followed our names.

Then Alicia hung up. Without a goodbye.

"Sorry," she murmured.

"No, *I'm* sorry," I told her. "I hope I didn't get you into any trouble."

"Nah," she reassured me, her gleaming smile back again. "I'm polishing my resumé anyway."

We thanked her once more for trying, as we stepped through the well-guarded glass doors at the end of the hall.

But Alicia just shook her head and waved away our thanks.

"There will never be another Sam Skyler," she declared, then swiveled on her high heels to head back down the long hallway.

And the glass doors slithered shut behind her.

€IGHTEEN

"**A**licia really adored Sam Skyler," I muttered as I drove home.

"But did Nathan?" Wayne muttered back. A quick glance told me he was back in brooding mode. Better than leering, I supposed. Anything was better than leering. I shook the image out of my mind and tried not to think about singing or bridesmaids or frilled lamb chop costumes. Or Tessa's bloodied head.

"Are you saying Nathan didn't adore his father?" I asked slowly. "Because everything he's said is consistent with a real affection, a real love, for Sam Skyler." I waved the hand that wasn't attached to my steering wheel, trying to explain. "It . . . it feels right."

"Feels too right," Wayne growled. "Too pat. Can you believe that being the son of Sam Skyler was really the wonderful experience Nathan described? Kate, you met the guru. How much attention do you think he was able to give his son with all that ego running through his veins?"

I didn't have an answer, except that people usually do love their parents in spite of those parents' deficiencies. Especially once death has ended all disputes.

But I had a lot of new questions. Like where Nathan was

today. Why wasn't he at the Institute? And then there were Helen Skyler's comments. Why did she feel compelled to defend her son before anyone accused him of anything? And the biggie. How would a man, even a man as apparently kind and caring as Nathan Skyler, feel about his father if he was in love with his father's fiancée, the beautiful Diana?

By the time we got home, Wayne and I were both in brooding mode. Too many suspects weighed on my brain like a too heavy meal on the stomach. And too many that I liked. Because I did like Nathan Skyler, a lot. For all the sweetness he hid under all the fur. For his compassion and his insights. For his openness. I didn't want him to be a murderer, damn it. But who I wanted the murderer to be didn't mean a whole lot. The person who'd pushed Sam Skyler over the bluff hadn't consulted me first.

Wayne and I ate a quick lunch of leftover spicy black beans with polenta. All in thoughtful silence. And then Wayne got up to go. He had work to do at La Fête à L'Oiel. At least that's what he said. And since I wasn't privy to his ever so thoughtful thoughts, I decided to suspend disbelief. To trust. Well, to try to trust.

I was still working on that resolve as I listened to Wayne open the front door and shut it behind him. Then I heard him roar.

I think I might have heard him if I'd been in the next county.

I ran to the front door and flung it open, nearly knocking Wayne over as I did. But he stepped back just in time. And pointed.

"What the . . ." I said, turning.

And then I saw it. A huge papier-mâché nose with a red bow and a "Big noses can be dangerous to the wearer" sign on it.

I yanked it off the door and stomped on it. So much for

preserving evidence. And then Wayne stomped on it. And then we both went at it, sweating and growling as we did.

"They put it on while we were eating," Wayne protested, his voice way too high as he crumbled the last of the papier-mâché chunks under the sole of his boot. "While we were eating!"

A sacrilege in Wayne's book. And pretty scary in mine. Because neither of us had heard a thing. The stealth artist had struck again. Was the papier-mâché bomber the murderer?

I had to convince Wayne that art didn't equal murder, before he'd leave. Then I tried to convince myself of the same thing as I sat down at my desk. And wondered if he'd been convinced at all. Just where was he really going now?

The minute Wayne's Jaguar pulled out of the driveway, I popped right back out of my office chair. The towering piles of paperwork on my desk would just have to tower, lonely and deserted, for a little while longer. I needed to talk to Tessa Johnson again, head injury or no head injury. I was tired of Tessa's secrets. I was ready to browbeat her mercilessly. At least this time I left a note on the kitchen table for Wayne before heading out.

"Browbeat" might not have been the best choice of words, I realized as I strode into the reception area of the Olcott Johnson Funeral Home and saw Tessa with a tasteful white patch peeking out from under her gray curls. But niggling over semantics wasn't about to stop me.

"Tell me," I demanded as I reached her. "Tell me what you—"

"Shush," Tessa hissed, pointing to the party of mourners viewing a body in the chapel. My mouth snapped shut. I hadn't even noticed the funeral party.

"Can we talk somewhere in private?" I asked after a guilty moment, whispering respectfully now.

Tessa called one of her assistants to take over for her and then escorted me to a place of privacy. The embalming room.

She couldn't have picked a better place. The smell of disinfectant and the slanting floor would have been disorienting enough. But the overlay of formaldehyde and the lab-coated woman doing something to a body mounted on the porcelain pedestal, something involving a trocar—

"Kate, are you all right?" came Tessa's voice into the haze of my mind.

"Me, oh sure," I squeaked, turning slowly, very slowly, away from the woman, and the body, to Tessa.

"You wanted to ask me something?" she enquired innocently, a glimmer of humor peeping through her serious demeanor.

That glimmer was enough to clear my mind. Tessa wasn't the murderer. At least I didn't think so. I was pretty sure she wouldn't have hit herself over the head with a brass candlestick. Couldn't have hit herself. But she *was* laughing at me. That I had no doubt of. And she *had* chosen the embalming room purposely to distract me. I was sure of that too. Those two facts stoked just enough anger to remind me why I was here with her in the embalming room in the first place.

"You know something," I accused, pointing my finger for emphasis.

"I know a lot of things," she replied, the glimmer growing even brighter.

"Tessa," I said, bringing my voice down to a lower register, "someone hit you over the head. They might have killed you."

That statement shut down the glimmer, but it didn't open the floodgates. Tessa only nodded.

"Last night you told me you thought it might have had to do with Sam Skyler's murder—"

"Kate," Tessa interrupted. "Please forget any strange

things I might have said last night. Just the ramblings of an old woman whose brains were scrambled by a candlestick. Being hit on the head made me silly. I really prefer not to talk about it anymore.''

"But—"

"The attack had nothing to do with Sam Skyler. Probably just someone who wanted money. I always leave the door open as long as I'm here. People often feel the need of the chapel for a few days after their loved ones have passed on. An open door, a thief hoping the place was empty." She shrugged, then smiled. "Whoever—whomever—hit me picked the wrong place to rob, that's for certain. There's no cash here. The poor guy was probably more scared then I was when he realized that someone was on the premises and it was a funeral parlor to boot." She laughed.

I wasn't laughing, though. Because I didn't believe in her anecdotal thief for a second. And I didn't think she did either.

"Tessa, tell me," I begged.

But of course, she didn't. No matter how many times I asked. Instead she told me stories. And more stories. There was the one seemingly endless tale about a woman who'd had her thighs reduced, her face lifted, her hair bleached, and her breasts enlarged—all as part of her burial request. A woman who'd wanted to go out like Dolly Parton instead of whatever her real name was, a name that Tessa didn't share with me. And then there was the one about a man she'd buried who turned out to be a woman. His co-workers at the bank had never noticed. Even his friends hadn't.

"Or maybe I should say 'her—' '' Tessa continued relentlessly.

"Why did you call me?" I tried one more time.

Tessa hesitated for an instant, but only an instant. Then she took my hot hand in her cool ones.

"Kate, don't worry anymore," she told me, her dark eyes

completely serious now. "There's nothing to know, nothing I can tell you. That's it."

I was excused.

For a while on my brief ride back home, I even considered the possibility that Tessa had been telling me the truth. Maybe the candlestick had been wielded by a startled thief. After all, Tessa hadn't been killed. Wouldn't the murderer have made sure she was dead if she really knew anything?

But by the time I was back at my desk plowing through invoices, order forms, and payroll ledgers, with C.C. snoring delicately in my lap, I was sure that Tessa Johnson was keeping back something she knew about someone in the Wedding Ritual seminar. Though maybe that something was something that had no bearing on Sam Skyler's murder. Why else would she keep quiet? She wouldn't keep quiet if she'd seen the killer in the act. Unless it was . . . Ray Zappa. I erased a number I'd placed in the wrong column, swearing under my breath.

Or was it something connected with her profession, with someone she'd buried? I knew Tessa had buried Liz Atherton's husband and Perry Kane's father, and God knew who else. If her secret was related to the funeral home business, she'd probably keep it confidential. She was that kind of woman. Even in her endless stories she hadn't told me the names of those involved, or probably the real stories for that matter. I put the same number in the same wrong column again. This time when I erased, I erased through the paper.

I decided to give up on Tessa as I strangled the paper with my bare hands and started over, cursing loud enough to wake C.C.

"There's got to be another way to work this," I told the cat earnestly. "A safe way. Forget Tessa. Forget Sam Skyler's manuscript. What's left?"

C.C. let out a yowl before abandoning the former comfort of my now wriggling lap.

Sam's second wife going off the balcony, that was what was left, I decided as C.C.'s furry backside disappeared through the doorway.

I left Wayne another note and went to the library. I wanted to know more about Sam Skyler's trial for the murder of Sally Skyler. But there was nothing on the city library's newly installed microfiche replacement computer that Wayne hadn't already told me. I scrolled past newspaper article after newspaper article. Sally Skyler had died. Sam Skyler had been found not guilty. Case closed.

Actually, the most interesting thing I found in the library was an advertisement in that week's local throwaway newspaper left on the computer desk in front of me. An ad for Diana Atherton's tantric yoga class that had been staring up at me unread the whole time I was scrolling through Sam Skyler's life.

"Explore the realms of sacred sexuality," it advised once my eyes landed on it. "Everyone deserves the ultimate orgasm, the divine orgasm." A photo of Diana, gorgeous and serene, and clearly potentially divinely orgasmic was the clincher. I wondered what the ratio of men to women was in her classes and got up to leave the library, but not before throwing the throwaway in the trash.

I was just hoping that Sam had received his well-deserved divine orgasm before he went over the bluff when I pulled into my driveway for the third time that day.

But then I forgot all about tantric sexuality, sacred or otherwise. Because I had company. Emma Jett and Campbell Barnhill. And Wayne wasn't home yet. Two against one, the programmed wuss in my brain pointed out helpfully. I considered backing out of the driveway, pretending I'd never seen them. They'd leave eventually, right? And then someone threw the wuss-override switch in my brain and I found myself walking up the stairs to greet the smiling couple. To greet the

Quiero Police Department's choice for Most Likely to Murder a Guru and his faithful sweetheart.

"Hey, Kate," Emma sang out, jumping out of her porch chair like she was spring-loaded.

"Hello there," Campbell's musical voiced chimed in from behind her.

I paused at my front door, wondering if it would be better to talk with them out here on the deck, in full view of the neighborhood.

A window shot up on the left, next door, underscoring the thought. So far I'd avoided explaining the recent comings and goings to my neighbors. Mainly by running every time I saw one. Literally. Maybe I'd keep it that way.

"I understand you and Wayne are still—" Campbell began, belatedly rising from his own chair, stroking his ginger beard.

"—nosing around this Sam Skyler thing," Emma finished for him, flipping the hank of her hair that wasn't cut to the scalp out of her face with a neck-wrenching swivel.

I squinted at her suspiciously. "Nosing around" was a common enough expression, maybe even more common for someone who actually had a pierced nose, but brass studs aside—

I heard the sound of another window sliding open, from the house on our right.

"Might as well come on in," I offered brusquely, unlocking the door. At least the neighbors would hear if I had to scream. Or would I need to open my own windows, too?

I didn't have time to open any windows. Within a moment, Emma and Campbell were settled on my denim couch as if they lived there. I didn't offer them tea. Instead I offered a question, as I lowered myself into one of the swinging chairs. My house, my question.

"Emma, did you know Sam Skyler before the Wedding Ritual class?" I threw out.

"Wow, you don't waste any time bullshitting, do you?"

she shot back. Was she temporizing to come up with an answer? A lie? She narrowed her eyes, reminding me of C.C. for a moment, then answered.

"Sam and his space-cadet girlfriend came to one of my Angie and the Angst shows, like, maybe a couple years ago. But I don't think he probably remembered me. I just remembered him 'cause of that weird body of his. He was way cool, you know, but kinda top-heavy."

What a eulogy.

"Emma is a really multitalented person," Campbell put in fondly. And irrelevantly. They still hadn't told me the reason for their impromptu visit.

He put his arm around Emma and she snuggled up in his embrace, once more reminding me of C.C. I wondered if she'd jump free the moment he wriggled.

"Emma can do anything. You should see her Connie the Condom series—"

"Yeah, too bad nobody appreciates it," the creator muttered.

"By Godfrey, lots of great artists weren't appreciated in their own times," Campbell assured her gently. I imagined he knew a lot about the past. Maybe he even lived there. But then there was Emma. She certainly wasn't from the past.

"In fact," he went on, "the more far-reaching the art, the less appreciation in the present—"

"Campbell's a really cool musician himself," Emma cut in. "He's with this Irish band. They're way cool, you know. He plays all these weird instruments—"

"Uilleann pipes, tin whistle, flute, fiddle, and bones," he interrupted helpfully, the hint of a blush on his undistinguished face. And then he was back to his favorite subject, his sweetie. "Emma does performance art. Once she tied up her legs and rolled herself around in a wheelchair like a paraplegic, trying to bounce a basketball painted like the world. Then she was

screaming, 'Save the world! Save the world!' while I video-
taped the people who helped.''

"And the jerks who turned away," Emma added.

"Listen, you guys," I said, taking advantage of the micro-
second of silence before the mutual admiration started up
again. "Why did you—"

But Campbell was not so easily distracted from listing the
contributions to world art by the object of his affections.

"And then once she went down to Golden Gate Park with
the Angie and the Angst crew and held up implements of self-
destruction and asked the crowd if the crew should kill themselves.''

"What did the crowd say?" I prompted, curious in spite of
myself.

"The reviews were mixed," Emma put in. "Some guys got
real, like, excited and yelled, 'Go, go!' But most of them told
us not to. Especially the women. It was a really cool gig.
People left us a whole pile of money, even though we didn't
ask.''

"And then there was this son of a goat who came into the
market and kept giving me a bad time—" Campbell said.

"An ex-boyfriend—" Emma explained, wriggling in the
enclosure of Campbell's arm.

"So she jury-rigged his revolving tie rack with all these
insulting messages on little slips of paper tied to pink rib-
bons—"

"That was just a practical joke," Emma said impatiently,
twisting completely away from Campbell's arm now.

A practical joke. An alarm was going off in my head. Faint,
but getting louder as it blew.

"Emma even has some ideas for your gag-gifts. Tell, her,
Emma."

"Well." Emma was blushing herself by now. "I thought

of this really cool doll, Hygiene Hyena, for dentists, you know, with these really big teeth—''

''Performance art!'' I yelped, my brain inventorying the papier-mâché, catsup, red bows, and notes and putting them all together in the same category. ''Like trocars?''

Emma slammed back against the unforgiving denim of the couch, her cat eyes widening.

''Like cockroaches and noses?'' I hissed, getting up from my swinging chair.

Emma didn't say a word. Campbell didn't either. He just looked at Emma and then at me, confusion scrunching up his bearded face.

''You did it, didn't you?'' I accused.

And for once, I got an answer to an accusation.

''Yeah, so what?'' Emma replied, crossing her arms defiantly.

''So what'?'' I parroted back, astounded as much by the fact of her admission as its wording.

''I was just trying to help Campbell,'' she muttered, not looking so cool now. Campbell didn't look too well either as he stared at his beloved.

''Listen,'' she insisted, uncrossing her arms as she leaned forward. ''I just wanted to get you and Wayne off his back.''

''But you're just making things worse for him,'' I told her, barely resisting the urge to take her by the scruff of the neck and shake some sense into her.

She blinked, looking all of ten years old for a moment.

''Emma, don't you see? Wayne and I didn't even suspect Campbell. It's the police who—'' I cut myself off as another thought occurred to me. ''You didn't do any 'performance art' for the police, did you?''

''Well,'' Emma muttered, ''just a dolphin and harpoon thingie. That guy Woolsey is nuts about dolphins. So I—''

''What in the holy blazes have you been doing?'' Campbell

demanded now, not looking anywhere near as affectionate as he had before. In fact, his face looked as distorted by anger as it had the day he'd shaken his fist in Sam Skyler's face.

"I was just trying to scare people," Emma came back, her voice rising in both timbre and volume. Her hands flew into the air, fingers splayed and shaking. "So they'd lay off this whole murder idea. So they'd just let it go as an accident or a suicide, a cry for self-help, you know—?"

"Why did you need to scare us off?" I asked, deepening my voice and lowering my brows in an unabashed imitation of Wayne's glare. I was one for one in forced admissions of guilt. Could I make it two for two?

"Did you kill Sam Skyler?"

NINETEEN

Now Campbell turned his angry face in *my* direction, leaping up from the denim couch a second later to hurtle toward me. And his face was breath-stopping scary, so contorted, it was almost unrecognizable from his ginger beard up. Not to mention scarlet.

That was when I remembered it was two against one. And that I hadn't ever opened my windows. I got ready to scream, anyway. But Campbell beat me to it.

"What!" he bellowed, stopping inches away from me as he clenched his fists convulsively.

"No, sweet-buns, no," Emma admonished, up and running from the couch a moment after Campbell to squeeze her body between his and mine. She waved a hand in front of his distorted face, then tugged on his short red hair like you'd tug on the fur of an out-of-control dog.

Campbell's shoulders slumped; he turned and shuffled back to the couch, dropping back down on the denim with his head in his hands. When he looked up again, there was shame on his face where the anger had been. I let out my breath, lungs aching.

Emma turned to me now, her slender shoulders as straight as she could hold them.

"The answer is no," she declared, her voice trembling. "I did not kill Sam Skyler." She paused. "And neither did Campbell."

I believed the first part. But I wasn't so certain about the second.

After a glimpse of Campbell's rage, however brief, I was about to join the Quiero Police Department in their assessment of Campbell Barnhill as prime murderer material.

"We were together, holding hands, the whole time the scuba wedding was happening," Emma told me. "And I wouldn't lie for a murderer, not even for Campbell."

Damn, if I didn't believe her, at least for that moment.

I looked again at Campbell, who muttered miserably, "It's true," as he stared at his feet.

One thing I was sure of, this odd couple was really in love.

"Well, do you have any idea who—" I began.

The doorbell cut off my question. It was just as well. If Emma did have any idea who'd killed Sam Skyler, I'm sure she would have spilled it by now. And, more important, no matter who was at the door, it wouldn't be two against one anymore. I answered the second ring, smiling inanely, glad to be alive and breathing.

The young woman on my doorstep was a tall, well-dressed brunette. She looked familiar, but I wasn't sure why until she pulled out her tape recorder and shoved it in my face. I dropped the smile.

"Hi, I'm Jeannette from the *San Ricardo Post*," she chirped brightly. "I'm a friend of Felix Byrne's."

Did Felix have friends among his fellow reporters? Somehow I doubted it. Friends shared. And I couldn't imagine Felix sharing a story. And if this woman knew Felix at all, how could she believe that being his friend would endear herself to me?

So I just said, "Felix who?" tilting my head as if in confusion.

I could hear Emma and Campbell stirring from behind me as Jeannette's bright smile struggled to remain attached to her face. Inspiration struck, telling me it was time for my own version of performance art.

"Oh, you must be here to speak to Emma Jett," I sang out enthusiastically. "Creator of the wonderful Connie the Condom series."

Bingo. Jennette's smile faltered, then crashed onto the redwood deck.

I turned to Emma, willing her to take her cue. She took it. And Campbell shared it.

They were both on their feet and crowding past me onto the deck with the reporter before I had to make any further introductions. Or fend off any.

"Emma Jett is an incredibly multitalented artist," Campbell began. "You can put that in your story. She's a musician—"

"A 'performance artist'—" I couldn't help inserting.

"And writes and illustrates the Connie the Condom books," Campbell finished up. His undistinguished features were gleaming proudly now, all anger forgotten.

"Hey, you two were there when Skyler—" Jeannette began. But she was out-mouthed.

"Connie the Condom is the heroine in my children's book series," Emma interrupted loudly. "A pink condom, you know, way cool, with blond curls. She, like, helps little kids get out of trouble."

"The books are very educational," Campbell added. "And beautifully illustrated, by Godfrey! The text and illustrations have been featured at the Newmind Gallery . . ."

Jeannette dropped her tape recorder in her bag and backed down the stairs. If she was a friend of Felix's, she sure hadn't picked up his pit bull instincts.

"If you want to, you can make an appointment for an interview," Emma yelled as Jeanette rushed down the driveway, got in her Honda, and drove away.

"Heh-heh-heh," Campbell leaked from behind his hand. And then we were all laughing. Hysterically. Bonding is a strange thing. A few minutes ago, I'd been waiting to feel the pressure of Campbell's hands around my neck. Or at the very least, the impact of a punch. And now I wanted to hug him and Emma.

Until the police showed up, anyway.

I was still in the doorway, and Emma and Campbell were still on the deck yukking it up, when we heard the clomping of nearby feet.

"Having a lot of fun, are we?" asked Chief Woolsey, crossing his arms, his lean features set in that perpetual expression of jaded disgruntlement.

"Yeah," Officer Fox put in, crossing his own arms.

Emma Jett shriveled before my eyes. She turned to me, her face clearly begging me to delete any references to performance art. Especially performance art of the "dolphin and harpoon thingie" school. Then Campbell turned to me with a pleading expression.

"We were just talking about Emma's Connie the Condom series," I said to Woolsey. No, I wouldn't mention the performance art. Woolsey would harpoon Emma himself if he ever found out.

Woolsey looked confused until Emma began to explain her book series and Campbell chimed in with good reviews.

Woolsey nodded sagely while they spoke.

"Sounds interesting," he said fifteen minutes later. "A good metaphor for safe sex. A condom who is capable of saving lives."

Emma's cat eyes widened slightly; then she went on more enthusiastically, chronicling the adventures of her heroine. I

guess she hadn't expected the chief of the Quiero Police Department to be such a good audience. Nor had Officer Fox
apparently, as he'd fidgeted and glared.

But now Fox himself nodded. And pretty soon the four of
them were discussing Connie's brave acts as they walked back
down the stairs.

Had Woolsey forgotten his reason for visiting me? Or had
he been following Emma and Campbell all along? Or was he
just enthralled?

I closed the door softly behind them and peeked out the
living room window as my uninvited visitors continued their
conversation for another good fifteen minutes, then got in their
respective vehicles and left. Woolsey was enthralled, I decided. And if that was so, it would be a good thing for Campbell. It couldn't hurt his image any if the chief approved of
his fiancée. I just hoped I was right in believing Emma when
she said Campbell wasn't a murderer.

I went back to my Jest Gifts paperwork. It was looking more
appealing to me suddenly. My mind was actually engaged by
the intricacies of payroll-tax charts when the doorbell rang
again, another fifteen minutes later. Damn. What if the Quiero
police hadn't forgotten me after all?

But when I opened the door, only Emma was there, looking
incredibly vulnerable for all the brass studs in her ears and
nostrils.

"I just wanted to thank you," she whispered and threw her
arms around me in a tight hug. Then she turned to run back
down the stairs.

"Emma," I shouted after her.

She turned.

"Be good," I told her sternly.

"At my art?" she threw back, winking.

Then a another possible piece fell into place.

"Are you the one who called the Skyler Institute and told

one of the puppet women that we knew who killed their leader?'' I asked.

Emma's face fell. ''Uh-huh,'' she admitted, hanging her head. Then she muttered, ''I'm sorry, Kate,'' before running the rest of the way down the stairs.

I went back to my desk, but my mind was distracted now as I plodded through the tax charts. Would a woman tell the truth about all the rotten things she'd done and then lie about murder? It was possible. I wanted to ask Wayne. I needed to ask Wayne.

And I couldn't resist asking Wayne when he walked in the door, even though it meant I had to admit to talking to suspects. Alone. Two against one, etc., etc.

But Wayne just sighed when I told him Emma and Campbell had come and gone, that long, deep sigh he was so good at. And he advised keeping any future visitors on the deck, nosy neighbors or no nosy neighbors.

I recounted the whole visit then, toning down Campbell's anger as much as I could while Wayne cooked something that smelled of fresh lemon grass and galanga and basil. Thai tonight. I alternately salivated and babbled until I was finished with my tale and had set the table, carefully omitting any mention of my earlier visit to the Olcott Johnson Funeral Home. Admitting to that trip would probably elicit more than a sigh.

One good sniff of the Thai vegetable curry over cellophane noodles, and Emma and Campbell slipped out of my mind as smoothly as the food went into my mouth. I savored a touch of red chili and coconut on my tongue, and then just let the flavors overwhelm me. I was still panting with pleasure when Wayne finally offered an opinion.

''I believe her,'' he said.

''Who?'' I asked, slurping bits of vegetables, noodles, and seitan, murder completely forgotten.

"Emma," he replied with a fond smile in my direction. The man still loved to watch me eat, earlier sighs notwithstanding.

He was a good man with a good heart. I took a quick break to circle the table and kiss him on his delicious mouth, before returning to stuff mine again.

Because I believed Emma too. At least I wanted to.

By Friday morning, my doubts and I were back at my desk while Wayne toiled away in the back room at his own administrivia. I signed a paycheck. *Performance art. Acting.* Could Emma have known that confessing to the minor sins would make me believe her when she said she wouldn't cover up for a murderer? I stabbed at the keys of my adding machine. Could she be just as calculating?

I even began to wonder about Tessa as I practiced my tai chi form that night surrounded by classmates. Had she hit *herself* on the head with that candlestick? As my body turned during the rollback sequence, my arm swinging back and over in the general direction of my own head, I realized *I* could bonk myself on the noggin. Easily. And the candlestick incident had certainly worked to put Tessa out of the running as a murder suspect. At least in my mind. Had the police come to the same conclusion?

And then there was Nathan, I thought, my body moving forward in the press movement. And Diana. And Martina. And . . . The circle of suspects dancing through my head became as complex and repetitive as the tai chi form itself. And just as difficult to master.

Saturday was a Wedding Ritual class day for Wayne and me again. It had been exactly one week since Sam Skyler died. I was ready for action, whether Wayne was or not. I would center myself and concentrate, the way I should have in my tai chi class the night before. But this time I'd concentrate on murder.

I didn't even let Yvonne O'Reilley's pot-bellied pig, chickens, and llama distract me as I closed the gate of the chainlink fence behind Wayne's Jaguar. At least not too much. Even averting my eyes, it was hard to ignore the competing sounds of wind chimes, grunts, clucks, moos, and other animal noises, a couple of which Old McDonald had probably never heard in his whole long life.

I patted the rough surface of the stone Buddha for luck before we went through Yvonne's open doorway. And shielded my eyes against the rainbow kitsch I knew would assault them.

"Hey, Kate," two voices said as one when Wayne and I stepped in. Emma Jett and Ray Zappa.

They both swiveled their heads at each other as if astounded to be sharing the same phrase. Tessa and Campbell were a little slower with their own sideways glances.

Then Ray shuffled my way, his hand outstretched, his handsome face a screen of conflicting emotions. But I couldn't have told you exactly what those emotions were. Or what their source was for that matter.

He shook my hand when he got to me, a careful sweaty handshake, whispering a brief thanks for "taking care of Tessa."

And then I got it. I'd helped the woman he was in love with. Friendliness, gratitude. But she had called me instead of him. Jealousy and anger. And then there was the built-in cop's suspicion of my actions. Maybe even of Tessa's actions. No wonder his face was twitching.

Campbell was next in line to thank me and shake my hand. At least his hand wasn't sweaty. I gave him a quick hug, embarrassed by all this gratitude, and pushed him back toward Emma. Because people were watching.

Ona squinted my way and then turned her gaze thoughtfully toward Emma. But Emma's eyes were on Yvonne now. And Yvonne was watching Martina, who was watching Tessa, who was eyeing Nathan. Nathan for his part seemed to be scanning the whole crowd. His eyes stopped when they reached Perry, however. I turned to Wayne. His gaze was firmly fixed on me. I hoped *he* at least was thinking of wedding ceremonies instead of murder. On second thought, I decided I'd rather he had his mind on murder.

"So Yvonne, how's it going?" I asked, poking a hole in the silence of the room.

She jerked her eyes back from Martina Monteil like a minister caught reading pornography. And then her face curved into her usual big smile.

"Oh, I'm just moving along at warp-speed," she sang out and proceeded across the room to hug Wayne and me, ankle and wrist bracelets jingling. "Everyone's here and ready to be energized. Except for Diana and Liz, of course." She paused for a moment, running her hand through her curly blond hair, colliding with a pink heart-shaped barrette. Was she thinking of the other missing person? "But love is a wondrous thing and we're all here to celebrate it!" she finished up enthusiastically.

"With the exception of one dead man," Ona muttered.

Martina Monteil shot her a warning glare that could have fried eggs. But Ona just returned the glare. They both drew back their shoulders.

"So, Martina," Yvonne went on quickly, her voice ascending even higher. "How are your plans for the Institute going?"

"And what exactly do you mean by that?" Martina demanded quietly, turning our class leader's way, glare still in place.

Yvonne threw her jingling arms into the air. "Oh, nothing," she squeaked.

So far the celebration of love wasn't going too well. I wondered just what had happened *before* we'd arrived.

"The Institute is healing," Nathan put in, his voice gentle and calming. "We are all healing."

"Healing, yes," Yvonne jumped in gratefully. "Cosmically healing. And growing. And remembering that death is merely a passage—"

"One-way ticket, though," Ona commented.

"Hey, how about that video you promised us," Ray Zappa cut in quickly. "Sounds hot."

"Thank you, Ray," Yvonne said and her gratitude sounded sincere. Desperately sincere. "Our video today is a sumptuous feast of love. Two lovers delighting in the bliss of their desire. A tango wedding. So everyone take a seat with your loved one."

I flinched at the phrase, shooting Tessa a quick glance as I thought of all the "loved ones" resting back at her funeral home. She caught the glance and grinned in return. Two minds with one thought? I took my opportunity and quickly stepped over to her to whisper in her ear.

"Can I tell the class what happened to you?" I asked. "Then we could find out where people were at the time you were—"

"No, Kate," she whispered back, shaking her still bandaged head. "No."

And then she sat herself down with Ray on the velvet cushions of the wicker love seat. I joined Wayne on the paisley throw rug, the molded neon-purple plastic couch being occupied, as well as the tiger-stripe pillows, and turned my head dutifully toward the video screen. But I couldn't help noticing that two of the love birds weren't roosting together. Nathan and Martina stood yards apart as Yvonne pushed the button and the wedding began.

Ray was right, the tango wedding was hot, so hot I wondered if the preacher should have replaced "You may kiss the bride" with "Have you already consummated the marriage right before our eyes?" All that slithering and swooning and undulating. Wow. I snuggled closer to Wayne, breathing in his scent. Maybe the two of us could take tango classes. It would probably take years, though, before we got that good. Now there was a cheery thought. Indefinite postponement of the wedding until we perfected the tango.

"Jesus!" Ona commented, turning her baby face toward Perry as Yvonne pushed the Off button.

"Way cool," Emma added, her arm tightening around Campbell's waist.

"Yes, indeed," Tessa agreed quietly. Ray threw his head back and laughed, then laid a big smacking kiss on her pinkening brown cheek.

Whatever had gone down before, Yvonne had her Wedding Ritual seminar back now. Except for Nathan and Martina. A quick glance told me they were still standing exactly where they'd been when the video began.

"Are you inspired?" Yvonne demanded of us, clapping her hands. "Are you ready?"

I don't know if I was ready for marriage, but I certainly wouldn't have minded making love. I stroked Wayne's chest and peered into his passion-glazed eyes.

And then Yvonne passed out the questionnaires. On individual clipboards, no less.

What was it that brought you together? was the first question.

Murder, I answered silently, the last chords of the tango fading from my mind.

Next on the list was: What is the passion that holds you together?

And I was ashamed that I didn't have an answer. Or maybe I had too many answers. My passion for Wayne didn't spring from a common interest like computers or art, but from a heartfelt appreciation of his love, his lovemaking, his kindness, his vulnerability, his wit, his intelligence . . . Just for starters. Not to mention the food. Somehow I couldn't think of Wayne without thinking of food.

I set down my clipboard and turned to the man who inspired my passion. Because he did inspire passion, even if I couldn't pinpoint its exact nature. Wayne's brows were pulled down low in thought. He chewed on the pencil in his hand, apparently as stumped as I was. I put my arms around him and squeezed.

We left not long after that, our questionnaires still as blank as the mental slate on which I'd planned to write the murderer's name.

But as Wayne pulled the Jaguar into our driveway, we came to the happy conclusion that forms weren't as important as love, and that form wasn't as important as substance. As commitment.

"You're right, Kate," Wayne growled and my ears tingled joyously. "The format of the wedding doesn't matter. Only its occurrence."

"Yes!" I shouted, throwing a high-five toward the ceiling of the Jag. "No long white veils, no steak costumes—"

"Steak costumes?" he said, tilting his head my way.

"Never mind."

"But the wedding will occur?" he prodded as he shut off the engine, his vulnerability peeking out from beneath his brows.

"Soon," I assured him and put my arms around him again.

We were still holding hands when we reached the top of the front stairs. Connected emotionally and physically. To the exclusion of all else.

So connected, I almost missed the sobs issuing from the

woman standing at our front door. So did Wayne. I felt his body jerk in recognition at the same time as mine.

Diana Atherton was at our door. Waiting.

And she was crying. And talking. Or trying to.

It was a few long minutes before I could make any sense at all of her mumbles and sobs. I heard "police" once, and "they think," and one or two other things. Then finally a string of words burst out in one full sentence.

"They think I did it!" she yelped.

"They who—" I began.

"The Quiero police. They think I killed Sam." Now she was loud and clear.

"But why?" I asked.

"Evidence!" she shrieked. "They say they have the evidence to convict me!"

TWENTY

I stood back, out of Diana's eardrum-blasting range. Just in time too.

"But I didn't do it!" she screamed on. "I didn't kill Sam. I didn't." And then she started sobbing again.

I stared at Wayne. He stared back. And finally we helped the weeping goddess into our house, each of us holding one arm very gently until we had guided her onto the denim couch.

Then we sat down on either side of her, acting very, very calm. At least I was just acting.

When she'd sobbed herself out for the moment—and I knew it might be only a moment—I leaned her way and quickly threw out my first question.

"What kind of evidence do the police say they have?" I asked, keeping my voice low and soothing.

"Massage oil!" she shouted, full volume.

Ouch, that was loud. I quickly drew away from her, rubbing my ringing ear. I kept forgetting her lung power.

But the volume was enough to click something in my brain. Hadn't Felix mentioned the police finding oily hand prints on Sam's jacket? But he'd also said that they'd found the imprints of Yvonne's vases on his shoulder blades. That had to make the oily hand prints irrelevant. Or did it?

"I always use this massage oil on my hands," Diana went on, her usual sweet voice lower now but still nasal and rasping. "It's honeysuckle scented, very natural. Organic and everything—"

"And they matched that with the oil on Sam's jacket?" I prompted.

She shot me a quick, suspicious glance. She hadn't mentioned the jacket yet.

But then the look was replaced with one of admiration. Did she think I was finally displaying my magical powers of deduction as per her expectations?

"Yes, on the jacket, exactly," she said, turning even further my way, putting her moist hand on mine. "But that was just because I was massaging his shoulders that day. I did it as often as I could. Sam's shoulders were always so tight. All his empathy, I think."

Or all his fears and ego, I thought back uncharitably. She withdrew her hand.

"But that doesn't mean I pushed him."

I nodded, and not insincerely. The person who'd pushed Sam Skyler had used the bottoms of Yvonne's vases. At least that's what I thought Felix had said. How else would the bruises have been so evident? That took force. Deadly force.

I glanced across at Wayne. We'd promised Felix not to talk about the evidence. And I didn't want to break that promise. Diana was still a suspect in my book. She could have massaged Sam first and then pushed him with the brass vases for all we knew. One action didn't preclude the other. But still, the Quiero police had her terrified. And probably for no better reason than to try to scare her into an admission. They were more likely to get a nervous breakdown at this point.

"The police are just trying to frighten you," Wayne finally put in. "Don't have enough evidence to convict."

"Really?" she said, her saucer blue eyes ready to believe

as they turned his way, her hands fluttering toward her face. I caught the scent of honeysuckle. Was she still using the oil, even now?

"Really," he assured her.

But then her eyes filled up with tears again. She clasped her fluttering hands together and pulled them down to her lap.

"There's more," she told us, her words clogged but discernible. "Someone told them I was really in love with Nathan. And they're right!" She looked at us both as if for forgiveness, one after another.

We both nodded slowly in turn. I felt like the Pope. Or half of the Pope.

"I've been falling in love with Nathan for months, but I didn't want to be disloyal to Sam. I mean, I loved Sam too. He was so kind, so good with people. But I wasn't in love anymore, I guess. But even so, how could I just drop him like that? And there was all the pressure from my mom not to marry Sam. I felt like I might just be caving in 'cause of her. I didn't know what to do—"

"And then Sam died," I finished up for her. How convenient for everyone, except, of course, for Sam.

"Oh, Sam," she murmured and then she was wailing again. Loudly.

I put a hand over my ear closest to Diana. And Wayne and I both started throwing desperate, reassuring words her way. About Sam, about the police, about her love for Nathan. Anything to stop the wailing.

The doorbell rang, succeeding in stopping Diana's tears where our words had failed. I trotted to the door thankfully.

I was even more thankful when I opened it. Diana's mother, Liz Atherton, stood there. No nonsense salt-and-pepper hair and all. All right! Mom to the rescue. *Our* rescue.

"Gary said Diana was headed over here," Liz explained brusquely. She rubbed her temple and looked away as if embarrassed to intrude. "Said she was upset. Thought I could help."

"I'm so glad to see you—" I began.

And then Diana cried, "Mom!" and jumped from the couch to run and throw herself into her mother's arms. For a moment, I thought she'd knock the smaller woman over.

Pretty soon, both Liz and Diana Atherton were seated on our denim couch, Wayne and I sitting on the futon across from them. Wayne offered Liz a succinct version of what Diana had told us, sans tears.

"They'll be wanting a scapegoat," Liz commented when Wayne had finished the part about the massage oil on Sam's jacket. She put her arm around her daughter's trembling shoulders. "But it won't be Diana."

"But Mom, they know I . . . I love Nathan," Diana announced tremulously.

"Nathan?" Liz said, drawing back from Diana. "But . . ." she stared at her daughter, as if she didn't recognize her for a moment, then seemed to pull herself back together as she closed her eyes and rubbed her temple some more. Obviously, she was hearing Diana's confession for the first time.

Then abruptly, Liz stood up from the couch. "Diana and I will be going," she announced. "Shouldn't be troubling you good people anymore."

Then Diana stood too, back yoga-straight.

The two women exited together, Liz's arm around her daughter's waist as they walked down the stairs, Diana's long black braid brushing the back of her mother's encircling arm as they went.

"Don't worry, honey," Liz said. "There is some justice in this world. The police won't arrest you for Sam's murder. I promise."

I just hoped she could keep that promise as I watched the two leave in their separate cars. I wasn't so sure. Liz had said it herself—the Quiero police needed a scapegoat. They were between a rock and a hard place, so to speak. Or a bluff and a hard place. Sam's spread-eagled body flashed into my mind in gruesome detail. I shook my head hard to rid myself of the vision. Think, I told myself. But my thoughts weren't much better. With the vase prints on Sam's shoulders, the police couldn't just explain away Sam's death as a suicide. And they probably didn't have any better idea of who really killed him than we did. Scapegoat season in Quiero had probably just begun.

Once mother and daughter were gone, Wayne and I flopped onto the couch, each of us lost in our own thoughts.

"Are we back on the case?" I asked after a few minutes of silence.

Wayne opened his mouth, probably to object, but then seemed to change his mind midway to verbalization. He closed his mouth, then opened it again. With obvious reluctance.

"Guess so," he sighed. "But together, okay?"

"Okay," I agreed and stood up. "Let's go see Nathan."

A call to the Institute got us Nathan this time. He was just leaving and agreed to see us at his home in half an hour.

It was a long half hour. Because Wayne and I both spilled out all our theories on the way to Nathan's, all the theories we weren't supposed to be working on. Perry as religious fanatic (Wayne's theory), Tessa as self head-bonker (mine), Nathan as playing out Oedipal feelings on his soon-to-be stepmother (Wayne's), Martina as ambitious to gain control of the Institute (mine), Liz as being in love with Sam herself (Wayne's), Ray as wanting the story (mine), and . . . We couldn't seem to stop as the theories cascaded from our minds via our mouths.

I was more confused than ever when we parked in front of Nathan's apartment building. Because, between us, Wayne and I had motives for each and every person who had been there

when Sam was pushed. Multiple motives. Except for ourselves. And I was sure we could have come up with those too
if necessary.

Nathan's apartment was a lot like his office. His living room
was stuffed with bookcases and filing cabinets. And his furniture might have come from the Salvation Army. In fact, it
probably did, I decided, lowering myself onto the lone, lumpy
brown couch next to Wayne. The major difference between
his office and home was the extra animals here. Not only Sigmund, the graying Labrador retriever we'd already met, but
an Irish setter, and three or four cats darting in and out and
around the stacks of papers and books on the floor. No wonder
Nathan cultivated such a furry face. He had to in order to fit
in with his menagerie. Nathan pulled a kitchen chair across
from us and sat down. A tabby with a well-chewed ear claimed
his lap immediately to the yowls of the remaining cats.

"You're here about my dad?" Nathan asked, his voice as
calm and mesmerizing as usual. He might have been a psychotherapist ready to listen. And then I remembered that a
psychotherapist was indeed what he would probably become
now that his father was gone.

"We came to ask about your father," I answered, trying to
put the same mesmerizing tone into my voice. Trying to switch
our roles. "But we came to see how you were doing too. Do
you still think you'll go after your Ph.D. in psychology now?"
I would work up to the harder questions later.

Nathan leaned back in his chair and absently stroked the cat
in his lap. The tabby half closed its eyes, smugly surveying
the restless feline underclass circling the chair.

"Probably," Nathan said after a few purrs from his lap.
"My mom thinks I should. And Martina is certainly proving
herself able and ready to take over the reins at the Institute.
She'll do a good job keeping it going."

"How does Diana feel about that?" Wayne asked softly.

Nathan's body jerked ever so slightly in his chair. I wouldn't have noticed except for the tabby who opened her eyes for a moment and hissed a swift reprimand before snuggling back down onto Nathan's khaki pants.

"Well," Nathan murmured, his face reddening in the few spots not covered in fur. "Um, Diana is okay with that. She didn't care that much about the Institute as the Institute anyway. She was more concerned with Dad."

"And with you," I prodded.

Nathan looked at the ground for a few moments.

"And with me," he whispered in agreement finally.

"Do the police know about you and Diana?" I asked, keeping my voice properly sympathetic.

"There isn't a whole lot to know," Nathan replied, his voice higher than before, but not by much. "Diana and I have certain feelings for each other, it's true. But we've never acted on them. It didn't seem right while Dad . . . while Dad was alive. And now, well . . ." He shrugged gently enough that the tabby didn't have to reprimand him.

Now I really was sympathetic. I certainly hoped he hadn't expressed himself in those particular words to the police. Unless he really was the murderer. Talk about your scapegoats. I squinted my eyes at him, trying to see what was beneath that kind, furry facade. And gave up. I would let Wayne be in charge of suspecting Nathan. I just couldn't get up the resolve to suspect a man petting a cat so gently, no matter how powerful his patricidal motives might be.

"Did your father ever tell you what really happened when your stepmother went over the railing?" Wayne asked quietly.

The feline encephalograph twitched, hissing as Nathan's body jerked again.

Nathan looked down for a moment at the cats on the floor and then lifted his head.

"Yes," he said, so softly the word was barely discernable.

We waited.

"You won't repeat any of this unless you have to?" he added a few moments later.

Wayne nodded. I added a quick, belated nod to Wayne's. Even the cats at Nathan's feet were staring up at him in suspense. All the animals in the room, including us, seemed to hold their breaths. And then Nathan spoke.

"I guess I already told you that Dad and Sally fought a lot," he began. "She'd throw a punch or a slap, and he'd hit her back sometimes. Too often. Oddly enough, he really liked her. Probably even loved her. That's why he put up with the physical stuff. When she wasn't angry, Sally was a witty and intelligent woman. Similar to my mother in some ways." He paused. "But Sally was a rage-aholic. And Dad . . . well, Dad just couldn't control his responses all the time. He talked to me a little about it, how he'd try to leave the room when she lashed out. Or to just breathe through it. But it wasn't just the physical stuff, it was the things she said with the blows. She called him a wimp and a nobody and all kinds of things that really hit him where he lived, in his ego."

Nathan got up suddenly, holding the tabby in his arms, then setting her gently on the floor before turning and walking to the window that looked out from his apartment. When he turned back he straightened his shoulders, not much but a little.

"I haven't told anyone this before, not even the police," he said, his voice stronger. "But Dad is dead now, so I guess it can't hurt. Dad and Sally lived in a house on top of a cliff in Eldora. They both drank too much. He stopped drinking after . . . after Sally died. After he pushed her." Nathan wrapped his arms around himself as if for the warmth. His normally calm voice sped up. "They were on the balcony. Sally was leaning up against the railing, ranting. She told Dad he was worthless, that he'd only married her for her money.

He told her it wasn't true. But she just kept going on. And then she hit him in the face, hard, screaming that he was a nobody and would always be a nobody. Dad shoved her then. And she went right over the railing.''

I felt a thud in my lap and for a minute I was sailing over that railing with Sally Skyler, feeling the cold air streaming by my sweating body. But it was only Nathan's tabby in my lap. Though the sweat was real. And the air felt cold now. I put my arms around myself the same way Nathan had.

''Dad literally couldn't believe he'd actually pushed her at first,'' Nathan went on. ''That's what he told me. He'd killed his wife. She was lying on the rocks below. He knew she had to be dead. But he was in complete shock. Drunk and frightened. But not too drunk to call the police. He dialed 911 and told them that his wife had jumped over the railing. He said he believed his own lie then, that she'd jumped. For a while. But then his nightmares began. And over the next few weeks, he remembered everything. In full detail.

''Lucky for Dad, Sally was so bruised by the rocks, the police couldn't really prove she'd been pushed. But they knew it. There was even a witness a couple of houses down who'd seen the flurry. So the prosecution took on the case. But Dad got on the stand with all he'd learned from his years of hypnosis classes and people skills and convinced the jury he didn't do it. Convinced twelve people that Sally had jumped off the balcony as he tried to stop her. That explained the bruise on *his* face. And the witness was too far away, his attorneys said. So he was found not guilty.''

Nathan walked back to his chair and put his head in his hands. When he brought it back up, I could see the tears streaming from beneath his wire-rimmed glasses.

''But Dad really did feel guilty. He kept having nightmares. He couldn't stop thinking about it. He cried all the time. He really was sorry.'' Nathan took off his glasses and wiped the tears from his eyes, his voice moving back toward its usual calm. "Though in his own narcissistic way, I think Dad was really more attuned to his own experience of grief than Sally's actual death. It was more as if something had been done to him, than as if he'd done something to her. Still, the experience changed his life completely. He went to a therapist who worked with him for nearly a year, partly with puppets, and out of his all too real guilt and grief for his crime came the book, *Grief Into Growth*. And the seminars. Then everyone felt sorry for the poor man who'd been unable to stop his wife from jumping onto the rocks. He made a fortune on the book and a fortune on the seminars. But he never got over his grief, his own self-generated hell."

A black and white cat jumped into Nathan's lap then and rubbed against him as if offering comfort. The psychotherapist's therapist. "Umh-humh," the cat purred.

"All the adoration in the world couldn't patch my Dad back together," Nathan finished. "But he put up a good show. And he really did believe in his own techniques. And he really did help others find some peace, I think."

No wonder Sam Skyler's shoulders had always been so tight, I thought. Not empathy, not even ego. Guilt. I felt a surge of pity for the man who'd murdered his wife. But that faded as I thought of Sally Skyler, dead all this time. I rubbed my arms, still too cold.

"Did your father ever tell any one else what really happened?" Wayne asked quietly.

I jumped in my seat, earning my own hiss from the tabby in my lap. I'd completely forgotten Wayne, forgotten the apartment we were in, forgotten everything but Nathan's story. Sam Skyler's story.

"No," Nathan answered. "At least, as far as I can tell. My mother doesn't seem to know. Dad didn't even tell me till a few years ago." He put his glasses back on. "You won't tell anyone, will you?"

No, we reassured him. Not unless necessary. As promised. Then we got up to leave.

"Wow," was all I could say ten minutes later as the Jaguar gobbled up the blacktop between Nathan's home and ours. "Sam Skyler really did kill his wife."

"And Nathan Skyler had all the more reason to kill his father," Wayne added.

"What?" I objected. "Nathan loved his father. Can't you see that?"

"Maybe he just inherited his father's good acting genes," Wayne pointed out.

I stared at Wayne, trying to figure out why he suspected Nathan Skyler, of all people. Kind, sweet Nathan Skyler. Kind, sweet Wayne, my mind echoed. Was that why? A case of like repelling like?

"Need to talk to Ona and Perry again," Wayne put in before I could voice the concept. "They've been to the seminars, seen Nathan and his father interact. They're perfect witnesses. Disinterested and observant bystanders."

"And mouthy," I added, thinking of Ona.

We were lucky again, with Ona and Perry. I phoned Ona from our house. She and Perry and their respective sets of children were all there. I could hear the lilt of kids' voices arguing in the background. And Ona was ready to talk. Itching to talk.

"Your car or mine?" I asked Wayne.

"Mine," he said. And we were on the road to Cebollas.

"Boy, am I glad you guys are still on the case," Ona greeted us as she opened her front door.

There were good smells coming from inside her kitchen. Perry was cooking again, I'd bet. I sniffed chilies and beans and maybe corn, something south of the border tonight. My stomach gurgled a little plea for food soon. But we weren't here to eat.

"That fatophobe, Woolsey, thinks I killed Skyler," Ona went on, leading us through the living room and into the kitchen as she spoke. "Because Skyler criticized my determination to be proud of my size. What a load of crap. If I murdered everyone who criticized my weight, there'd be a lot more dead folks out there."

"Including us," Pammy murmured under her breath, rolling her dark brown eyes.

"Don't you talk that way about my mother," Ogden warned, puffing up his burly blond teenaged body.

Ona ignored them as they went on arguing in muted mutters and squawks.

"Have a seat," she ordered us.

So Wayne and I sat down at the teak kitchen table. Perry picked up a pot from the stove and set it on the glazed blue tile of the counter. God, it smelled good. Maybe they'd invite us to dinner. He threw us a friendly wave over his shoulder.

"If they really think Skyler was murdered, they ought to be looking at Yvonne O'Reilley not Ona," Perry commented as he stirred the contents of another pot. "I've been on the Golden Valley City Council for years. That O'Reilley woman is compassionate about most things, but she has a real wild streak when it comes to preserving Golden Valley—"

"And that's just where Skyler stuck his rocket ship Institute," Ona finished for him. "Though it's kinda hard to take Yvonne seriously about preserving the character of Golden Valley with that zoo she has up there." She put her hands on her ample hips. "I can't believe they'd elect a woman to the City Planning Commission who has metallic madras wallpaper in her living room."

"Not to mention the chickens and llamas and cows," Perry added.

"Do you really think Yvonne murdered Sam Skyler?" Wayne asked.

"No, no," Perry backtracked as Ona shrugged her shoulders. "Yvonne really does seem like a kind, caring woman. She ranted a lot about the Institute when it was built, and then got herself elected to the planning commission, though too late to stop Skyler's Institute. But still, I can't imagine her actually killing someone. I just meant she had a greater motive in comparison to Ona. I'm afraid the man probably jumped. Sad but believable."

"Probably looked out over that bluff and felt guilty about killing his wife," Ona added, crossing her arms. And this time Martina Monteil wasn't there to contradict her.

I shivered in the warmly scented kitchen, remembering what Nathan had just told us. Had Sam Skyler jumped after all? Unable to bear his grief and guilt? But what about the bruises from Yvonne's vases?

"Wanted to ask you about Sam Skyler's relationship to his son Nathan," Wayne put in, and I remembered why we were here. "You both must have observed the two of them before the Wedding Ritual class, before Sam's death. Do you think Nathan really cared for his father or—"

But the rest of Wayne's words were lost in a high-pitched scream that bounced off the redwood rafters.

ꝖWENTY-ONE

Ꝗ whipped my head around in time to see Ona's burly son Ogden pinned to the floor by Pammy of the beautiful dark eyes, her slender brown hands around his thick pink throat.

"You can't talk about my mom like that!" Ogden yelled. Pammy's hands obviously weren't squeezing hard enough.

"You big fat moron!" Pammy screamed back. "You big blond piece of . . . you big . . . you . . ." Her voice faltered to a stop.

Within one hot breath, Ogden's face reddened. Then suddenly Pammy jumped off the boy as if someone had stuck a burning wedge between the two of them. Ogden jumped up too, backing away in a pre-Neanderthal crouch.

"I, um, I . . ." he babbled, his eyes still fixed on the young woman standing in front of him.

Pammy looked back at him and suddenly her beautiful dark eyes seemed to see something in Ogden's burly blond body that escaped the rest of us.

And then she was mumbling too. And her flawless skin was a pinkening mauve.

"Oh, God," Ona whispered from behind me.

But the two teenagers just stared at each other without moving. Had they just noticed they were of the opposite sex?

"I'm sorry," they both mumbled in unison.

"Oh, shit," Ona said. "We wondered when they'd go from bickering to lusting."

Yup. They had just noticed.

"Hey, Ogden," Orestes objected, his shrill little voice indignant. "You're not gonna let her get away with that, are you?"

But Ogden didn't even glance at his younger brother. His eyes were still riveted on Pammy, the Pammy he was seeing now.

Perry and Ona looked past their children at each other, their eyes wide with worry. Or was it panic?

Then Page reached out and slapped Orestes. Hard. For no obvious reason. And no one seemed to notice but Orestes who squealed with outrage. Pammy and Ogden certainly didn't care.

"Time out for a Talk," Ona announced.

Orestes and Page and Perry all turned her way, a mixture of resignation and fear reflected on each of their faces, but Ogden and Pammy's eyes didn't waver.

"TIME OUT FOR A TALK!" Ona shouted.

And then Perry sprang into action, inserting his body between the two teenagers, waving his hands as if to stop an oncoming train. I'd have placed my bet on the train.

"Guess we'll be going now," Wayne said to no one in particular.

We both rose unnoticed from our places at the teak table and scurried away from the family tableau. As we crossed the living room, I sent a sympathetic backwards glance at the worried parents.

"Good luck," I mumbled, knowing they were beyond hearing, and then Wayne and I were out through the living room into the cool evening air.

"Whew!" I said, waving my hot face as we walked toward the Jaguar. "Pheromone fever."

"Do you think it's catching?" Wayne asked, a smile tugging at his soft mouth.

"Yeah," I answered huskily, launching myself against his solid body like a torpedo, lips landing on lips.

Luckily, Wayne's good at catching. Torpedoes and lips included.

I wasn't sure if I was glad or not when my stomach started growling mid-clinch before our even baser instincts could take over in Ona's driveway.

"Dinner?" Wayne inquired reasonably.

My stomach gurgled a loud Yes while other parts of my anatomy shouted silently in disagreement. My stomach won.

We ended up at the Grazie, a little Italian restaurant in San Ricardo where the owners really spoke Italian. And really cooked. It was one of Wayne's favorite restaurants, next to his own. He stuffed himself with a sausage-and mushroom-loaded calazone, while I twirled my fettucini with veggies, basil, garlic, and chilies. And we exchanged more theories than the *Grazie*'s menu had selections.

I was sopping up the sauce left on my plate with the restaurant's own chewy sourdough bread when I thought of Sally Skyler again.

"Someone must have cared whether Sally Skyler lived or died," I said finally.

"Yumph," Wayne agreed through his last mouthful of calazone.

"And we still haven't figured out whether any of our Wedding Ritual class members was a friend of hers."

"Or family," Wayne added, bending forward eagerly over the table.

But then he shook his head and leaned back in his chair.

"Doesn't make sense, Kate," he growled. "Not ten years later."

But the idea wouldn't leave my mind in peace. I dreamt of Sally Skyler that night, tangled in seaweed and soundlessly mouthing her request to be avenged as the tides rolled her body to and fro, never quite reaching the slippery rock I stood on.

Sunday morning, "It's gotta be about Sally Skyler," were the first words out of my mouth. Well, not quite the first words, to be honest, but that was only because of Wayne's warm body beside me. There's something about unexplained death that brings out the carnal side of my nature. Embarrassing, but true. Happily, Wayne's temperament matches my own in that regard, just as well as his body fits mine.

But by breakfast, we really were both talking about Sally again.

"Who would know?" I asked Wayne over the peanut butter-oatmeal muffins and hot apple tea he'd made for me.

"Yvonne probably knows all the members of the class better than anyone else," he suggested warily. "She might have an idea who Sally knew in the class. If there *was* anyone besides Nathan."

"Yeah," I breathed, setting my tea down with a splash. "Yvonne O'Reilley, rabid preservationist of Golden Valley."

"Only according to Perry Kane," Wayne added moderately.

But I wanted to talk to Yvonne, immoderately. Unfortunately, we weren't able to schedule our visit to the defender of Golden Valley until later that afternoon between her Creative Office Spacing class from two to four and her Guardian Angels of the Menopause class beginning at five.

So we both worked until it was time to make her four o'clock afternoon slot. And we thought. And worked and thought some more. Our respective levels of paperwork went down, but as we drove in my Toyota to Yvonne's we found that we'd both been just as busy piling up new murder theories upon new murder theories in our minds. And the theoretical towers were ready to topple.

"This is ridiculous," I said as Wayne got out to open the gate to Yvonne's chainlink fence.

"What's ridiculous?" he asked once we were safely in, with the gate locked behind us.

"All these theories," I told him, climbing out of the Toyota to stare into the glazed eyes of a spaced-out llama. I lifted my hand carefully toward its muzzle, palm up. The llama turned and ambled away, rubbing up against a marble statue of Aphrodite on the way. Maybe carnality was in the air. "Do you think the police have this many theories?" I finished.

"Nope," Wayne answered succinctly as Yvonne came bursting out the door with her last Creative Office Spacing class member. Or maybe her only Creative Office Spacing class member, an older man with a gray goatee and stacks of binders and manila envelopes in his arms.

"Aren't you just cosmically charged?" Yvonne demanded of the man. "Now just go to your office and laser thorough it all. Remember, keep thinking creatively!"

The goateed man nodded, but his eyes were as glazed as the llama's as he walked to his car. Quails and chickens scattered as he backed out of the enclosure.

"Kate, Wayne!" Yvonne greeted us enthusiastically. She raised her arms, jingling with bracelets as usual, and embraced each of us in turn before swiveling around to lead us into her house, silken rainbow fringes fluttering from the shoulders of her jacket as the wind chimes rang in accompaniment.

Yvonne's place looked even stranger without the Wedding Ritual class members—the white wicker love seat, molded neon-purple plastic couch, paisley throw rug, and tiger-stripe pillows all empty. Our teacher sat on her tall rattan throne and motioned us to sit down too. At least we had a choice of accommodation.

We shot each other glances and chose the wicker love seat, appropriately, I hoped.

Yvonne squeezed her curvy face into a big smile as her hands danced in the air.

"I'm just so energized," she told us. "So blissed . . ."

I watched her as she spoke, dazed by the electric flow of her words, thinking that if energy was required for murder, this woman had all that was necessary. I tried to remember if I'd ever seen her down, even in the aftermath of Sam Skyler's fall.

". . . starting a new class," she buzzed on. "For Adult Children of the Paranormally Gifted. They need help, my help. My own mother was highly attuned to the paranormal. So few people really appreciate its potential." She leaned forward, her eyes zooming in on me like a dental drill. "But you do, don't you, Kate?" she finished.

"Huh?" I said, startled by her sudden attention.

"You practice tai chi," she accused, leaning further forward and pointing her waltzing finger my way. "Chi kung masters can push people without using their hands, just with their chi. But you know that, don't you?"

"Huh?" I said again. But I was beginning to come out of my daze. Clearly, Wayne and I weren't the only ones with theories.

"Of course you know. It's called 'empty force.' It can hurl a person right over. Right over—"

"Well, Diana does tai chi, too," I cut in defensively. Then I shook my head. Why was I getting defensive? This was not a theory the Quiero police were going to accept. I thought of Chief Woolsey and his earring. At least I hoped not.

"But that's fascinating about chi kung," I added, lowering

my voice in an imitation of relaxed interest. "I hadn't heard of that aspect before."

Yvonne leaned back in her chair, still squinting her eyes at me. One of her hands tangoed up to her curly hair and then she opened her mouth again.

"So, I understand you're on the Golden Valley Planning Commission," I put in quickly, feeling Wayne stir impatiently beside me.

"Oh, yes!" she caroled, clasping her hands together. "I love this land so much. It must be preserved. Did you know that redwood trees entwine their roots and share water in times of drought? And people treat the nonanimal species as if they have no feelings—"

"The Skyler Institute for Essential Manifestation must have plowed down a few redwoods to clear a space for their building," I interrupted.

That stopped her. She even frowned. At least for a second.

"Well, actually, they were pines," she came back after a quick breath. "Oh, I was pretty tinkled at first, especially when I looked at the plans. They weren't harmonic at all. But the contractors did end up erecting the Institute with some respect for the environment, you know, like leaving the oldest trees standing. And actually, the building was kinda cosmic when it finally went up, with all those skylights and solar collectors and neat shapes. Of course, the interior is pretty boring." She scanned the rainbows of kitsch and metallic madras wallpaper surrounding her with an expression of fondness softening her curvy face, then patted the nearest brass Shiva statue. "But Sam had to appeal to the masses, I suppose."

"Were you still angry—" I began.

A long *moooo* from behind us stopped my interrogation. It practically stopped my heart. Wayne and I turned to face a pair of big brown eyes and a thick, exploring pink tongue. I ducked the tongue, wishing I could use chi kung to move the cow away. Far way. Wayne dodged the cow's next swipe. When the hell had she wandered in? Or had she been in the house the whole time? I was pretty sure I'd shut the door behind us.

"Oh, Isis, sweetie pie," Yvonne chirped. "Are you hungry?"

And then Yvonne rose from her chair with a quick apology to us humans.

She was back even more quickly, with a handful of alfalfa sprouts for Isis. I nodded in approval. At least Yvonne had that right. I always thought alfalfa sprouts were made for cows, not people.

After kissing Isis on the forehead, Yvonne escorted her out the front door, which had indeed been shut, and came back to sit on her rattan throne.

"Isn't Isis wonderful?" she asked us. "She's figured out how to open the back door. I think she's psychic." I hoped we weren't back to a discussion of the paranormal. I shot Wayne a pleading glance. But he was busy eyeing his watch. Right, time was running out in our less-than-an-hour slot, and so far we'd only elicited accusations and attempted cow licks.

"Sally Skyler," Wayne interjected just as the words were about to come out of my mouth. More paranormal behavior? "Wondered if anyone in our class knew her besides Nathan?"

Yvonne looked at Wayne for a moment as if he'd just arrived from Mars, but she did answer his question.

"Not anyone on this plane," she said. I assumed she meant the earthly one since we weren't flying at the moment. Physically, that was. I couldn't even imagine where Yvonne's mind was.

"Do you know anyone at all I could ask about Sally Skyler?" I probed desperately. "Anyone who knew her. Maybe a friend?"

"Or a family member?" Wayne added.

"Well, there's always Karma Irvine," Yvonne answered.

"What's a karma irvine?" I asked.

"Oh, Karma was Sally's best friend back then, maybe her only friend." Yvonne paused. "I never met her, but from what Karma said, Sally wasn't always so, um, cosmically attuned. She kinda rubbed people the wrong way."

That was probably an understatement, I thought, remembering Nathan's description of his stepmother. But still . . .

"Do you know how I might get in touch with Karma?" I asked, hoping my wording didn't get me a lecture on past lives.

"Oh, that's easy," Yvonne assured me. "She owns the Karma Boutique in Hutton. It's a wonderful store. The most sumptuous adornments." She stroked her silken streamers. "I get all my clothes there."

"Thanks," I said, looking at my own watch. Only twenty minutes left. And I wanted to talk to this Karma person.

"Speaking of karma," Yvonne said enthusiastically. "Sally Skyler on the rocks, then Sam. That has to be karma at work, don't you think?"

"You mean Karma avenged her friend?" I asked eagerly.

"No, no, I mean real karma," Yvonne corrected me. "The force of Sam's actions determining his destiny. I think Sally Skyler's spirit must have channeled through someone's body."

"Whose?" Wayne and I demanded simultaneously.

Yvonne leaned back in her chair, steepled her hands, and closed her eyes.

"I don't know, but I can meditate on it," she assured us. Maybe her cow could help with the psychic stuff.

But Yvonne's doorbell chimed before she got very far in her meditation.

I expected a glowingly menopausal woman with a guardian

angel on her shoulder to walk through the door. But it was
Park Ranger Yasuda who was doing the visiting. His eyes
were glowing, though, but with what looked like infatuation
to me, not menopause.

"David," Yvonne breathed.

"Ms. O'Reilley," Yasuda breathed back.

More pheromones. The moon must have been in lust or
something. I'm sure an astrologer could have explained it. Or
maybe even Yvonne could have, but her attention was otherwise occupied.

Wayne and I looked at each other, rolled our eyes simultaneously, and left. Yvonne and Yasuda barely registered our
disappearance. Though Isis managed to give me a lick before
I made it back inside the Toyota.

"How do we know Yvonne O'Reilley and Ranger Yasuda
really met arranging the scuba wedding?" Wayne murmured
as I guided the car back home.

Damn. The beginnings of a new theory. Just what we
needed. Were Yvonne and Yasuda in it together? Maybe they
knew Sally and loved her. Or maybe Sam's Institute competed
with Yvonne's seminars. Or maybe . . .

Wayne must have heard what was in my mind as it buzzed
through the permutations like a chain saw through pine trees.

"Sorry," he said. "Gotta stop this speculation."

"Do you think there's a twelve-step program for unbridled
murder theorists," I asked him. "Theorists Anonymous?"

He shot me an "I'm serious" look.

But it didn't stop my mind from buzzing.

And it didn't stop me from finding Karma's Boutique in the
phone book when I got home. Or from punching in the number.

Karma answered personally on the second ring, her voice
turning very friendly once she heard I was a "friend" of
Yvonne's. Until we got to Sally Skyler.

"Oh, I stopped worrying about Sally years ago," she informed me briskly. "What's done is done. Take my boutique, for instance. I've been looking for the right partner to invest. That's now. That's today. Or someone to buy it outright. Maybe you might be interested."

I never did get the conversation steered back to Sally Skyler. I felt like I'd dived into a swimming pool only to find myself in the jaws of a solicitor. Karma kept on trying to sell me her boutique even when I swore I was broke. She suggested I take out a loan. Then I fought fire with fire. I tried to sell her Jest Gifts. Her efforts faltered. C.C. jumped on the back of my chair and yowled for food into the phone. And I let her yowl until I heard the click on the other end. Too bad. Karma and C.C. were clearly soulmates, both equally ruthless and single-minded.

I looked up at Wayne in defeat as I replaced the limp receiver in its cradle, my ear sore from solicitation, my throat sore from protesting.

"Let's just leave it alone," Wayne suggested. "We'll think on it."

I wanted to object, but he was right. We had talked to everyone, discussed everything, and imagined every single suspect murdering Sam Skyler. There was nothing left to do but think.

"Gotta go to work now," he followed up. "Sunday night crowd."

One last hug and Wayne was gone. I fed C.C., and then I was staring at my stacks of paperwork again.

Ten minutes later, the doorbell rang.

I knew the minute I heard the sobbing that Diana was on the other side of the door. Oh joy. But I opened the door, anyway. Cautiously.

Diana held her face in her hands, mumbling through her fingers.

"What?" I asked impatiently.

"Mama," she gurgled.

"What about your mother?" I prompted, my pulse speeding up a little. "Have the police accused her now?"

"No, no." Diana wept on, shaking her face, a face I couldn't see since it was still hidden in her hands.

Time for a little shock treatment, I decided.

"Did your mother kill Sam Skyler?" I tried.

Diana's face popped up, out of her hands finally. "Noooo!" she wailed.

"Then what?" I demanded.

"I . . . she . . . I . . ."

I took Diana by the shoulders and shook her. And it felt good. Too good.

ᵠWENTY-TWO

ᵠ jerked my hands away from Diana's shoulders and stepped back guiltily.

"Oh, Kate," she burbled.

And then she threw herself at me, like a child casting herself into a willing parent's arms. Unfortunately, I'm not as good as Wayne at catching. And Diana wasn't a child. At least not in size. She almost knocked me over with the unexpected move. But all those years of tai chi came in handy, allowing me to absorb the blow of her tall body and catch her before she bounced back off.

Once I had a stiff grip on the weeping yoga goddess, I led her into the house and onto the denim couch, only resisting the urge to shout at her by biting my lip hard enough that I tasted blood. She smelled of honeysuckle oil and gamy sweat, the latter scent new to my nostrils, at least on Diana's body. Even her long black hair was mussed, strands sticking out at random from her usually smooth braid. A tingle of fear tickled my chest. What *had* happened to Diana's mother? Was it really something serious this time? Had Liz Atherton been murdered like Sam Skyler?

But I knew I wouldn't get an answer till Diana calmed down. So I sat and clenched my jaw as Diana continued to weep, loudly enough that even C.C. came out for a good look before turning tail and ambling away. I wished I could have followed her to lie in the dirty laundry basket, or wherever else she might have been headed. But I remained dutifully next to Diana on the denim couch until her wailing quieted into subdued sobbing.

"Could you tell me now what you wanted to say?" I asked then, as gently as I could.

"My mother!" she yelped.

I jumped back, my ears ringing. Once again, I'd forgotten how loud this woman could yell.

"What about your mother?" I persisted.

"SHE'S GOING TO KILL HERSELF!" Diana shrieked.

Luckily, this time I was far enough away that my ears weren't blasted. But my mind was.

"Why?" I asked in a daze. The tingle of fear was a pounding now. "Why would your mother want to kill herself?"

"I don't know!" Diana wailed.

Had Liz Atherton killed Sam Skyler after all? I hadn't meant it seriously when I'd asked before, but now . . .

"All right," I said sternly, speaking as much to myself as to Diana. "Calm down. What makes you think your mother's going to kill herself?"

Diana's story came out in bits and pieces, actually in wails and murmurs and yelps. And finally a coherent stream.

"There was a message on my answering machine," she babbled. "From my mom. And she said she was going to kill herself. But that everything was going to be all right. That everything would be as it should be. She said not to worry."

"Are you sure that's what she said?"

"Yes!" Diana shouted.

"All right, all right," I soothed her, as my brain spun through possibilities. If Diana was telling the truth, we had to find Liz Atherton quickly, before she carried out her threat.

Then we'd try to figure out why she wanted to kill herself. First things first. "Have you been to her house?"

"I went, but she wasn't there, Kate. She wasn't there. And she wasn't at Gary's. And she wasn't at work. And she wasn't at any of her friends'."

"Where else would she go?"

"I don't know." Diana's voice rose again. "I don't know!"

But I did. At least I thought I did. The ocean bluff in Quiero. That's it, my pounding blood answered. The same bluff where Sam Skyler had stood as we'd watched the scuba divers rise from the surf.

"Could she have gone to Quiero?" I asked, keeping my voice as soothing as morphine.

Diana's eyes widened, wet blue saucers streaked with red.

"Yes!" she cried and jumped from the couch. "Yes, you're right, that's where she is. She must be."

It was all I could do to restrain Diana's wriggling body with one hand as I called Wayne's number at La Fête à L'Oiel with the other. I needed to call Wayne and tell him where I was going. But I didn't want Diana driving. She'd probably go off a cliff in her car, and then I'd have two dead bodies on my conscience.

The restaurant phone was busy. I slammed it down in frustration.

"Please, Kate," Diana begged softly. "Please. We have to stop her."

She was right. I scribbled a quick note to Wayne, then Diana and I were out of there.

As we sprinted for the Toyota, I wished once more that I'd bought a mobile phone like everyone else.

The steel-blue sky was already beginning to shimmer with twilight as we jumped into my car. I stuck the key in the ignition, and one more theory occurred to me. What if Diana was setting me up? I looked at her panic-stricken face. No, I told myself. No. I wouldn't even think it.

Still, I backed out of the driveway knowing that Wayne would kill me if I let this woman murder me.

The Toyota fishtailed as I took the turn onto Highway 1 leading to Quiero, thinking of the endless blacktop between us and there. What if I was wrong in my guess? Damn, I should have kept trying to call Wayne. He could have checked the other possibilities while I drove to the bluff. I pressed harder on the gas pedal.

"Has your mother ever threatened suicide before?" I asked Diana, suddenly wondering if the whole thing was a wild goose chase.

"No," she whispered. "My mom wouldn't threaten something she wouldn't do. It wouldn't feel right to her. She . . . she does the right thing. She believes in right and wrong, and all of that."

The right thing. Was the right thing murder as well as suicide? But why? Liz Atherton hadn't liked Sam Skyler, hadn't wanted her daughter to marry him, that was clear. But would a person who believed in the right thing believe in murder? Had Wayne been on the money with his theory? Had Liz Atherton loved Sam Skyler herself and been spurned? Or—

"I think Mom might be sick," Diana said quietly, more like the Diana I had known in tai chi, soft and sweet and spaced. "She hasn't done her sculpture in months. And she just doesn't feel like she's . . . I don't know . . . connected to me anymore. I can't seem to touch her like I could. And she's so tired all the time. And she keeps rubbing her head. I've asked her if she was ill, but she just changes the subject. What if she's . . ." Diana's voice dropped even lower. "What if she's dying, Kate?"

"Do you think she is?" I asked back, my voice almost as low as Diana's. Oh God, I hoped Liz wasn't dying.

"I don't know," Diana answered and then she was sobbing again. Softly, though. She gulped through her sobs to speak. "Mom's been acting strangely for months. She loves me and Gary, I know, but she'll just run off in the middle of a conversation. And she's so distracted. And her hair and her clothes, Kate. Neatness is important to her. Really important. She even dresses before breakfast. But she's been going out with her hair messed up and—"

"Would she kill herself if she was dying?" I asked as blandly as I could, keeping my eyes on the road, taking the curves as fast as possible while the sky darkened ahead.

Diana snuffled awhile before answering. I wanted to take a look at her face but I couldn't, not at the rate I was speeding. I could smell her, though, new acrid sweat over the honeysuckle scent. Fear. It was fear I was smelling. On the woman I'd thought was a goddess. I wanted to put out a hand to touch her, to comfort her, but I kept my hands on the wheel as I took the next hairpin turn.

"No," Diana said finally. "I don't think Mom would kill herself if she was dying. It wouldn't feel right to her. Unless . . ."

"Unless what?" I demanded. Again, I wanted to look at Diana, to see what her face revealed, but I was going too fast. Way too fast. I let up a little on the gas. I had to keep control of the Toyota. Diana remained silent.

"What?" I said again. But she still didn't answer.

And then my brain sent me another bulletin.

"Are you sure it was your mother's voice on your answering machine?" I asked. What if it wasn't Diana setting me up, but someone else, setting *her* up. But for what? What would a phony caller hope to elicit by such a cruel prank? Could Emma have—

"No," Diana answered, but I could hear uncertainty in her

tone. Then her voice got stronger. "No, It was Mom. No one else could sound like her."

At least Diana was talking again.

"I remembered more of my dreams," she added, her voice a whisper.

Dreams. This whole thing had started with Diana's dreams. I peered out into the darkening sky, underlit by an apricot glow now. For a moment I wondered if *I* was dreaming. The shimmying of my back tires on pavement told me I wasn't. I clamped my hands tighter on the steering wheel.

"There was a lot of violence between my parents," Diana went on, her voice trembling. "Between my mom and dad. See, I slept in their bedroom. I remember . . . I remember . . ."

"What?" I prompted, keeping my eyes focused on the road by pure force of will.

"My father beat my mother," she answered. "And . . ."

Was this what it was like to be a therapist? I wanted to reach out and pull Diana's words from her mouth now. But I was having a hard enough time keeping the car on the road. Seconds might count. I couldn't slow down.

So I said, "Uh-huh?" as invitingly as possible.

And it worked.

"He beat her and he beat her." Diana's voice was rising now, in pitch and volume. I braced myself for a blast.

But her next words were so low I couldn't hear them over the sound of the Toyota's rush toward Quiero.

"What did you say?" I prodded.

"I think she smothered him," she shot back.

"She what?" I said, forgetting to moderate my tone. And then I did turn to see Diana's face. I'd heard her words, but I couldn't believe I'd understood them correctly. The car skidded with my sideways glance. And all my look got me was a glimpse of the face of a dreamer. A dreamer with her blue eyes wide open and unfocused. Maybe not a dreamer, I thought, maybe a madwoman. I pulled my eyes back to the road as I pulled the Toyota out of the skid, my mouth as dry as drought.

"She did it with a pillow," Diana went on, her words as fast as the car now. "I think she couldn't stand the beatings anymore, so she killed him. She killed him, and I saw it happen. I tried not to remember all these years, but I saw it. And I dreamed it. And dreamed it. I couldn't help myself. I—"

"She killed your father because he beat her," I interrupted, my own thoughts speeding now, too fast to control. "And then you told her you were going to marry Sam Skyler. A man who beat his former wife. A man who killed his former wife—"

"But Sam—"

I stopped her. "It doesn't matter what Sam did or didn't do, what he was or wasn't. Not if your mother *believed* he killed his wife. Was your mother a court reporter when Skyler was being tried for murder?"

"I . . . I think so. She's been a court reporter for years—"

"Did she ever mention Sam Skyler's trial?" I breathed.

"I can't remember." The whine was returning to Diana's voice. "I don't know!"

I kept my thoughts to myself then. And kept on driving. We were nearly there. What if Liz Atherton had been a court reporter while Sam was on trial, maybe even *the* court reporter for his trial? She would have heard the rumors permeating the legal community like corruption, the rumors that Sam Skyler had killed his wife and gotten away with it. Even Ona had gotten the scuttlebutt from her bailiff boyfriend. And then Liz's daughter decides to marry this man, a man Liz believes is a wife-beater and wife-killer, no matter what Diana says in his defense. So she decides to stop him. She believes in justice. Her own justice.

The sun had almost set as I turned onto the side road that would take us to Yvonne's friend's house on the bluff.

"Are you sure your mother didn't kill Sam?" I asked, slowing down now, not absolutely sure which driveway was the one that would take us to the right house.

"I don't know," Diana answered, but her tears were flowing again.

Maybe I was wrong, I told myself, straining my eyes for the driveway. It had been paved, I remembered, not gravel. And on the left.

"After you told your mother about the police suspecting you, about the massage oil—" I began.

"Oh, God!" Diana cried. I felt her body jerk beside me. "Mom said she'd fix everything. That's what she said."

"Would your mother fix everything by confessing falsely and killing herself?" I asked, gentling my voice again.

"No, not Mom," Diana whispered. "Not my mom. She believes in truth. In justice."

And then I saw the driveway I was looking for in the waning light. I yanked the steering wheel to make the turn, my back wheels flying as I did, and drove as far down the pavement as I could.

I was stopped by a wooden gate. It was so dark, I almost went through it before I hit the brakes.

Diana was out of the car before me, tearing open the gate. And then we both ran alongside the house, toward the bluff, the wet cold smacking our faces.

As we rounded the corner of the house, I thought how foolish I'd feel if Liz Atherton wasn't there. But she was. She stood straight and tall as her small body allowed and then leaned over to place something the size of her hand on the deck chair behind her. I couldn't see what it was. But there was still enough light that I could see Liz herself as she sprinted the last long yards across the rough ground and climbed onto the two-by-four railing that guarded the length of the bluff.

"Stop!" Liz ordered, turning and crouching like an animal, hands and knees on the top of the railing. Her voice rang out calm and clear above the roar of the ocean. "Both of you stop right now."

TWENTY-THREE

We made it as far as the deck chair before Liz Atherton shouted again.

This time, we only heard pieces of what she said. The booming of the ocean and the shrieking of the wind sucked all the rest away.

"Don't come any nearer, honey . . . I've made . . ."

Diana started to run again. I watched Liz, backlit against the shimmering darkness as she lifted one hand off the railing that overlooked the rocks below. I leapt and caught Diana's arm, pulling her toward me.

"Thank . . ." Liz said. I lost her next words, then heard ". . . on there . . ." She pointed toward the object she'd laid on the deck chair. I picked it up, only recognizing it as a miniature hand-held tape recorder when I touched it.

Diana used that diversion to run once more.

"Don't!" Liz ordered and began to stand, wobbling like a tightrope walker on the weathered two-by-four. She lifted her hand as if to steady herself and then, mid-gesture, moved it to rub her temple.

I caught up with Diana in two steps and grabbed her by the shoulder. She was shaking. I was too. I took a big breath of chilled sea air, tasting salt. And fear.

"Listen to your mother," I told Diana urgently. "Don't rush her. Our only hope is to talk her down."

"But she's going to jump!" Diana cried.

"She will if you rush her." I'd worked in a mental hospital long enough to know that. Whether Liz would jump even if we didn't rush her was another question.

I tightened my grip on Diana's shoulder as a moist gust of wind helpfully tilted her trembling body my way.

"Diana!" Liz yelled above the wind, crouching once more. I let my breath out slowly, wiping my already cold, dripping nose with the back of my hand, the hand that held the tape recorder. "I transcribed what you need to know. I love you. Everything will be as it should be. Please, don't try to stop me."

"Mom!" Diana cried out and tried to run again. I caught her with both hands this time, jamming the tape recorder I still held into her flesh inadvertently, hitting the Play button as I did.

"To my two children," the tape began in Liz's distinct no-nonsense voice. Diana and I both jumped, startled, but I kept my grip on her. "Diana and Gary, this is a tape for you." The words were tinny but just audible against the screaming wind and ocean. "There are also three written transcripts. The Quiero police should have one by tomorrow. And there will be one for each of you two. I haven't been a court reporter all these years for nothing." A chuckle crackled through the speaker. "I love you . . ."

As the taped words poured out like the dubbing of a bad movie, the words, "I love you," echoed from the real Liz's mouth once more. I looked up to see her still crouched on the railing, the sky growing darker behind her. "I killed Skyler . . ." And then I couldn't hear anything more from the live Liz.

But the tape kept on running.

". . . I had to kill him. At least, I thought I had to kill him. I knew he'd murdered his former wife. Everyone at the court-house knew. Everyone except the jurors. And I knew he'd hit her. I couldn't let that happen to you, Diana. I couldn't let you go through that. Though from what his son said, perhaps I was wrong. The second most important decision in my life, and I might have been wrong." There was no chuckle during this pause. "I got the idea from all the talk about tai chi. I realized how easily someone could be shoved over that low railing, especially a man as top-heavy as Sam Skyler . . ."

I looked up to see Liz still perched on that low railing, waiting. Waiting until we heard the entire tape as it rolled on? Or until the last glimmer of light left the darkening sky?

". . . everyone else was mesmerized by the scuba wedding going on below, but when I looked over the bluff all I could see was Sally Skyler's body lying crushed on the rocks. She deserved avenging, even if it hadn't been for you, Diana . . ."

Diana sobbed next to me as the tape continued. I pulled her closer and wrapped my arm around her shivering shoul-ders. And smelled honeysuckle and sweat against the fishy salt spray.

". . . didn't want to leave hand prints, so I picked up the two brass vases from the railing near Skyler. He never even turned my way. I held them up over my head and struck him with all my strength. After all those years with the chain saw, my strength is considerable. Skyler went over without a sound. Or if there was one, it was swallowed by the ocean. I wiped my fingerprints off and threw the vases after him. Good rub-bish after bad."

"Why?" Diana shouted over the wind. "Why?"

"I killed your father!" Liz shouted back, and the tape took over again, echoing eerily in the wind.

". . . killed your father. Lennie Atherton, the drunken, big-oted cop on the take. Talk about your stereotypes. I thought I was marrying law and order, but I married corruption. And violence. So I pushed a pillow over his face while he was dead drunk . . .''

The tape continued in detail as the live Liz yelled, "The sudden freedom, I can't tell you how it felt! I'll never forget. But I didn't stop to think that you were there too, Diana, that you might see! I'd hoped you'd never remember . . ." And then the rest of her words were snatched away as the wind changed course. But the tape was still running.

". . . couldn't kill Tessa, though. I was convinced she knew everything. I'm sure she knew I killed your father. How many widows are covered with bruises? How many widows have black eyes? How many wife beaters die of natural causes at such a young age? Tessa looked at me over twenty years ago and she knew. But she never said anything. Lennie's cop friends knew too, but they'd have to talk about motive if they arrested me. They'd have to talk about all the times they'd found me and brought me back to Lennie when I took you kids and tried to run away. So they said he had a heart attack, 'what a shame.' It was a small town, easy to get the doctor to sign the death certificate . . ."

"It's okay, Mom," Diana cried out. "I still love you."

I couldn't tell whether Liz had heard her daughter from the railing, but she looked up and lifted one hand in a gesture that might have been blowing a kiss our way. The tape rolled on.

". . . and then at Skyler's funeral, when Tessa made the re-mark about the relief that mourners feel, I thought she was talking to me, telling me she knew. I thought she had figured out that I killed Skyler so he wouldn't beat Diana the way Lennie beat me. So I went to the mortuary to talk to her, to beg her not to tell, to tell her I was dying anyway. To ask her to wait. I walked into the chapel and saw the back of Tessa's head. She was bent over, probably praying. She never heard me. And then I saw the brass candlestick. And I went mad. I grabbed the candlestick and hit her. The minute I did it, I knew it was wrong. Terribly wrong. Tessa slumped over, her head bleeding. But I felt her wrist and there was still a pulse. I even thought of killing her then, of finishing her off. But that would have been unjustifiable. Lennie and Skyler were evil. Tessa wasn't. I couldn't kill her. So I just wiped my prints from the candlestick and ran, grateful she wasn't badly hurt. She was already regaining consciousness when I left. And then I went home and waited for the police to arrest me. I was sure Tessa would tell them everything. But she didn't. I don't know why.''

I thought I heard the sound of brakes screeching, somewhere behind us, but then it was gone again. Maybe it was just a gull.

The live Liz jerked her head up. Had she heard it too?

''. . . I'm dying anyway . . .'' the tape pushed on.

''No, Mom, no!'' Diana screamed.

''Mom!'' echoed behind me.

I turned to see two figures storming through the gate in the darkness.

''Kate!'' shouted the largest one.

Wayne and Gary. Relief washed over me. But not for long.

Because Gary kept running, straight toward his mother. My mouth went dry in all the wet and cold.

''Stop!'' Liz's voice rang out.

I swiveled around and saw her rise to a standing position again, swaying as she did. I braced myself, as if centering my own body could stop hers from swaying.

''I have no regrets!'' Liz shouted as Gary rushed on, passing us.

Wayne grabbed at him, just missing his collar. He picked up his own pace, running almost as fast as Gary.

The forgotten tape was still spinning, though.

''. . . I'm dying of a brain tumor . . .'' it said.

Gary stopped and looked around.

"Mom?" he said in confusion.

"She says she killed Sam and Daddy," Diana told him.

Gary nodded impatiently as he looked at his mother, then jerked his head around to check behind him for her double. How long had he known that his mother had killed two men? Or suspected? From his and Diana's first visit to us? Had he been the one to tell Diana to call us off? Wayne caught up with him and reached out. Gary shook off his hand. Wayne respected the gesture and stood back.

"... Lennie's revenge." Another chuckle. "The doctor doesn't agree, but I'm sure the tumor began back then from all those times Lennie hit my head. And now it's killing me. Inoperable, they say . . ."

Gary turned back to the live Liz.

"Mom, don't jump!" he bellowed. "We'll find a way."

Liz shifted her feet carefully on the railing, turning toward the ocean, as the tape ran on about medical opinions on how long she had left, about alternative treatments, and about her own opinion that the tumor wasn't worth treating, not even the pain.

"No, no!" Gary yelled and made a sudden dash toward her, too sudden for Wayne to even grab for him. Bile filled my mouth.

Gary had almost reached the railing when Liz turned her head to look over her shoulder.

"I love you both," she said, her calm voice suddenly clear over the sound of waves and wind.

An instant later, the tape echoed, "I love you both."

And finally the tape clicked to an end as Gary ran, stretching out his hand.

And Liz Atherton jumped.

ᛏWENTY-FOUR

⁘

We all stood on the wooden pier watching a ferry boat
aglow from stem to stern with candlelit lanterns floating toward us under the cool, moist night sky. At least this time I
was dressed for the occasion, in two pairs of socks, a long
parka, and a knit cap. I leaned against Wayne for a little more
warmth and sighed contentedly. The scene was breathtakingly
beautiful, the golden lanterns reflected on the bay waters, the
night sky clear and starry. The sound of the revelers was just
beginning to reach us in high-pitched laughter and low shouts.
Frying garlic from a nearby restaurant, fishy bay smells, and
Wayne's unique herb-musk scent intermingled deliciously. Tonight was the last meeting of the Wedding Ritual class. And
yes, the ferry wedding was as sumptuous and wondrous as
Yvonne had promised. Though not as hot as the tango wedding. But then, nothing was ever going to be as hot as the
tango wedding. Unless Wayne and I thought up something
really good.

Little starbursts of conversation competed all around us
from the remaining members of the class. Martina Monteil
wasn't there for the last class, but Nathan Skyler was. Maybe
to show he forgave the group for their part in his father's
death. ''For closure,'' he'd probably say once he became a

psychologist. Tessa and Ray, Emma and Campbell, and Ona and Perry had all stuck it out too. And—surprise, surprise—we had a new member in our group, Park Ranger David Yasuda, who stood grinning absurdly and holding hands with our fearless leader, Yvonne O'Reilley.

A gull shrieked, and my thoughts bounced back to Diana Atherton. And Liz Atherton. Nathan had told us Diana was already in therapy. She was remembering everything now and stronger for it, he insisted. She was going to make it. I hoped so.

Wayne had spent long hours closeted with Gary Atherton. Gary had told Wayne he'd always known his mother had killed his father. Since he was all of eleven years old. It was his little sister, Diana, only seven herself, who had wandered sleepily out of his parents' bedroom over twenty years ago, murmuring, "Mommy put a pillow over Daddy's head and now he's really, really quiet," before she made her way back into the room where her father lay so silently. When Liz had announced their father's death the next day, Gary knew she'd killed him, and had been grateful. Very grateful, but worried about Diana who'd never mentioned the pillow again. Or her father. So Gary had kept a watchful eye on his little sister all those years, waiting for her to remember. Waiting for her to explode. But it was Liz who finally exploded.

I shook my head as hard as I could. I didn't want to think about Liz Atherton now. It had been only one night since she'd jumped and landed on the same rock as Sam Skyler. With the same result. I forced my eyes back out over the bay, banishing the image of Liz Atherton's spread-eagled body.

The glowing ferry was finally docking, the celebrants spilling out, laughing and chattering, some of them even singing. And finally the bride and groom emerged, their faces as luminous as the candlelit lanterns on the boat. The happy pair were decked out in full Navy whites, an oversized bow tie on the groom's neck and the same oversized bow atop the bride's head with a couple of yards of white lace trailing from it. The wind caught the lace, wrapping it around the grooms's shoulders. The two of them laughed and ran for shelter into the restaurant where the reception was being held, while our group watched from the deck. And talked.

Emma told us she was going to mortician's school next semester as Campbell nodded proudly, his face pink from the cold under his ginger beard.

"What could be more cool than death?" Emma asked beneath the night sky. I shivered a little in my parka as she flung out her arms as if to embrace the universe, darkness as well as light. "Life, death. Yin, yang . . ."

Tessa smiled gently and gave the younger woman's shoulders a little squeeze, before turning her head away. Was Tessa thinking of Liz, too?

"Did you know Liz killed Sam?" I asked her. I had to find out.

Tessa sighed, her narrow face somber in the dim light.

"I was fairly certain Liz had killed her husband," Tessa began, her hushed voice just audible over the bay noises.

All the members of the Wedding Ritual class turned her way. I wasn't the only curious one in the group.

"I was only an assistant all those years ago when Liz brought her husband to the Olcott Funeral Home to be buried," Tessa murmured, her dark eyes losing focus to memory. "I saw a woman covered with bruises." She paused. "And pinpoint hemorrhages in the eyes of her dead husband. Among other things. I wondered then if he'd been smothered. But the police were calling it a heart attack. So I kept my mouth shut."

She shook her head slowly, as if still there.

When she spoke again, I flinched, startled by the steel in her soft voice.

"But Sam Skyler?" Tessa sighed and shrugged. "I never

saw the connection. This woman might have killed her husband over twenty years ago. But I just didn't see a relationship to Sam Skyler's murder.'' She paused for another moment. I sucked in a chestful of cold air. ''I've seen a lot of death over the last twenty-five years.''

There was an even longer silence from Tessa as the bay waters lapped at the pier and little spurts of laughter and conversation peppered the night air.

''Tessa,'' I asked finally, unable not to. ''Why wouldn't you talk about the night you were attacked? Why wouldn't you let me ask people where they'd been that night?''

Tessa seemed to come out of her reverie then. She even laughed lightly.

''Because I assumed the police were doing the necessary detective work,'' she answered.

''Oh,'' I mumbled, embarrassed by my own assumption that *I* had been the detective. Some detective.

She must have seen the ''duh'' look on my face, because she laughed again and whispered in my ear, ''and to keep the peace with Ray,'' so quickly I wasn't even sure I'd heard her until she'd finished and turned away again.

Time to change the subject, I decided, swiveling my head in Ray Zappa's direction.

''So, how are your memoirs going?'' I asked.

Ray's handsome face went scarlet under the night sky.

''Um,'' he muttered. ''Uh . . .'' And abruptly I tried to remember if I was even supposed to know about his memoirs. Nope. I remembered what Tessa had said about keeping her mouth shut and decided to try that method for a change as Tessa stood on tiptoe and kissed her stammering fiancé into silence.

''Ah, love,'' Ona commented with a wink, snuggling up to Perry like the Persian cat I'd always see when I thought of her.

I opened my mouth to ask Ona how Perry's daughter and her son were coping with their teenage romance, then shut it again. How many seconds had expired before I'd forgotten the Tessa method?

"Pammy and Ogden were in love for all of eight hours before they started arguing again," Ona said, as if she'd heard me, anyway. So much for keeping my mouth shut. My mind was probably wide-open. At least that's what the psychics always told me. "What a hoot! But they'll probably fall in love again. We're talking a lot about safe sex now—right, Perry? Damned if we know what else to do. Kids." Ona squirmed closer to Perry as he nodded and nuzzled the top of her head. Then she suddenly whipped around in Nathan's direction.

"Hey, where's Martina the Malevolent?" she demanded.

Nathan jumped in place, but answered her calmly enough.

"Martina and I have split up," he said, rubbing his hands together softly.

"Good for you!" Ona said and gave him a congratualtory pat on the back that almost sent him sprawling.

"Well, Martina *will* be the acting president of the Institute," he added quietly.

"Hey, don't let that barracuda push you around," Ona advised, shaking a finger in Nathan's face. "She's a real ball-buster—"

"It's fine," Nathan interrupted, raising his hands as if in surrender. "Everything's fine. Martina has no signatory control at the Institute. She's merely the figurehead." I thought I saw him grin. "I'm not completely naive. The Institute was really who Martina wanted to marry in the first place."

"And you?" Ona prodded.

Nathan looked down at his feet. Or maybe he suddenly saw something of interest in the wooden slats of the pier.

"Diana," Yvonne murmured dreamily. And Park Ranger

Yasuda's absurd smile grew even wider, a Cheshire cat's grin in the darkness.

"Well," Nathan muttered, still looking down. "Diana's really healing. You know, she won't touch Dad's money. She's using it to set up a trust fund for battered women's counseling with it. And one for battering men." He brought his head up, but his eyes were still hidden by his thick glasses, the condensed mist of the bay shrouding them even further. "The irony is that my father would have never hit her, I'm sure. My dad dead, her mom dead. I just don't know . . ."

"No, Nathan," Yvonne piped up, her high voice tinkling in the cold air. She reached out the hand that wasn't holding Yasuda's and her bracelets tinkled in harmony. "It's cosmic, really, all that karma played out in each of their lifetimes. Sam pushes, he's pushed. Liz's husband hits, he's killed. Liz leaps from the same bluff as Sam. They'll all go clean into the next lifetime. You see, it's really just wondrous. Just perfect. You can let it go."

Nathan looked into the curving lines of her face for a few laps of the bay waters against the pier. Then she released his hand.

"Interesting," he murmured thoughtfully. "Really interesting." His stooped shoulders straightened a little.

I gave Yvonne a big hug. Her logic may not have been exactly in the right place, but her heart certainly was. I hoped it worked out with her park ranger. Wayne and I still didn't have a wedding ceremony planned, but still . . .

I snuggled up to my sweetie and whispered in his ear, "Let's go home."

And then Wayne and I quietly exited the Wedding Ritual class, waving goodbye to the remaining members on the pier.

We were back in the Jaguar, on our way home before I spoke again.

"How's Gary?" I asked.

"He'll be okay," Wayne said.

Then I asked the question I'd wanted to ask from the beginning.

"Were you in love with Diana?" I whispered softly.

"Diana?" Wayne barked, jerking his head around. "You mean Diana Atherton?"

I just nodded.

"Good God, no!" he spat out, staring at me, eyebrows raised as the Jaguar veered ever so slightly to the right. He turned his eyes back to the road, his voice softening to a low growl. "I love you, Kate. And even if I were to fall for anyone but you, it'd never be Diana. She's too . . . too young. She's too scatterbrained. And she's too damned skinny!"

The words rattled around in the back of my brain for a moment, tickling a forgotten memory. Hadn't Barbara used those same words an eternity ago to assure me of Wayne's lack of interest in Diana?

I leaned my head back and laughed, unable to stop for five or ten miles of blacktop despite Wayne's sidelong glances.

Until, finally, I was all laughed out. Only then did I put my cold hand gently on my sweetie's warm thigh. And kept it there as we rolled home under the starry night sky.

Do It Yourself:
Grief Into Growth Puppet

INSTRUCTIONS

1. Cut along dotted lines.
2. Fold and tape, leaving bottom open.
3. Follow the arrow for personal transformation.
4. Share the experience!